D1374329

Getting Out

HENRY HOLT AND COMPANY | NEW YORK

GWENDOLEN GROSS Getting Out

A NOVEL

Henry Holt and Company, LLC
Publishers since 1866
115 West 18th Street
New York, New York 10011

Henry Holt® is a registered trademark of Henry Holt and Company, LLC.

Library of Congress Cataloging-in-Publication Data

Gross, Gwendolen, date.
    Getting out : a novel / Gwendolen Gross.—1st ed.
        p. cm.
    ISBN 0-8050-6834-1 (hb)
        1. Children of divorced parents—Fiction. 2. Terminally ill parents—Fiction.
    3. Parent and adult child—Fiction. 4. Brothers and sisters—Fiction. 5. Outdoor
    recreation—Fiction. 6. Young women—Fiction. I. Title.

    PS3557.R568 G76 2002
    813'.6—dc21   2001051643

First Edition 2002

Designed by Fritz Metsch

Printed in the United States of America
10 9 8 7 6 5 4 3 2 1

For my family, adventurers all

Getting Out

One / I didn't expect to love it so much, to come to need it, going out, the trees lit with green or bare as fingers, the open palm of the sky from a peak, the cheese-flavored camp-stove mash, mornings in rocky-bottomed tents with a cold nose and warm feet, or outside, waking up in new air. I never imagined I'd willingly squeeze through the pitch and silty hollow legs of Spider Cave, belly down in an underground river; that I'd walk backward over the edge of a crevasse; that I'd strap teeth to my feet and cut ice-ax steps into the face of a glacier. That I would long for the smells of cedar and old oak leaves and the woody tang of sassafras twigs against my tongue. I didn't realize I would have to keep going, staying out longer and longer until I could see myself clearly enough to come back inside.

In the beginning, it was an excuse to escape my father's silent gravitational pull. It was a way out of the monotony of family, food, work, sex, and comfort, something to keep me busy when my boyfriend, Ben, had to work weekends.

I am short, five foot one, with brown hair and brown eyes that look quite nice together, I think, now that I've forgiven genetics for not making me a green-eyed redhead. Despite my height, I have always been very strong. My butterfly sprint brought the Carleton College swim team reliable firsts and seconds in the relay. I was never the New Cult type; I didn't have the will to try my friends' gym fads: spinning classes and kick boxing and power yoga. Bars rarely enticed me, either, because I got lost in them, standing in a sea of sweaters and elbows.

I joined the Adventurers' Club in October, when my sister, Marla, had just started seeing Reed, and my brother, Ted, and his wife, Abby, were still together and seemed as strong as a single oak. I was working at a design firm where I conjured indoor spaces and displays, signage, and corporate newsletters for businesses. Despite its location in a swank refurbished brownstone on Beacon Hill, the office housed a potent scent of mouse and dust. The partners had called in cleaners and *feng shui* consultants and exterminators and aromatherapists, and, for a while, overwhelming blasts of Orange Julius emanated from the copy room, but ultimately the underlying dusty mouse funk clung.

Sometimes I designed whole interiors, crafting spectacular rooms to walk through on my computer, and then later I would visit the disappointing coffee shop where they'd replaced my silvery orange and brushed chrome with plain brown paint. At first the projects always looked like they had meat, and I stayed late and woke up thinking about the details: the metal filigree over the menu board, pickled wainscoting, a tongue-in-groove wood ceiling. Then it all got dulled down over a course of meetings—long toxic affairs with donuts staining paper plates and corpulent handouts with endless columns of numbers that, if you squinted, looked like ants sliding down the pages.

The day I found out about the Adventurers' Club, I'd just fled a particularly protracted and sad meeting, in which I had to cut all the velvet wallpaper from my original design and the project manager reminded me of a balloon slowly losing its air. I went back to my cube and spun around in my chair, deciding whether to call Ben. If I called, all peevish, he would probably comfort me, maybe offer to meet me after work at Boston Common. On the other hand, if he was peevish himself, exhausted from having to raise funds for the museum instead of spending them to make exhibits, the bitter price of his recent promotion, he might act dismissive.

Ben was usually wonderful: patient and calm. He never acted dismissive on purpose, but sometimes it slipped out. He said stuff like "Jeez, you'd think you had to live in that coffee shop" or "You know, you could stand to design your own apartment a little more" or even "So what, you hate your job." If I looked at him as he said these mean little things, he got a surprised look on his face, his blue eyes slightly glassy, as if someone had stepped into his body for a second and used his voice.

Maybe his naked opinions were part of the reason he managed such swift promotion at work, but he didn't work for me. I knew he didn't mean what he said, but he would never take it back, so I got mad. Later, after I sulked for a while and tried to get him to apologize, he'd say, "I'm sorry you got upset." I'd say, "I'm sorry you got me upset," and then we'd have a great time relieving the tension of the fight by chasing each other around my apartment.

I was holding my phone but not dialing when my boss

slid in my cube's insubstantial doorframe and leaned. My boss, with her short gelled red hair, thought she was arty. She wore faux-bohemian open-toed sandals and tight suits of slightly iridescent fabrics that cost a fortune and made her look like firmly packaged leftovers. She leaned on walls and words and applied posh scents that were not made for her; they warmed against her reptilian skin when she grew excited, and she smelled like an overripe cantaloupe. She got things done, all kinds of things, and kept clients happy. She got promoted. She got my goat. Maybe I was jealous.

"Um," I said, not sure whether to put the phone down.

"Hannah," she said. "I *need* you."

I noticed the long shadow of her new client from the bike shop on my carpeted wall. Clyde's was a minor account, so at first I hadn't understood her fuss over him. But then I noticed the tilt of her shiny head, the way she always shifted her hips when she was with him. She was deep in lust. Clyde didn't seem to mind the attention.

"Hm?" I said. Clyde sidled up behind her. His grease-stained finger brushed an invisible piece of lint from her shoulder.

"I *need* you to get coffee for us." She held out a twenty, tipping it from the air into my hand, which I hadn't yet volunteered. It wasn't my job, coffee. It hadn't ever been my job at the firm. I wasn't her secretary, and I wanted to say so, and I wanted to take her twenty and slap it across her painted cheeks like a glove in a forties movie. But I also wanted to keep my job.

"Bev's out," she said, referring to her most recent secretary. She gave me her plaintive look, which was frightening. The gloss on her mouth cracked, and her eyes shed scales of Bite-Me Bronze shadow.

My throat itched with obscenities. I commanded my

hand to take the bill, but it wouldn't obey and the twenty fell to the floor.

"Skim vanilla double-shot latte for me." She forced a gruntlike giggle. "And I believe Clyde likes plain coffee. With lots of *cream*."

Clyde started to reach for the bill, but my boss took his hand instead and led him down the hall to her lair. I wanted to scream.

I put down the phone, picked up the bill, and stormed down to the coffee shop. I ordered my boss's drink decaf, out of spite, but then changed the order: somehow, she'd know, and she'd know whom to blame.

Back at the office, her door was shut, so I marched the coffees into the copy room, where we'd all cool off. I made a quick color copy of her change, wanting to waste something at company expense. The quarters came out black from the reflected light. Then I noticed a stack of photographs by the machine, and something about them was clearly not of the workplace—maybe it was their small size, their lack of super gloss. And I could see from the top one that the subjects were not a new branch of a bank or a ficus-filled restaurant in Back Bay. The top photograph featured a blond man attached to a harness and ropes, a cliff and a huge blue sky above him. His mouth was tight with concentration, his body tense with effort. His fingers gripped the thinnest sliver of rock, and somehow I knew he'd bring himself up.

I flipped through the stack. More people, climbing. In every one, the sunshine was fierce, lighting hair and eyes. The man from the first photograph, tall and lean, was joined by an older man with a long nose. They scaled rock faces, peeking over the edge from above, spidermen. There was a woman, who looked slightly familiar, lowering herself over a precipice in successive photographs; there was another woman, with pale hair, stepping backward over the same cliff. She had a scrape on her leg, and the line of blood thickened and spread as her descent progressed.

I was engrossed. Not one of them looked tired or worried. An Indian man had wrapped himself in a red rope; his head was tilted back and his mouth open with laughter. Sun spilled inside his lips.

The scent of crushed leaves wafted around me as I finished flipping through the stack. I almost forgot the coffee.

"If you're so interested," said a woman's voice, "maybe you'd like to come to a meeting tonight."

I looked up to find one of the women from the photographs; she was tall—close to six feet—and wore black slacks and a soft green sweater with an apostrophe-shaped stain on the cuff. She didn't come all the way into the copy room.

"You're Hannah Blue, right?" she said. "I'm Linda from marketing. And I believe those are mine." She gestured toward the photographs, which I was smudging with my voyeur's fingerprints.

"Um, yes," I said.

"It's kind of an adventure club. We're meeting tonight to talk about winter trips. Want to come?" She had small brown eyes surrounded by an expressive network of creases.

"Oh," I said. Guilty. "Oh, okay." Why would I want to climb backward over a cliff? But I still had her pictures, so I felt obliged.

She smiled, and I handed over the photos.

"If you're not interested—" She took one step and was outside the door.

"Oh, no!" I said. I couldn't let her disappear back into the maw of marketing. "I'm interested. Really. Tell me more."

And that was how I joined the Adventurers' Club, by letting the kind-looking Linda woman take me to a meeting at the Caffè Paradiso in Cambridge, where a group of people who looked normal enough in their button-downs and boiled wool passed around more photographs, from hiking trips and a white-water rafting expedition. All afternoon I had fretted—a meeting. It had sounded so dangerously clubby or cultish. It had sounded like commitment. But as I matched many of the faces to the climbing shots, they struck me as perfectly ordinary people. The trips sounded as thrilling as the photos, though. And as distant. I drank too much coffee for evening and they invited me along on the next excursion: hiking in the Adirondacks.

I hadn't anticipated the very early morning and the very long drive. I'd heard the time-to-meet at the café, and I'd registered the New York destination, but it hadn't really sunk in. I was too excited by the prospect of unearthing my old hiking boots and getting a good whiff of the Great Outdoors; I pictured a dazzle of foliage and hot chocolate by an ember-rich campfire, a star-punctuated arc of night sky. But when my alarm clicked on a Spanish pop station at 4:45 A.M., I assumed it was a bad layer in my dream, one that would soon transition to a chase scene with a sheepdog or the rescue of blue marine crabs from the angry gods of the sea.

I love sleep. I am habitually late for work, or anywhere I have to go in the morning, though come afternoon I become Girl Promptness, arriving at the exact designated minute. But the Adventurers' Club met at 5:30 A.M. at the city hall parking lot in Newton, the suburb where I grew up, and where my mom still lived in her wide-hipped Victorian with curved-glass windows and a dramatic mahogany front door and too many rooms for just her and her second husband.

I had to extricate myself from bed at five to make it from Brookline to Newton, in my unreliable inherited Saab named Lemon. Lemon was once my stepfather's car, and even when new it was likely to let loose a hose clamp on the highway. Owning it was a matter of hope and duct tape and trips to the junkyard for spare parts. I kept an extra rearview mirror and a mysterious clamp in my closet.

Ben was still asleep in my bed. He rolled over, heavy with sleep, his big arm claiming my pillow, as I was trying to untangle my legs from the nest of sheet. Ben always said I danced in my dreams and also that I stole all the bedding, but clearly he was the comforter hog—I could see the mound he'd hoarded even with the shades drawn.

Luckily, I got Lemon to start after only three tries. Also luckily, I hadn't signed up to drive on the trip, but unfortunately this meant I had to park on my mother's street and walk half a mile lugging an enormous borrowed frame pack with too much stuffed into its left side. Everything was empty and asleep in the sharp blue transition between night and morning. It was as if I owned all of it, suburban streets and flashing yellow traffic lights, houses with their eye-shades drawn: Greek revivals with Corinthian entrance columns, square-jawed Colonials, the occasional ranch, bland as a plain white T-shirt among the party dresses of velvet and tulle. I jaywalked happily.

But I was exhausted. So tired, that even among strangers I fell asleep in the backseat of Linda's Volvo station wagon and didn't wake up until it was time to eat lunch and hit the trail. My face was hot and Frankensteined by the seat seams. I had drooled, my arm wedged against the door and my sweatshirt pulled up, baring my back, yet somehow I was sleepy enough not to care.

We had lunch at the trailhead, squeezing peanut butter and honey from tubes onto bread and slicing up cheese and apples with the Swiss Army knives everyone carried. Everyone except me. The air smelled of cedar and oak, and the trail was a tunnel of gold and green. I couldn't believe how lucky I was, how long it had been since I'd been in the woods, real woods. It was cool and sunny and a hawk screamed overhead. I sat on my pack and looked at all these people: Linda, who looked even kinder in the bright afternoon light with woods all around us; her husband, Alan, a biologist she'd met through the club; a Chinese man shaped like Popeye, Shing, who squeezed peanut butter from the tube onto his finger and skipped the bread; wiry Nicky; fair-haired Camilla, about my age; and Noah, who was beautiful, very tall and sinewy with short straight blond hair and pastel eyes that might be blue and might be green, depending on the light. His ears got red as he talked and ate.

It felt very comfortable and chummy and safe at the trailhead. The comfortable part faded, though, as soon as we hit the trail up Mount Marcy. Sure, the leaves were blushing and the creek sang softly beside us. Yes, the air was clean and Linda's happy voice burbled along at the head of the group. But my feet hurt. My back hurt. The boots I'd dug out of my storage bin in the apartment eaves were old but stiff. I could feel the leather cutting into my skin, lacerating it with each step. The pack was hugely heavy. I had packed according to the list Linda gave me: socks (two pair per day), long underwear (preferably silk or polypropylene; I had mothball-stinky cotton), wool sweater, light shell, down vest, raincoat (I figured my dress coat would do, though it was rather bulky), sleeping bag, sleeping bag pad (Linda lent me an extra), flashlight, gloves, hat, fork and spoon, bowl, et cetera. I didn't have a down vest, so I'd borrowed Ben's massive down jacket. It made me look like a blueberry stuck on twig legs, but it was warm. I couldn't find a plastic bowl, so I'd packed one of my father's sturdy ceramic ones. I wasn't really thinking about weight. I had added in a few extras: a little bit of hair gel since there wouldn't be showers, a cotton sweater that looked nicer than the old wool, a book for reading by the campfire. I'd forgotten, in packing, what the term *backpack* meant.

So by the time we took a break for gorp and water, I was ready to quit. I'd been talking to myself along the steep stretch of trail we'd just finished, counting the rocks and then counting the steps and then telling myself that if I lived through this I would never do it again. I could quit nature completely, except for the occasional walk through the Public Gardens with lightweight sandals and a diaphanous dress, my arm in Ben's so he could help me keep my balance if a pebble disrupted my step. The ceramic bowl was denting my spine. My toes were numb, but that was a blessing, because the other parts of my feet were on fire. I had been watching the backs of Noah's boots, and I could tell he wasn't walking as fast as he could, that he was my designated baby-sitter, because everyone else was at least a mile ahead.

He turned back to look at me, and I knew my face was plum from exertion. I tried to say something. It came out as a wheeze. "Um, is this what it's usually like?" I paused and leaned on my knee to slow my breath.

"Oh." Noah smiled. A quick smile. Beautiful, like the rest of him. Even kernel teeth. His eyes were in a green phase. I hated his ease. "Oh, well, every trip is different. It's sort of an adjustment at first, but it's really great."

I grunted and put my head down again to count the rocks. The second time he looked back I think I grimaced, but neither of us said anything. I was sure he could hear my panting as I stopped, leaned on my knees, and faced the ground, thinking about how ugly rocks could look, like massive insect eggs. About how autumn leaves were very lovely from the passenger seat of a car, but underfoot they were simply more stuff in the way of my boots.

The gorp break was short. Actually, it was probably very long, but since Noah and I didn't catch up until half the M&Ms had been picked from Linda's and Nicky's bags, I guessed they'd been waiting awhile. I could feel all the eyes on me as I bent forward, leaning into the steep steps to make it up the last bit of trail, and half fell onto the rock where they were parked.

"Hey, kiddo," said Alan, "it's great to have you along. New blood." He was the one with the grayish hair and a beaky nose. He looked like my high school math teacher and I was afraid he was going to ask me to recite the quadratic formula.

"Thanks." I groaned.

Noah moved around to the back of the group and started to stretch his long long legs. He didn't bother to take off his pack, which was the bright yellow and black of a bumblebee and looked like about as much bother to him as a wallet.

Trying to shrug the great animal of my own pack off onto the rock, I slipped backward and lay on the trail, arms stuck in the straps and legs splayed, like an upside-down turtle. Camilla laughed. She had a musical laugh and pale blond hair and I was lying near her ankle, which I wanted to bite. I looked up at the silvery birch trunks and the sky. If I borrowed someone's keys and turned around now, I could be home by the middle of the night. I could take a shower and get Ben to administer first aid to my bloody feet and bruised shoulders. I could stand in the shower for an hour. I could sit in the shower for an hour. I could take a nap in the shower. I'd get out in time for breakfast.

"Let me help you with that," said Alan. He extricated me from the straps. Camilla rubbed my shoulders and Linda gave me gorp. I hated them all.

The second half of the climb was better, because my feet and legs had grown numb. Also, the scenery changed as we climbed, moving from the tall maples into a thick zone of Christmas-tree heaven. We'd never had a Christmas tree— though only my mother was Jewish—because my father considered it a waste of a perfectly good tree.

Noah was still with me. I followed his boots. I could tell he was waiting because his boots moved ahead, then paused. I was thinking maybe soon we'd take another break and I could fall down again and make a fool of myself in front of six strangers.

"I don't think I can go any farther," I said, to the backs of Noah's boots.

"Once," said Noah, as if he hadn't heard me, "I lost a pair of boots to a porcupine."

"Uh?" I said, hoping to sound interested. Actually, I was interested. It was a distraction, imagining tall blond Noah in sock feet, wrestling with a porcupine.

"Before I knew better," he said. "I was in a lean-to, and I left my boots outside. Of course there was the usual night-time scuffling, but I'd set up a bear bag so I wasn't worried about anything. In the morning, nothing but soles."

"Bear bag?" I panted.

"You know, you hang the food in a bag between trees, so bears don't get it. If you keep it inside, you might find some furry company in your sleeping bag." His boots kept going. The pace was easier when I was listening.

"Why porcupines? And how did you know?"

"They like leather. Soles aren't too tasty. And they left evidence."

"Little porcupine signatures in the dirt?"

"Well, probably there were tracks. But I meant scat."

Of course.

"Break," said Noah. I hadn't even seen it coming or heard the chatter of the flock as they waited.

After the break, Camilla and Nicky joined on as my baby-sitters. This was okay, because they liked to talk, and I didn't even have to waste breath answering, since they had each other. They gossiped. Gossip, when it involves people you don't know, is like listening to people speak another language.

"He's not such a peak-bagger, now that Vijay's gone," said Nicky. Nicky was sandy-haired, wiry, and slight. He had brown eyes and heavy brows, big feet, and peaked lips that made him look like someone's little boy. I might have found him charming if he wasn't so fast. He looked like he might accidentally burst into a run at any moment. He'd had time to pick out a walking stick and start whittling a curve in the top while we walked.

"Let's not," said Camilla, her voice low. I tripped and caught myself. Her voice brightened. "At least he packs good stuff sometimes, instead of the ubiquitous mac 'n' hack."

Ubiquitous, I thought. I know that word. Not only was Camilla swift and beautiful, she was also a vocabulary queen. At least I knew mac 'n' hack was box macaroni and cheese— and I was not looking forward to eating it. I wondered if they would notice if I stopped. I sat down on a rock to wait for tomorrow.

"Hey," said Noah. "You found some wild raisin." He walked back to my resting place.

"Are you sure these are really edible?" Camilla pursed her lips at Noah. She gave his shoulder a light shove, as he scooped up some blackish berries, currant-sized and dry-looking. I wondered whether they were a couple. It was hard to tell in this group. Linda and Alan didn't touch each other any more than the others.

She turned to me. "He has this thing for wild edibles. Most of the time he's right—when he has his *guidebook*." She took the berry he offered and crushed it between her teeth.

"Just because you gave it to me doesn't mean I always have to weigh down my pack," Noah said. Nicky tossed his berry in the air and caught it in his mouth.

"Here," Noah said, holding a single tiny berry out to me.

"Oh, thank you, I'm full."

Camilla giggled. "Smart one," she said. "It tasted like bird poo."

Then, sadly, we started up the trail again.

By the time we reached the campsite, it was almost sunset. As we'd climbed, I'd collected a layer of sweat inside my clothes and a layer of cold on the outside. When we stopped, the cold sank in, so I felt chilled and soggy. The Adventurers' Club knew how to set up camp—when Noah, Camilla, Nicky, and I arrived, the first tent was already up, the stoves and pots out. As I sat down, Linda and Shing appeared at the top of a hill lugging a five-gallon plastic container of water and an armload of twigs.

"Only take what's fallen," said Shing. He smiled at me as I sat slumped against my pack, too tired to remove it as I froze to the ground.

"And if I were you, I'd get out some dry layers."

"Oh, thanks," I said. I couldn't move. My body was congealing, a mass of ache and sweat and blister and ooze. I watched Noah and Camilla set up a tent; I'd be sleeping with them. I could hardly imagine what this would be like. Would I be squashed in a corner? Probably not. They were nice. Too nice. Too fast, too strong, and too patient. I felt like a spoiled child.

"Hey, Hannah," said Nicky, at work on another tent. "Come help me with this."

I knew he didn't need my help. He just wanted to make me feel useful.

" 'K," I said. I shrugged off my pack and dug out the cotton sweater. I pulled the boots off my pulverized feet and walked over in socks. I held a pole while Nicky made expert work of the tent, tying the fly to two trees and driving stakes into the ground with his boot heel.

"You need more clothes," he said, and he took off the thick gray sweater he was wearing and pulled it down over my head. "Cotton isn't very warm."

This seemed clear to me now. I remembered, a long time ago, my father saying, "Wool is warm when wet." The sweater was full of Nicky's heat, and it helped.

"But you'll freeze," I said.

"Nah, I'm toasty." He hugged his arms in their thin fleece shirt.

"Peak run," said Linda. "C'mon, Hannah, get your boots back on."

"Excuse me?"

"You've *got* to see it," said Nicky. He put his hand on my back. "It's less than a mile, and we can be there for sunset."

I pulled my sneakers out of the hateful pack and tugged them on.

"Coat," said Linda, smiling. I couldn't believe I was going to move again, ever. But they were all already on the trail, and if bears and porcupines were lurking around the campsite, I preferred not to meet them alone.

We started to hike again, but this time I kept up with the group. My legs burned and I kept dropping Ben's big blueberry jacket, but as the trees thinned I could make out slashes of blue sky. And without the pack, I felt light, despite my muscles' ache.

"So, if you start a list, this is your first four-thousand-footer with the club," said Linda.

"Mount Marcy is five thousand three hundred and forty-four feet," said Alan. His nose was pink. "New York's tallest."

"He's such a teacher," said Linda, grinning.

The trees got shorter and shorter until they were miniature trees, like bonsai.

"Real alpine zone," said Alan.

The sky opened into the sharp light of just-before-sunset. We were mostly walking on rock, now, and could see bands of orange and yellow forest down below.

Camilla and Nicky started to jog.

"Show-offs," said Linda.

"Careful!" yelled Alan.

They looked like goats, trotting along the rock. Strong, long legs, perfect balance—they were backlit. The light grew more intense, and the sky was a fantastic blue that even jellyfish can only dream. Then we'd caught up with them, standing in a circle of boulders slightly taller than us. Camilla pointed to a metal plate in the rock. USGS, it said. United States Geological Survey. This mountain had been counted. It felt, to me, as if we were the first ones there.

I could see everything. It didn't erase the pain, but for that second I forgot that I wanted home and bed. The sunset, the roads cutting across the landscape like snakes, the bands of greens and golds.

"Come up here," said Noah. He was on top of a boulder,

reaching his hand down. I took it. Sitting on the boulder, there was even more to see, the pink and orange expanse of sky and, below it, a wedge of blue lake. Mountains huddled all the way out to the horizon, hunched shadows of green and gray.

"Lake Champlain." Noah pointed at the lake.

He wore a wool hat and gloves and he looked warm, and dry, as if he hadn't exerted himself all day. His thighs touched mine; I was almost in his lap, because there was no more room on the rock. I started to shiver, even in Nicky's sweater.

"And behind that, more Adirondacks. I've climbed most of them, even though they're not fancy four-Ks. And behind that, the Green Mountains. Vermont."

The sky grew richer, as if it wanted to show us its full array of colors before shutting off for the night.

"Gotta get going," said Shing. He reached up and helped me off the rock.

I put on Ben's jacket and continued shivering as we started back down the peak to the campsite. Camilla and Nicky moved ahead again.

"Start dinner," Shing yelled after them. I couldn't imagine anything more necessary, at that moment, than food.

Camilla and Nicky worked their magic on the camp stoves and produced two great orange mounds of macaroni and cheese. Shing and Noah tossed the salad by throwing a garbage bag filled with torn iceberg lettuce and sliced cucumbers and carrots back and forth.

"Tossed," yelled Shing.

"Salad," answered Noah.

I couldn't believe there'd been all this food in their packs, along with tents and stoves. I'd only carried my own stuff, and my back felt like I'd been the doormat at the public library for a week. I piled the food into my ceramic bowl and shivered by Alan's fire while I ate it. Box macaroni and cheese. It was delicious.

"Hey, you carried *that*?" Noah pointed at my bowl.

"Whoa, girl, what are you, in training?" Camilla laughed. She had two plastic cups and a pair of chopsticks.

"She's going gourmet on us," said Noah.

"Right," said Linda. "Mac 'n' hack gourmet."

"When you're food planner, you can change the menu," said Camilla, waving a noodle in her chopsticks.

"I'm so beat," I said. Even speaking was an enormous effort. "Can I go to sleep?"

"Give me your bowl," said Noah. "I'll wash it out for you."

"No," I said, "I can do it. What do I have to do?"

He led me down to the stream, where I scrubbed out the cheese with leaves and water. Noah was quiet again. He had on and off moods, it seemed. Or maybe he was shy.

"Um, thanks for all your help," I said. I slipped and grabbed a tree branch behind him as we clambered back up.

"We all need help at first," said Noah. "Give me your toothpaste and anything else you've got that might smell. I'll put it in the bear bag."

I fell asleep to the murmur of voices by the campfire. At first, I thought they might say something about me, so I tried to listen. But to get warm enough, I had to wear my hat and coat, get inside the sleeping bag, and pull it over my head. I put my dress coat on top of the sleeping bag, and didn't even hear Noah and Camilla come in. But I did hear them breathing, long, loud exhalations, when I woke up in the middle of the night wondering why Ben wasn't there and why I was so wet. I was sweating inside my bag, getting sticky and colder.

I shivered. I wanted to go back to sleep and wake up to Ben's big arms, the smell of coffee and croissants in the warm oven. I pulled off the soggy down coat and started counting. But as the numbers passed all I could think of was yesterday's climb, and I realized I had to go back down every inch I'd gone up. Still, I finally fell asleep again, and when I woke up, a tree root under my head, there was green light coming in through the tent, and I smelled woods, the nylon of the tent, and some very bad breath that belonged to Camilla or Noah or else, quite possibly, to me.

Two / The odd thing is, after I came home and looked at my fresh white walls, after a bath and a nap with a real pillow and a long-awaited dinner out with Ben at Clio to celebrate his promotion at the museum, I wanted to go back. The lobster risotto slipped, salt, butter, sweet meat, across my tongue. I sipped Spanish wine. I toasted my boyfriend, thinking maybe he'd come along sometime on an Adventurers' trip, maybe when he wasn't so busy.

When I told him about it, I stuck to the highlights: the view, the piney scent, Camilla and Nicky sprinting. I de-emphasized my war wounds and didn't even show off my battered feet. Ben was too busy at work, and for once I didn't mind. I let him complain about how his new secretary had purposely Xeroxed the wrong files so he'd have to do the work himself, how he had to go to a fund-raiser while I was on my trip and wear a tuxedo, and how he felt like a pimp, selling bronze plaques in a place invented for play. I let him steal the covers, and on weekends when he slept late I watched him sleeping and thought that he looked very tired. That he could use some getting out himself.

Benjamin Shepard and I had met six months ago, when the Children's Museum hired my firm to make new booths for the entrance. It wasn't originally my assignment, but then the designer in charge quit and eloped all in one weekend, and I had to finish his work. I hated it at first: he'd planned a child-ish scrawl for the signage and hidden the admission prices inside the booths behind layers of glass. I made a few alter-ations so the signs were playful but not condescending and the booths became one long open desk with mini-exhibits built in at kid height for line-time entertainment, and Ben was so happy he kissed my forehead when I showed him the new design. My forehead had been waiting for that kiss. I'd put a lot of overtime into the project, because it was a worthy chal-lenge and possibly because Ben, with his deep blue eyes and dark hair, kept coming into the office to check on my progress. Later I learned he looked really handsome dressed up. He looked fine in sweats, too, but somehow the tie and button-down made him appear larger and brighter than life, the way a peacock with plumage spread seems to have a flock's worth of dazzling eyes. He didn't ask me out, so I had to go all the way back to the museum twice to check on the installation.

He still didn't ask me out, even when we were standing by the gigantic milk bottle that sold take-out near the pier and the moment seemed exactly right. The bay embraced the pilings; the sky peeled off a woolly layer to reveal clear blue.

"So, Hannah," he said, smoothing his grape-print tie. The guy inside the milk bottle pretended not to watch but we were the only show, parked right in front of him.

"Yes," I said. "Ben." I smiled in an open way, invitingly, I hoped.

"Yes. Well. Thank you so much. If I didn't have to go—"
He gestured toward the museum doors as if his mother were
calling from within.

"It's okay," I said, stupidly. I wanted to be braver, to simply ask him to dinner. It was obvious. But, pathetically, I
wanted him to do the asking.

So I gave up and said yes instead to gawky long-blond-
haired Ken Cillia from accounting, who turned out to be
way too tall for me and was still completely in love with the
girlfriend who'd left him two months before. He kissed like
a fish. His sweaty hands grasped my fingers all night like
they were lucky dice. I kept thinking of Ben and wondering
whether I should call him. But I couldn't think of a reasonable excuse. *Are the signs working out? Do people still come
to the museum?*

It seemed hopeless, and I mourned the missed opportunity for weeks. Then I saw Ben at a Mexican restaurant, Sol
Azteca, with his two roommates. Ben lived in a three-bedroom
apartment in Somerville with two other guys who were
never home; Mark worked at a bar and Fish was a phle-
botomist. The apartment smelled like cheese and feet, odors
that emanated from Mark and Fish's rooms, respectively.

At Sol Azteca, he stared and stared from their table
behind the pinball machines, and my friends Lora and Beth
kidded me like high schoolers. Lora was sure everyone was
interested in me, and Beth was sure everyone was interested
in Lora, and we all got along best when none of us had
boyfriends. Beth was seeing someone at the time, so she
said, "Go, Hannah, profess your true love. Or at least ask
him out."

"I think you should wait for him to ask you," said Lora,
running her finger around the rim of her margarita glass.
"He's going to."

"He isn't," I said. "Maybe I've just got cilantro on my tooth."

"Told you," whispered Lora, as Ben finally ambled over.

I had never seen him so shy. He was wearing an old sweatshirt with holes at the elbows, and he leaned so hard on our table he spilled the salsa.

"Would you like to—" he started.

"Yes," I said.

On our first date, a rainy Saturday, we went to the Boston Museum of Science.

"Isn't this too much like work?" I asked him, as we waded through a throng of families by the space capsule.

"I like museums," he said. "They're like telescopes, or microscopes, directed for you within the vast universe of possible interest."

"My goodness," I said, waiting for a punch line. But he was charmingly, earnestly serious.

I planned our second date, a trip to Walden Pond. We had to park about a mile away, because the lots were full. We walked along the poison ivy–infested breakdown lane; Ben lugged an overloaded picnic basket. He offered me his jacket as we ate bagels in the drizzle and watched insect-hopeful fish rise to meet the raindrops on the pond. He didn't complain about the walk or the weather, but the quarter-sized patch of poison ivy welts on his arm plagued him for almost a month.

On our third date, we went to the Museum of Fine Arts. We wandered through the Egyptian exhibit and then ate chicken salad with grapes in the café. The crowds clamored by on the way to a sold-out Pop Art show, and Ben told me what, as a child, he wanted to be when he grew up: a space engineer.

"I spent hours designing colonies for the different planets. Mom got me rolls of butcher paper so I could spread out in the living room. I liked making domes," he said, tracing the shape on the table. "They were like windows for looking out, but they also made the inside finite: a single drop on the planet."

"Sounds confining," I said.

"Not really; it was more about perspective—you know, how we are each just a speck on this planet, and the planet is barely a point in the Milky Way, and, at least in my imagination, the whole Virgo Supercluster is just a mote behind the left ear of a god."

He reached across and touched my ear.

"Or goddess," he said.

Ben wasn't always serious. At the movies, during the previews, he crept his hand along my thigh, holding one finger up like the head of a horse and whinnying quietly. We missed most of the features, playing, then kissing. His mouth was inquisitive and always deliciously minty, even after popcorn. On our fourth date, he gave me a hickey my friends teased me about all week.

At five-foot-six, Ben was hardly tall, but he seemed so to me, at least when we were both standing. He had a broad chest, a tiny bit more stomach than he liked, and wavy hair, which looked boyish and adorably sloppy when he didn't get it cut regularly. Since his promotion, he'd been religious about haircuts, and I missed his sudden cowlicks.

"Hey," I said, when at last he woke up. "Hey, Sleepy."

"Mmm," said Ben. He pulled at my pajamas. I loved days like this, Saturdays when we didn't have to go anywhere.

"I really think this club is for me," I said, letting him unbutton the top and skate his warm hands inside.

"Mmmm," he said.

I thought about inviting him along on the next trip so he could see for himself, but instead I slid back inside the covers.

Home was the same. I still had three flights of worn stone stairs to walk up to the tiny rent-controlled apartment in Coolidge Corner I inherited from my brother, Ted, after he got married. It had curved glass windows and a view of Beacon Street, where I watched cars weaving around one another like a herd of panicked antelopes. The radiators still hissed and clunked at night. The kitchen floor still sagged. My sister had left two messages on my machine telling me all about how she thought her new boyfriend Reed was the One because of his cute little ways and how he really loved her, unlike her last boyfriend, whom she'd dumped last month, who had only loved the idea of her and maybe her bright blond hair.

At twenty-one, my sister, Marla Blue, had never had a regular job. I thought it was time for her to have one, and I worried that Reed might be a fresh excuse. She'd never really been out in the world, having gone to a private girls' school after Mom made her money and our parents divorced. They thought Marla would be too distracted by boys in a regular school, and besides, she was a great lacrosse player, and the public school didn't have a team. Then she went to college, not a women's college, which would've trained her in something, but a girls' college, where she decided that maybe she'd become an artist, *you know, like Dad,* and that she ought to have a substantial library, because having books around you is important. Even if you haven't read very many of them.

I thought the schools were partly to blame, because Marla was not dumb. She was a decent student, and she could fix

anything: toasters, truck engines, my father's kiln thermo-
stat, the icemaker on my mother's testy fridge. She worked
with a deep concentration that changed her face, spread seri-
ousness across her eyes, and set her mouth.

I also blamed the timing of the divorce, which was right
before her eighth birthday, for her arrested development. She
seemed to take it personally—as if it were possible not to, as
if anyone could let it not be about them when their parents
divided the house's contents, living and still. Even if they
were finally on good terms; even if my father, Wolf, borrowed streams of money from my mother and ate the cookies my mother's husband, Marty Schwartz, baked in gluts.
Most of the time he talked with our mother like a decent
human now, with no more gruffness than he used with the
rest of the world. But we each bore a thousand little wounds
from the drama of that time, and I sometimes thought Marla
understood her scars the least.

When we were little, my father, an artist with waves of
moderate sales success and corresponding creative frustration, was *around*. His thick-fingered hands smelled of clay,
and crumbs of terracotta let loose from his arm hairs when
he picked me up and swung me above his head. His stubbly
cheeks darkened minutes after shaving. He had brown eyes
and lashes that were too lovely and long—like a hint of con-
cession in his plainly masculine, angular face. Dad took time
out from teaching pottery classes for teens and moms on
their evening escapes from home, or from his studio work, to
build us rope swings and to play tag with as much enthusiasm and desire to win as the next six-year-old.

He was fun and he was reckless, often making us late for
dinner, as we finished installing a sundial in the yard or a
birdhouse made from birch bark shed by a tree, or building a

two-inch-high dry-stone wall around the Japanese maple seedling by the driveway. Helping meant we held tape measures, nails, glue guns, and levels, for long half hours; it meant standing by appreciatively as he worked and gave a running narrative of how-to.

My father was chronically late. Often he was late alone, and we worried that something had happened: car wreck, train crash, heart attack. Sometimes he kept Ted and me too, and we were caught in the viscous time of his trying-to-leave trying-to-finish; I understood, in those moments, how indecision and stubbornness kept him from the ceremony at my cousin's wedding, from meeting Mom at the T before she walked home in heels and frustration. I understood how it happened to him, I hated being drawn in, and I was powerless to pull away. I missed my brother's sixth-grade play (he was Harry the Horse in *Guys and Dolls*) because I was "learning"—bored, anxious about being late, chewing my cuticle—how to hang a door properly on the garage. Dad cut his hand with the planer.

"See, Hannah," he had said, holding up his sliced hand. "See how rushing never pays?"

He put his head on his good hand for a second, clearly woozy from seeing the blood, before wrapping an old oily rag around the sawdusted wound. I was my mother's daughter, concerned about infection, but my father seemed proud of the rusty stain on his shirt as we drove too fast to the elementary school and walked into the emptying auditorium. My brother never complained about his lateness; my mother cried in public.

My mother couldn't tickle me; only my father could, practically making me pee in my pants with terror and delight just by waving his fingers in a tickly manner, five feet from my armpits. He was generally gentle, but at the time of the divorce, both our parents became livid, boisterous fighters and dragged their fights into the street.

Probably, I hadn't recovered from being afraid of my father then. We were never his targets in the war, but he vented his fury on innocent objects and always seemed as capable of cutting flesh as he was of his actual assaults—slicing coat seams with an X-acto knife, slamming the door to the library so hard a hinge broke and the wood cracked. I could imagine him flinging us the way he flung his pots, powdering his basement studio with overworked and ruined earth.

The winter of the divorce, the family outerwear was always strewn about the lawn. I don't remember seeing my parents throwing those things, but there they were when I came home from school: unmatched gloves gossiped beneath the stick-figure dogwood; scarves draped the bushes like decorations, their stitches quietly unknitting among the red yew berries.

The divorce wasn't the only possible source of Marla's arrested development; she was also a victim of her own good looks. Marla had always been gorgeous. I knew it when she was first born—even as a soft bald infant she had a glow. Only five, I still knew it was something I didn't have. In high school she was on the swim team, as I had been, but she switched to diving because she liked standing on the platform before all those eyes. I went to a meet at her school's indoor double-Olympic once, to watch and cheer. She was perfect, poised on the platform, but she dove imperfectly every time, leaving a long gash in the pool's surface as her feet flipped back. Her body was so exquisite, though, I felt

she should be given a perfect score regardless. Or maybe a
horrendous one, because what had she done to deserve it?
She got eights and nines, scores that were only slightly too
generous.

Marla was a genetic wonder. She kept her silky blond hair
long, and her eyes were clear unadulterated blue. Her lashes
were dark, so it always looked as if she were wearing mas-
cara. She was long and lean, taller than our father—five ten.
She had a scar on the back of her thigh from the time she fell
out of the car when our parents were fighting. As my mother
backed out of the driveway, Marla leaned on the door and
her knee hit the latch—or maybe she'd done it on purpose.
We were supposed to wear seat belts, and I always felt guilty
about not checking hers. She spilled onto the driveway
stones, splitting her lip and gouging her thigh on the sharp
corner of the car door. It stopped our parents, but only for a
minute. Once the wound healed, the thin silver line only
added to Marla's allure.

I was afraid Reed Scrum was the result of Marla's lack of
exposure to many men. Here she was, fresh out of college,
living in a mom-subsidized apartment, collecting books for
her library and Reed for her bedroom. She'd told me he
worked for a small software company, routing calls to the
microsupport department and managing payroll. "But
really," she'd confided in the second message, her voice high
with excitement, "he's going to be a model." I couldn't bring
myself to call her back, because the taunt, *What does Dad
think?* sat just behind my silence, waiting to make its ugly
appearance. Dad was unpredictable in judgments; he'd hated
my first serious boyfriend because he wanted to be a photog-
rapher, he'd adored my second, who was awful to me,
because he knew all about cheese, having worked in a cheese

shop in Paris one summer. I never knew whether my choices would please or upset him, but it still mattered.

My job was the same. I came back to six deadlines and a memo from the coffee chain about the coffee-picker portrait I'd selected for the wall above the comfy chairs. The hands holding the coffee cherries were too dirty and needed air-brushing, and while I was at it could I make the skin look a little lighter?

I remembered how, in college, majoring in Art History, I'd told my mother I planned to be practical—her wish for all of us being, of course, practicality and steady brilliance. Since I wasn't sure I could carry out the second part, I said I might like to work on book design or maybe even architecture. My mother wanted simultaneously to pay attention to us and to let us go: a by-product of the motherhood/desire for success conundrum that had plagued her when we were small. She was willing to worry about us—so we begrudged her hovering—and she was willing to be proud, upon occasion. My mother hauled around her guilt about the divorce and her own choice to work when we were young like an enormous essential suitcase.

Dad never seemed to feel guilt, though maybe he just hid it as well as he hid pride in his children. Dad hadn't ever expressed interest in any sort of career-minded behavior from us, though secretly I imagined designing or building something so exotic and noteworthy that even he would be incapable of withholding his pride. When I told him about the position I'd landed, just out of college, I might have exaggerated a little about the design work involved. He sighed and held up one hand as if to wave the job away.

"I guess that's one way to squander your talents," he said.

At the time, I was fiercely insulted, but it was the closest thing to a compliment I'd heard from him that I could remember.

I kept thinking about the trip, about the forest scent. The view. My heels were blistered for a week, and I had to wear sensible shoes to work, but I kept remembering the peak, sitting on that boulder with Noah, higher than anything, and recalling the moment when I had slumped against my pack at the campsite, too tired to take it off. My memory had already reduced the discomforts to a thin bitterness that enhanced the sweet; I couldn't wait for the next time.

November and December. Two expeditions. They were what I looked forward to most, when I was standing on the T on the way to work or trying to get Lemon to start so I could repark it on the opposite side of the street to avoid another ticket. The night of the next meeting, I skipped a movie with Lora to go to Caffè Paradiso. Lora complained that Beth had a date and I was getting too caught up in Ben, that I didn't have time for her anymore. I didn't correct her; I just apologized. For the November trip, winter camping at Lonesome Lake, I missed meeting Ben's pregnant sister, who was in town for the weekend.

I rode to New Hampshire in Noah's car. I was trying not to feel guilty, as if I'd chosen Noah over Ben, when, at 5:30 A.M., I met Noah's girlfriend, Jenni with an *i*. She was almost gorgeous, except for a too-small nose, and she was surely too young for him—about Marla's age, I guessed. Jenni stank up the car with rose perfume, and they sat in the front and I sat in back with the food supplies. I wanted to sleep, but the perfume kept me from drifting off—that and knowing what I was in for. I was still the same sluggish wimp among the androids. And who would baby-sit me while Noah was busy with Jenni?

By the time we stopped for gas and breakfast at Franconia Notch in New Hampshire, I was exhausted from being awake. I gave myself a silent pep talk as we ate greasy diner eggs and Linda and Alan showed us the route and Jenni held onto Noah's arm like a lost child. I would keep up this time. I would show them Hannah Blue was tough enough for the Adventurers' Club. At the trailhead, I stuffed more than my share of food supplies in my pack to show I could take the weight.

I was much better prepared this time. I'd procured improved gear—I found my old Girl Scout backpack in my mother's basement and bought a new giant bag for the frame. A child-size frame, adult gear space; it was just right for me. I wore silk liners and wool socks so I wouldn't get blisters, and I started out fast, matching two of my steps to one of Noah's long strides. But by the time I was overlooking the Pemigewasset River on the Lonesome Lake Trail, my pace was almost half the speed of the others. The river was a churn of dead leaves and stones. We had to cross on stepping stones; I slipped and soaked one foot to the cuff, but I didn't fall. I imagined it the whole time, falling on my face, pinned by my pack, drowning in a foot of icy water.

"Hey, Hannah," said Linda, as she watched me slip, "don't think about it. Just keep walking."

"Okay," I said, thinking very hard.

After the crossing, the group took off again, Noah's bumblebee pack one of the first to vanish into the woods ahead. I found myself walking with Jenni and discovered I didn't hate her, despite her perfume. She was slower, even, than I was, and it turned out she was thirty-five and had met Noah at a bar and she was a lawyer and probably would never go hiking again. She kept asking me questions about him, as if I knew him better.

"He's so quiet," she said. "Cute but quiet. I thought maybe I'd get to know him on this hike. I—" She stopped and leaned against her knee in a familiar pose of fatigue. "I had no *idea*," she finished.

I was the fast and brave one, keeping her company, and it made me feel almost as good as the view from Kinsman Peak.

In December, I almost didn't go. The night before, I was packing up my gear—plastic cup and chopsticks, wool sweater, Ben's trusty jacket, and a brand-new compass and topographical map of the White Mountains Crawford Notch area—when the phone rang. Ben was away on a museum retreat, so I wavered. If it was Ben, he'd start talking into the machine. If it was my father—well, it wasn't; my father never called. If it was Marla, she'd keep talking about Reed forever and I'd never get my new Gore-Tex raincoat properly seam-sealed or my boots dried out with newspaper blotters. I had let everything molder in my pack by the door during the month since Franconia.

"Hel-*lo*," said my mother, shouting into the machine. "Hannah Blue, you need to talk to your mother." She sounded important, as usual. She had a rich round voice: compelling, commanding. The voice of guilt and pleasure all rolled into one short stout body.

"Hi," I said, picking up. "I couldn't get to the phone—"

"Right, you had to run all the way across your giant living room." My mother loved the tiny apartment but thought I should borrow money to buy it and then buy the place next door, so I could knock down walls and expand. She even offered to give me a loan, which is the last thing I wanted. I wondered what she thought I needed all that space for. She and Marty slid around in her great house like the last sips of milk in an almost-empty container. The high ceilings made my mother look like a midget.

"So?" I didn't invite more discussion of the apartment.

"So," my mother intoned. On the phone, you'd think my mother was a thirty-year-old opera star. In person, she was a sixty-one-year-old surgeon and professor who had made a lot of money by inventing a special slow-dissolving material for muscle repair sutures. She was Important and Busy and Grand and looked like me, short and strong, only about a hundred pounds heavier, with green eyes like my brother, Ted.

"So you need to come for dinner."

I tried to breathe slowly. *Need* to come. As always, I almost asked the wrong first question: Is Dad okay?

Family dinner was always a torturous evening, with my father agitating around the edges of his old house while Marty was civil and still. It couldn't be urgent, I told myself; in the case of accident or death my mother would call crying; she wouldn't offer chicken with pearl onions and polenta with roasted peppers and Marty's special chocolate layer cake. Still, I didn't like mandatory family dinner; we'd been "invited" to family therapy and later told about the divorce over family dinner.

When Ted and Abby announced their engagement over family dinner, my mother drew me into her kitchen to express her concerns because Abby was "a very nice *goy-isheh* girl." As if my mother herself hadn't married a goy, my father. But then she'd married Marty Schwartz next. Still, I noticed, she'd never changed her name back to the original Weinberg or on to Schwartz. She was still Maridel Blue. She made jokes about Marty and herself as being black and blue. But she kept my father's name. And my father—well, he had flirted gruffly with Abby at the rehearsal dinner but sat at the back of the room during the ceremony, cleaning his camera lens with an ancient tissue.

"Okay," I said, pointedly not asking why I needed to come to dinner.

I was afraid it might be one of my father's staged dramas. Once he'd called us all together at my mother's house to announce that he was *done* with art; once he'd given us each a precious belonging (I received a dented metal mini-globe from his childhood) because his own father had died unexpectedly at fifty-two and my father had turned that same age the week before and expected the worst. He'd made it past the age of crisis, of course.

I was exhausted from twenty-six years of worrying about my father, and recently, while we sat together at an awkward party for Marla's completion of college and he explained how lead glazes had poisoned him, I decided I was through practicing distress over his imagined crises.

"But I can't come this weekend, I have a trip."

"A trip? What kind of trip?"

"A hiking trip. Let's do it when I come back. Unless someone's dying."

"In December?"

"Don't change the subject."

"The Saturday after next, then. I'll call back if your brother or sister can't make it." She wouldn't mention Dad, though probably it was about Dad. Everything was about Dad.

Ted and Marla always made it to my mother's dinners, though usually Ted was very late, unless Abby came. When Abby came, he was almost on time, and he was even able to talk sometimes. She squeezed and tickled him at the table to crack his special family shellac. We all loved Abby, even my father. She was Ted's height, about five-seven, and pale beside his dark Semitic looks, with long sandy hair she kept in a braid down her back. She never wore makeup but always looked clean and fresh. It was easy to imagine her as someone's mother, though Ted said they weren't going to do that: parenthood. Abby looked like the grade-school teacher you truly loved. And, in fact, she taught third grade and her car was full of children's first love letters. *Be mine, Miss Bloom.*

After I got off the phone it occurred to me that the crisis must be Marla and Reed. Marla must be planning to marry Reed Scrum, and in my mother's mind that was an enormous disaster. Not only did Reed Scrum sound like a dud, but Marla was only twenty-one. My father would not tolerate it. He'd probably blame my mother. Or, worse, he'd say nothing. And my mother, with her needle-sharp intelligence, couldn't bear her children doing things that were really stupid. After all, she'd only been twenty-one when she and my father married, and it took her thirteen years to get around to medical school, and another ten to make her fortune.

This time, I had to agree. I hadn't met Reed, though he sounded emptier than a hand puppet. I wrote FAMILY on the appropriate Saturday block of my date book. Then I sighed and went back to drying my boots.

Camilla, Shing, and Noah all brought snowshoes to Mount Isolation. Jenni hadn't returned, so I was at the back of the pack again. I was so proud of my new raincoat and the rain pants I'd borrowed, I hadn't even thought about the snow. I crunched and sank along behind Linda on the Dry River Trail in a persistent drizzle that painted shimmering slicks on the crusty three-foot-deep drifts. At least my jacket kept the top half of my body from getting excessively wet. But Shing and Camilla and Noah were making waffle prints along the surface, leaving Linda and me far behind. Alan was somewhere in between, even though he had no snowshoes. I was beginning to think I would never catch up on any trip; I had obviously chosen the wrong hobby. Maybe Ben and I would take up Rollerblading.

"Um, Linda?"

I was talking to the back of her jacket. With each step she sank to her knees. With each step I sank to my crotch.

"Um, Linda?" I said it louder. I longed for something to interrupt the quiet drilling sound of rain on my hood.

"Oh, did you say something, Hannah?" Linda stopped, with effort, and turned around to face me.

"I, uh, wondered when you went on your first club trip."

"Oh. Alan invited me." The sliver of her face that was visible through the hood, neck gaiter, and pulled-up turtleneck was shining and pink. "It was caving. I was terrified. I'm not big on cramped spaces."

I imagined Linda falling down Alice's rabbit hole.

"And there were bats. Alan loves bats. But I'm kind of afraid of them, at least I used to be." She turned and started trudging again, so her story was muffled in the crush of our steps. "But something kept me coming back. Not just Alan. Though he was certainly an incentive."

Adventurers' romance. I wondered how many of the people I'd met had been couples, or had had crushes. Still, the club's driving force had to be the trips, not the romance.

"Is it pretty much always the same people?" I asked. This trip had a smaller subset of members—no Nicky or Jenni. I'd met everyone from the photographs I'd spied in the copy room, except the laughing Indian man. At a meeting, I'd asked Linda about him. "Vijay," she'd said, in a muted voice. Then she cleared her throat and started talking about food planning.

"Oh, some people are only interested in spring and summer trips. Fair-weather hikers. Not as brave as us. Though the summer trip is pretty much always the same group."

"Summer trip?"

"We have a big trip in the summer, two weeks. Last year we went to the Wind Rivers in Wyoming; the year before that was Peru."

"And next summer?"

"I think the Olympics and Baker."

"Which are?"

"Oh, in Washington State. Some day trips, a little ice climbing, rope work, mostly backpacking."

For the rest of our trudge, I knew what I wanted to do. I wanted to go on the summer trip. If it took jogging every day to get into shape, if it took begging for the block of time off from work, if it meant quitting my job—a sudden gleaming thought—I'd have to do it. I needed that candy at the end of my maze.

"According to the guidebook," said Camilla, rubbing her bare hands together, "water is plentiful everywhere except here, the top of Montalban Ridge."

"Let me help you." Noah took her hands and put them inside his jacket, lifting his sweater. I wanted to be those hands.

"Hah," said Alan. "Water, water, everywhere." I was working with him, trying to stomp an even platform for the tent into the wet snow. We'd borrowed the others' snowshoes and I felt giddy, walking over the snow instead of sinking through it. My legs were soaked despite the rain pants. My lips were chapped from licking. But Linda and I had made it together, even if I was slightly behind her; no one had had to baby-sit me.

And after the tents were set up, I helped Camilla make the spaghetti. The stove started and stopped, belching like an ancient boat motor.

"Ooh, going gourmet," said Shing. He'd already promised something better, something different, when he was on chow duty. The spaghetti was the work of Linda and Alan. Next trip I'd do the food planning with Shing. We'd collect the money and go shopping. I felt like I was starting to belong.

I tore the lettuce and washed it with snow melted on another stove. The ice chunks hurt my hands, and I watched the skin fade from red to white.

"Hey, put your gloves on," Shing said to me, his voice surprisingly sharp.

Noah looked up at Shing with a quick enigmatic expression. Then he resumed flipping through his wild edibles guide from his perch on a folding seat.

"Find us any snowberries?" Camilla waved a chopstick at Noah.

"Dingleberries?" said Shing, who was trying to ignite wet wood. His voice was casual again.

"Yuck," said Noah. He took my hands, as he had with Camilla's, and put them inside his shirt. He pulled them up against his very warm, smooth chest. Somehow I'd imagined he'd be hairy, but there was no more than a fine fuzz on his hot skin. My hands felt so good, warming against him, such a simple comfort, that I shoved any guilt for other pleasures down deep, under the snow, where it would have to wait for spring.

In the morning, I woke with my face pressed against the tent and Linda crushing me from above. We'd melted our tent platform with body heat and were rolling down the ridge in slow motion. I wadded my waterlogged bag into my pack and we ate wet granola and started the slog back down. At the bottom of the trail, as afternoon started its squeeze on early evening, Noah and Camilla were waiting by the trail-head sign, stripped down to T-shirts and rain pants, their snowshoes strapped to their packs. Everything had melted; at the bottom of the mountain, the trail had become a muddy river. There was a tenuous glow to the fading sunshine.

The Boston Globe, waiting in my mailbox, told me that while we'd been slogging up Mount Isolation, the Boston weekend had seen record high temperatures for December. Some fool forsythias had bloomed, and the parks had been full of couples on Rollerblades.

Three / My brother, Ted Bloom, made obscene sculptures out of shrubbery for a living. He started out in landscape design when he and Abby lived in New York and he'd just given up the idea of vet school, because his undergraduate grades from Cornell were a few points too low and because he didn't really like blood or cysts or needles, he merely loved animals. He and Abby had recently gotten married, and they combined their surnames, Blue and Throm, to make Bloom—an auspicious name for Ted, given the profession he was about to happen upon. Abby was in graduate school at Columbia for teaching, and Ted found himself wandering in the New York Botanical Gardens in the Bronx. Then he found himself in school there.

Ted did a lot of finding; he always had. It surprised me, because he didn't have the look of someone lost. He wasn't very tall or very loud, and, inexplicably, he had the lone Boston accent in the family. It only intensified when he moved to New York and came back again. He said *way-ah* for where and *wick-it* for wicked, meaning very. Ted made a prickly first impression; some people thought he was cold or snobbish, but I believed it was the coating that kept him safe from the world.

Ted took care of us during the divorce, while Mom and Dad were lost in their respective battles and passions. Ted kept Marla and me from falling too far into the rift. Marla was almost eight, I was thirteen, and Ted was the most adult sixteen-year-old in Newton, Massachusetts. He made lunches and signed notes for school. A shaky learner's-permit driver, he took us out for dinner in Dad's car while Dad was buried in his ceramics studio and Mom was at another conference or meeting or appointment with her first post-Dad love, her lawyer. We went to International House of Pancakes and ordered grand envelopes of crepes with blueberries and whipped cream, and French fries on the side. Ted paid with the change he harvested from the dog dishful Mom kept on the mail table in the front hall.

Now Ted knew about Boston's secret gardens. As we walked down an urban street with him, he might point to a curved metal gate revealing only a heavy wood door and whisper, "There's a courtyard—Blanche sweet lilac and Korean spice viburnum." Then, almost as punctuation, he'd add, *"Syringa hyacinthiflora, Viburnum carlesi,"* as if the Latin were necessary to finish his sentence. Sometimes, in ordinary conversation, he'd mask the Latin incantation with his fist over his mouth, as if coughing. But the more nervous he got, the more Latin you'd hear. Our father hated it; I was never sure whether he was embarrassed or just jealous that he didn't know the names himself.

After private gardens of the ordinary, Ted was known for

his talent in fulfilling garden fetishes. He worked wonders with espalier shapes: fuchsia, magnolia, and dwarf fruit trees trained into candelabras, vast fans, and faux fountains along walls or grafted into English fences. His topiary work won all sorts of awards, and he was willing to make great phalluses or mating nymphs in addition to life-size elephants and elegant green horses. He went to California to design a massive orgy of men, carved into a circle of sweet bay and Kaffir lime in a ring around a fountain. Three times a year he flew to San Diego to trim the sculpture back into submission.

The last time Ted and I had talked, right before the trip to Mount Isolation, he had been commissioned to make a weed garden for a private company's courtyard. Usually, he planted and tended the expensive and rare, or at least cultivated, so it was fun, he said, to see what he could do with the generally unloved. The company chair thought weeds would make a statement about their environmental consciousness. Ted thought it was hilarious to be planting cattails and cinquefoil and scarlet pimpernel in a glassed-in courtyard with a timed watering system and a fake waterfall, but he was always up for a challenge.

Ben was also up for a challenge. We were talking from our offices, each leaning into our padded chairs. I imagined him as we spoke, swinging his chair in lazy half-circles, one finger rubbing behind his ear, his eyes bright despite the dull fluorescent light.

"So, tomorrow's Saturday night, does that mean we should be doing something wild?"

"I'm sick of the whole holiday business," I said. "Let's go somewhere with no soggy Christmas music and no left-over New Year's drivel. Let's go to the Bahamas."

"Okay," said Ben. "I'll see if I can get a table for two."

I opened the new page in my date book and doodled on the squares. "Oh, shit," I said.

"I guess that means the whole island's booked."

"Hah. I wish. I have to go to my mother's on Saturday."

"Okay," said Ben. "How 'bout I come along?"

Ben had met my mother once. We went to dinner in a former nunnery in Newton and Ben charmed her, despite the dank air and the too-buttery food. Ben liked my mother. He ducked his head slightly when he spoke to her, grinning and blushing. Her research was fascinating, he said, and the two of them launched an elaborate plan to use her suture material for temporary space shuttle repairs or, alternatively, in a museum exhibit to teach children about surgery. She called him honey and kissed his cheek good-bye, leaving her indelible lipstick signature. My father was the one I worried about. So far, he had canceled two dates with me and Ben. He had a show to go to once, and the second time he called after we'd left to meet him and told the machine, "Hannah, I can't make it." We got the message after waiting at No Name Seafood for three hours. Then, slightly drunk from our three beers of waiting, we bought take-out chowder and came home. My father never explained and never said he was sorry.

"You're so good, but it's a horrible family thing, and I don't think it'll be fun."

"You'll be there, so it can't be too bad."

I sighed. He was being obliging, but I wasn't sure which was worse, family dinner with Ben or without.

"It's a family thing."

"Well, that's okay," he said, with an almost imperceptible sigh. "I didn't mean to invite myself."

"So Sunday, instead?"

"Yes. Gotta go."

After we hung up, Ted called.

"I don't want to go," he said. His voice was flat.

"So," I said, "don't."

"Right," said Ted. "And miss Marty's cheese toasts and Mom and Dad together?"

"Sounds lovely to me."

"I think I have to be there for this one," he said. "Oh, and Mom said it's going to be catered."

"Catered? Why does she bother?"

"I can't tell you." He sighed.

"Any new weeds?" I asked, trying to alleviate his doldrums.

"I don't think there's any such thing as a new weed. I just added yellow dock," he said. "*Rumex persicarioides*. The stem sheaths look exactly like labia."

"Oh, goody. Perfect for the corporate world."

"Plus you can eat the leaves."

It made me think of Noah and his wild edibles. Which reminded me of his smooth chest thawing my hands. And I heard the echo of Ben's tiny sigh.

I called Ben back.

"Please please please come with me to my horrible awful family dinner," I said. "My brother told me my mother's having it catered."

"Well, catered!" said Ben. "And a chance to meet the elusive Wolfgang Blue." He laughed. "If you put it that way, I'll even wear a tie."

We drove to Newton in Ben's new black VW. I felt itchy everywhere, my hands, my stocking-clad feet, under my skin. My father called Volkswagens "Nazi cars" with a personal vengeance, though the Blues were safely, Waspishly ensconced in Boston during World War II. My father's presence at my mother's house always made me nervous. Of course, it used to be his house. He'd hung his many coats in the massive closet in the entryway; he'd shared the queen cherrywood bed, which was now my mother's bed with Marty. He'd kept his kilns and clay and wheels and the wide concrete slab on which he sculpted in the basement, and even though he'd moved out most of the equipment and my mother had replaced it with bookshelves crowded with medical journals, the basement still held the smell of clay and glazes. My father held the smell of clay and glazes, earth and elements, in his powdery, thick hands, in his squally, mostly white hair.

My father's art was sculpture, or pottery, depending on how you looked at it. He made clay vessels—usually hand built and exquisite in their minute detail and seamless shapes—that couldn't hold anything. Deliberate gaps in the seams or bottom slits ruined any attempt at containment. It was his specialty: useless beauty. At first, a lot of his work found its way into galleries, but he didn't change his concept over time, and the idea grew less fresh. He could make gorgeous functional objects on the wheel and sometimes did. He made Ted and Abby a whole set of luminous moth-silver porcelain bowls and handleless mugs for the wedding. But mostly he made his vessels—when he was working and not brooding.

I could still envision him leaning over his concrete table, a smear of slip from lip to cheekbone, smoothing a seam with his finger, his whole body attentive to the task.

"Close the door," he'd call gruffly, as I stood at the top of the stairs. I'd been glad he'd managed to notice me, even if it was only the result of the light and draft I'd introduced as interruption.

One of the big fights my father used to have with my mother was about getting treatment for his depression. He felt that leaning on medicine for relief from one's woes was a sign of weakness. He also believed that most surgeries were unnecessary, most doctors suspiciously interested in drugs and cutting.

Mom was practical; until they divorced, she could be relied on to put his and our worries before any of her own. She once missed an exam she needed to pass to finish her premed work, because he was having trouble working and I had a cold. Sometimes I wondered whether she now longed for the excuse of us; despite all her successes, our father could still derail her. I wondered what their conversations were like, how he'd convinced her to organize that dinner when he announced he was giving up art. Did he tell her what he planned? It was a ludicrous exercise; all he really wanted was the dramatic weather we made when assembled like elements of a storm.

My father took huge loans from Marty and Mom—they insisted they didn't mind—and he lived in a cramped apartment in Watertown. I worried about him; he generated a sense of constant danger, as if we might lose him if one of us stopped thinking about him, as if somehow he needed us for all that anxious animation. Only Marla seemed immune to the worry.

"So, will he like me?" Ben had been joking, all the way over, about the different names of the Newtons—Newton Centre and Newton Upper Falls and Newton Highlands and Newtonville and Newton Corner and West Newton—so his question caught me in a silent brood.

"Oh," I said.

"Wait, is this Newton Lower Falls? South Newton Square?"

"Upper Falls. I told you."

"Is there a Middle Falls?"

"He's not at his best at her house. I'm sorry. Don't let him bother you." I was saying it for myself as much as for Ben.

"I'll do *my* best," he said, as we wound down the drive.

My mother's house squatted on its lot at the bottom of a hill like a fat spider in a web. It was gray, with fine filigree woodwork and a widow's walk. When we first moved in, the gutters were ruined and the roof had soggy spots. We'd been living in rented houses and my parents wanted something grand for their first home, so they bought a fixer-upper. Neither of them qualified for the job, though, so for the first five or six years we lived there many rooms were uninhabitable.

There was a ballroom on the third floor, someone's fantasy, with a slick black-and-white-square marble floor. We weren't supposed to go inside because the marble had cracked and the exposed ceiling beams were loose, but Marla and I used to play Broadway Stars in the ballroom anyway. I was nine, still young enough to let a four-year-old play with me, to imagine with her for an hour or so. We slid on the marble floor and sang out what show tunes we knew, "The Sound of Music" and "Gonna Wash That Man Right Out of My Hair," and swung each other around by both arms.

We never went into the attic, because we didn't need the space for anything and because my parents were afraid of what damage they might discover, water or insect hives or bats or the secrets of past residents. We each chose a bedroom and my father helped us decorate, using an unorthodox method of spray paint and papier-mâché collages, and we nested in other rooms when we got bored. Ten bedrooms, four bathrooms, the ballroom, two living rooms, a den, a library, six fireplaces. And thousands and thousands of dollars in necessary repairs. By the time our parents split, though, my mother had the money to start. Even now, she still called the carpenter monthly for dry rot, beam restoration, or unfinished molding, and last year she'd had a huge crew come in to replace the ancient asbestos-wrapped furnace with a more modern model.

My father used to build things in the yard—uneven benches and cairns marking out his idea of hiking trails through the little birch woods and past the algae-wadded pond. He erected bird feeders and birdhouses everywhere on the acre and a half, but since he'd moved out they had been empty. He was always threatening to fill them, as if that might insult my mother's new fancy landscaping: she'd hired my brother to create a hedge maze with a fountain at the center and a grove of cherries and figs. Each year he updated with annuals. Mom bought stone benches and had an irrigation system installed in the pond. But she'd left my father's bird feeders empty, like ghosts among the new life of the yard.

I kept a key to my mother's house on my chain, but out of respect—and maybe fear of finding something I didn't want to see—I always rang the bell. It felt odd, ringing my own old doorbell. I felt shut out, but also older and safer than when I lived there.

"I just hope she isn't pregnant," my mom whispered as she kissed me. "Hello, dear Benjamin," she said, salmon-lipsticking his ear. She was wearing red pumps and a red suit, and her hair looked newly brown. I hadn't really thought about it before, but her hair probably required regular coloring to obscure the gray.

She whisked back into the kitchen, leaving me to look at my sister, Marla, lounging on the portly ivy-pattern couch with one of her legs draped over Reed's lap. Reed looked so young I almost laughed. He had a chiseled chin with a centered dimple and smooth skin and icy eyes.

"At last," said Marla. "You're here, Hannah! This is Reed."

Reed nodded at me.

"This is Hannah and Ben, and if Hannah marries Ben, she can change her name to Hannah Shepard. It would be so much nicer than *Blue*. I keep telling her she should." Marla winked at Ben.

I sighed, unable to reply except by shaking Reed's hand and kissing Marla's cheek.

"Cream cheese," said Ted, slouching in from the kitchen. "Hi, everyone."

A woman wearing a little black serving outfit, complete with hat and apron, followed him with a tray. Ted had phyllo flaking off his lips.

"Dad's not here," said Marla. "And Abby isn't even coming." She was nervous. Her leg twitched in Reed's lap.

"Hey, Ben," said Ted. "The mushroom caps are pretty tasty."

"Why not?" I looked at Marla, then at Ted. I took two crab cakes off the waitress's proffered doily. They were sweet and oily and delicious. My back itched, but I couldn't reach the spot.

"Why not what?" said Marla. She let the waitress bend to offer her appetizers, then inspected and took nothing. Reed nodded. I wondered whether he was mute.

"Why isn't Abby here?"

"Can we talk about something else?" Ted murmured.

"Well!" said my mother, sweeping back into the room.

"Mom," said Marla. "Reed's a vegetarian. Hannah, what do you think of changing your name? I mean, really. Would you?"

Obviously, she had marriage on the brain. But to this statue of a boy?

"Reed," I said. I was trying to think of something to say. "Um, so."

"Look," said Ted. "Dad's here, out in the yard."

I looked out the wide new window at the naked birches and the sweep of cold-bleached grass that led down to the pond. My father was stumping around the lawn, heaving a hefty paper sack. He looked dark against the backdrop of silvery trees; wrapped in an old overcoat, with his big barrel chest, he looked more like a moving monument than a man.

"What is he doing?" At last Reed spoke. His voice matched his name: skinny and hollow. He had a Boston accent, which I found a tiny bit endearing.

My father, as if answering his question, spilled an outburst of birdseed on the ground as he reached up to fill one of his orphaned feeders.

Dinner was served in multiple courses. There were delicious, slightly bitter, grapefruit palate-cleansing sorbets. The thin lobster bisque was salty, too salty for me, and served with an orange nasturtium blossom as garnish. I picked up the flower after tasting the soup.

"You can eat it," said Ted. I realized he was talking to Ben, not me, that Ben was holding his flower in his spoon, looking contemplative. I reached under the table and squeezed his solid knee. My father kept getting up from the table to stand at the living room window.

"Wolf," said my mother. "Stop that. Come sit down."

"Really?" Ben lifted his nasturtium suspiciously and took a tiny nibble.

"It's okay, Mare," said Marty. He looked dwarfed by my mother, his gray sweater flanking her red suit.

"But it isn't," she said.

My father sat again, picking seeds from his sleeve. He placed them carefully beside his fork.

"You let them starve," he said. "They came expecting food." He stood up again and went to the window.

"It's been years, Wolf. I think they've learned," said my mother.

Reed cracked ice cubes in his teeth. He hadn't eaten anything but the salad.

"The goldfinches may never return," my father continued, as if she'd said nothing.

"Peppery," said Ben.

"Well, I'm sorry your precious birds suffered," said my mother. "Maybe you shouldn't have given them such grand expectations." Marty squeezed her hand and smiled apologetically.

"*Tropaeolum majus*," whispered Ted. I wondered why he was so nervous and why Abby wasn't there. I knew he'd tell me if we had a moment alone.

We used to play sardines in the house, with my friends and sometimes Ted's, though he had few. And with Marla, but only because she begged. One person would hide and everyone else would seek, cramming themselves in along with the hider in one of the many window seats, in the slanted fourth-floor closets, in the dumbwaiter that ran from kitchen to basement, in the splintery pantry closets that rose from floor to fourteen-foot ceiling; less imaginatively, in the claw-foot tub in my parents' bathroom. Sometimes we forgot to tell Marla to stop looking after everyone else had discovered the hiding place. We'd have moved on to tormenting wasps under the rhododendron or Truth or Dare, and Marla would wander out from the house with a worried look on her face. "Did I find it?" she'd ask.

"Mom, did you read that article in the *Globe* about hospital management?" I was trying to distract her. I still felt a primal need to distract my parents from each other. When they fought, before the first official separation, I used to make noise, yell something loud. Sometimes I even pretended to hurt myself, or that Marla was hurt. "Baby!" I'd cry. "The baby's *crying*." Sometimes Marla obliged, even when she was seven and hardly a baby anymore. Sometimes my mother looked over blankly, a perfunctory check, before resuming their fight.

I wondered whether Marla was pregnant. My mother was pregnant when she and my father got married, but she'd had a miscarriage in the second trimester.

"We stopped getting the *Globe*," said Marty.

"*The New York Times* is so much better," said my mother. She looked as if she wanted to get up and tackle my father, but Marty held her hand fast.

"No comics," said my father, sitting down and placing his napkin on his lap with a gesture of finality. He smiled as he dug into his salmon-and-braised-leek frittata, which he hadn't let the waitress clear before the soup.

"I know." Marty grinned, conspiratorial.

My father had had girlfriends for a while after the divorce, but they were all completely wrong, and I was relieved when none of them stuck. Mom dated a huge array of men—they'd accompanied her to benefits, to greasy spoons, and to movies at Chestnut Hill Mall—and when she settled with Marty, I was surprised, in a way, that he wasn't

younger or somehow more dramatic. But he could make
pierogi. Her mother would have loved him. He wasn't my
father, and he was exactly right.

Over the decorous chocolate sampler plates—miniature
chocolate mousse with mint sprigs, individual warm chocolate cakes, chocolate finger cookies, and chocolate-dipped
strawberries, white and dark, a candied violet in the plate's
center—my mother tapped her fork against her water glass. I
felt the tone in my stomach like a quick jab. First Marla
would make her announcement, then Mom her reproach,
then Marla would turn to Ben and me, growing shrill. My
father would make some pronouncement with great authority, something subtly rude and unpredictable. Ted would grow
quieter and quieter and then let loose an explosion of broth-
erly protection. Reed would probably say something unbear-
ably stupid: declare his undying love. Dad would bellow;
Reed would duck. I scratched at my ankle, then my wrist.

"So, I believe we all know we aren't just here for fabulous
food." Mom's lipstick had dulled.

"I'd hoped Abby would join us tonight," said my father,
directing that terrifying beam of attention across the table at
his son. My father cleared his throat, and we all stiffened.

I wanted to rescue Ted. I used to rescue him at school
sometimes, when we overlapped in elementary, and then a
single year in high school. I'd see Ted out by the back steps
where all the leather jackets went to smoke cigarettes or pot
and pick fights. He was hovering. Sometimes they asked him
to be lookout. Usually this was when someone was going to
get caught, and Ted was smart enough to know he'd be the
sacrificial lamb, but he did it anyway, just to please them.

It wasn't that he didn't have the occasional friend; it was
that they were never anything like him: one jock, a football

player named, sadly, Jock, who got help with his chemistry homework and told Ted about his girlfriend woes; Jimmy Zeek, whom Ted tried to save from a cocaine habit; thin smart girls who wore baggy black clothes and heavy eyeliner and followed him around talking about music in scratched, sexy voices.

Out by the school's back steps I would call to Ted. When I needed him, he came. That was how I saved him, by needing him. But protecting him against my father was another matter.

Maybe the divorce was hardest on Ted. He had to take three jobs to make it through college, because they were fighting about money and he couldn't get much in the way of loans because of Mom's income. She wanted to pay, but it was part of the battle. Or maybe it was hardest for Marla, because she got everything, so she never really understood what had happened.

"Actually," said Ted, talking to the candied violet left on his dessert plate, "Abby had a great suggestion for the weed garden. Indian tobacco for the blue." He paused and looked quickly at my father. "*Lobelia inflata*," he said.

"So," said my father, slamming his big hand on the table. The spoons jumped and his smile was odd. "I'm dying," he said.

"Hm. Do you mean something new"—Ted's hands hovered close to my father's, by the sip-stained wineglasses—"or just that you're getting older?"

"Lupus," my father said.

He was always proclaiming diseases. Once he was sure he had skin cancer, but my mother's dermatologist friend discovered only a plain mole grown with age and two skin tags. He wasn't a hypochondriac, exactly, but he did declare dramatic diagnoses for minor symptoms.

"Are you sure, Dad?" I felt like I had to say something.

"Lupus is highly treatable," said my mother.

"Expert opinion says I'm dying," Dad said, and smiled sardonically.

"Who's your doc?" Mom asked, sounding solicitous. Marty wiped his mouth, squared his chair, and went into the kitchen.

Ben turned to me, his mouth tight with concern, and gripped my hand.

"He's always okay," I said quietly. "It's never as bad as he makes it sound."

Ben's mouth relaxed a little, while my parents talked disease details.

"Eminently treatable," my mother said. She looked sure.

Ted twirled his fork and Reed folded his napkin into squares, shook it out, and folded it again. Marla leaned in, as if memorizing the information.

I was tired of expecting the worst. Always, the worry was wasted. This time, I vowed to believe my mother's off-the-cuff prognosis, if my father did in fact have the disease he'd selected.

Ben was quiet on the ride home. I wasn't sure whether to excuse my family, whether to mention them at all. I said something about work as we clumped up the stairs. Ben asked whether he could stay over and followed me as I crumpled on the couch.

"Nice weather," I said.

"Yes indeedy," said Ben.

"They're not always this bad," I said, closing my eyes. "But sometimes they're worse."

"I think he likes me," Ben sat beside me and folded his arms around me like a blanket.

"Yeah, at least Marty's easy," I said.

"No, I mean your dad," said Ben. He laughed weakly. "He was very attentive."

Silently, I thanked him for not asking about the possible medical outcomes, for not making me repeat the truth of my father's overreaction. "Sure," I said, forcing a small laugh. "I told you your girlfriend came from crazies."

"They're not that bad. Ted's funny, and Reed seemed nice enough."

"He's always so *angry*. As if Ted were trying to embarrass him. And Reed looks like a piece of wheat; he didn't say anything. They *are* that bad."

"Every family comes with its—well, history. Did you always eat like that? How come you're not fat?"

"My father is always okay," I said. Ben swayed as he held me, rocking. It wasn't soothing, though it should have been.

Four / The Thursday before the January cross-country skiing trip in Vermont, I woke up with that rush of energy from childhood, the thrill of realizing it's a snow day without even having to look out the window. My alarm hummed half Spanish pop, half static. The light was muted by snow, remote and bright as starlight.

"Don't get up," said Ben, pulling me closer to him.

I wanted to turn off the alarm, but he held me tight. I kissed him and tried to roll away. I had to wrench my neck to squirm loose and shut off the music.

"So," said Ben, as if continuing an established conversation. "Do you want to come along next time I go to my sister's?" I wondered whether this was something he'd been storing, waiting to ask.

"Sure, if I can get away," I said. I wasn't fooling him. Ben's sister Kate lived in New Jersey with her husband John, a very involved father and history professor at Rutgers, and two children. Three children—she'd have the third one soon. Ben adored his niece and nephew, and whenever he came back from a trip to New Jersey, he glowed with father potential. I heard about crawling and baby teeth and new words and adorable bargainings at bedtime. It made me happy and it made me nervous. I knew that wasn't what I wanted now and felt I shouldn't have to decide whether I wanted it, ever. I liked kids, they were fresh and elastic and said things you didn't expect, but that didn't mean I was equipped for parenting. My own parents hadn't exactly been ideal models. Ben's were. During Ben's cookie-scented tender years, his mother had a part-time job as a children's librarian, guiding giant picture books around the circle and singing songs at story hour. Now she took care of her grandchildren; she'd assembled all the gear in her own house: crib, high chair, playpen, baby gates. His father wrote weekly e-mails and called regularly from Westchester, and when they talked he and Ben seemed to really *talk*. Ben even shut the bedroom door once so they could have a private conversation when I was at his apartment. I'd sat out in the living room with Fish's guitar collection, looking at the wood veneers and plastic commas, nervously wondering whether they were talking about me. He was close to his sister, too. They'd fought as kids, but only enough to feel tragic when their mother sent them to their separate rooms.

I'd been dreading the day he invited me along on a family visit. "I mean, I can try to plan it sometime you know you can get away." He had one eye under the comforter.

"Okay," I said. "What about the club?" It came out fast, a subject change I hadn't planned. "Would you like to come along on a trip?"

"Of course," said Ben. I felt wretched. "I mean"—he turned and kissed me—"if I can get away."

Ben went back to his apartment to finish some grant proposals. I was sorry he wouldn't stay with me all day, because even though the snowstorm had quieted the city, I still felt like I was playing hooky, and I wanted to share it with someone. I watched Ben wading out to the curb to get his taxi; he slipped and caught himself. I sighed for my poor lonely self.

I bittered my mouth with coffee and mulled in my tiny living room. The quiet had shifted from pleasing and full of luck to plain and empty. I put on layers: my new red silk long underwear, a cotton shirt and wool sweater, and coat and hat and gaiters and boots and scarf and mittens.

Just as I was at the door, trying to mitten my keys into my zipper pocket, the phone rang.

"You still want to do the shopping today?" asked Shing. He didn't announce himself. He'd never called me before, and his disembodied voice made the whole thing seem unreal: the slogging along the trails, the tents, this weekend's trip. I'd never been cross-country skiing with a backpack, but I'd gone out a lot when I was at Carleton, so I felt fairly confident. I knew how to herringbone and snowplow; I could lean from side to side and glide along trails without a lot of tipping over into snowbanks.

"Snow day for you?"

"No work," said Shing. "Do you think Bread and Circus is open?"

"Don't you think that would break the club piggy bank?" I hadn't done the shopping before, but that market was for the deep-pocket gourmet.

"Just for a few things. We'll get the rest at Star—I've already called, and the Brookline store said they wouldn't close even for an earthquake. Want to come over and make a list?"

I was sweating in my gear, holding the bulky wool hat in my mitten. "Um, I doubt my car will start, and the T isn't running. Where do you live, anyway?"

I realized I hadn't ever imagined Shing sleeping somewhere, sitting in a living room. So far, for me, he'd lived in tents and the Caffè Paradiso.

"Cambridge. You're in Brookline, right? I'll come get you. Half an hour."

"Okay. I live—"

"I know," said Shing. I wondered how. Then I remembered our club list, addresses and everything. I peeled off all my gear and had some more coffee. I flipped through the pages of my clean cookbooks, looking for ideas. Pasta primavera. Crab cakes. Cheese fondue. It seemed so silly to me, the elaborate construction of camping: minimizing what we carried, dismissing the tradition of collecting, hunting, gathering, and storing kitchen goods and clothes and beds. Giving up the house. Then again, it was just temporary, just traveling light for a time. I wondered, though, which world was more real to me, in or out. Probably inside, I thought, leafing past raspberry chocolate layer cake and tiramisu.

A half hour later, I was bored with waiting. I put all my gear back on and clomped down the slippery stone stairs. As I passed the closed apartment doors I heard children shrieking and voices filling rooms; more people were around, it seemed, than on any weekend day.

I watched for Shing's red minivan, the one he'd brought on every trip so we could pile our gear on the extra seats. The streets still hadn't been plowed, but there were packed tracks from a dozen or so cars. I sat on my building's front steps and listened as wind cracked icy twigs from the sidewalk maples. A grumbling sound made its way down the block, and a motorcycle tobogganed along the snowy street.

It stopped in front of my house, and a man wearing a leather jacket, rain pants, and tall leather boots and a helmet waved at me. I waved back. He waved again, holding out another helmet. It was Shing.

We did our menu planning and shopping at the same time. Shing walked down the aisles in his leather, with his slight swaggering gait, like a man on a serious mission. I said so.

"Well, this *is* serious," he said. "I want to prove we don't always have to have Camilla and Nicky's orange slop, just because we're packing it all in."

All he wanted in the fancy market was produce.

"Winter melon," he said. "For winter."

"You're going to carry a melon?"

"Sure, builds stamina. No, I'll cut it first. Tomorrow night. You want to come over and help make fruit salad?" He held up a kiwi between thumb and forefinger. "Ripe enough," he said, cradling it among the mangoes and bananas in the cart.

"Oh, okay," I said.

"Unless you have big Friday-night plans."

"I kind of—well, I guess I have some plans, but I'm not sure what." I wasn't exactly keeping Ben *secret*. Linda knew about him, and Alan and Camilla and Nicky, but I'd never mentioned him to Shing or to Noah.

"It's okay, I'll do it myself this time," he said. "Boyfriends." He humphed and smiled. I wondered, for a second, whether Shing was gay. Maybe Vijay was an ex-boyfriend.

"Almost as bad as girlfriends," he added, eating a grape off the still-life ready, dewy mound.

"Oh?" I wanted a grape but felt too self-conscious to pluck one from the store's selection. I ran my finger along the cold lip of the metal case. "Hey, Shing, do you go on the summer trips?"

"Of course," he said, swallowing. "They're the best: no showers for days, peaks and views, and no phones or bills. It's really different to get out for weeks instead of just a few days. Incredible—as long as no one does anything stupid." His last few words were laced with contempt, or else he'd bitten into a bitter grape seed.

Shing swung the cart away from the fruit, racing down the aisle. I gave in to desire and grabbed a grape. I had to jog to catch up with him. Shing didn't look prepared to elaborate, so I didn't ask, for fear I might be the kind of person who did stupid things. The split skin of the sweet grape felt like a purple grin in my mouth.

On Friday night, Ben and I had an early pizza dinner at Pizzeria Regina in the North End, orange soda in a bottle for me, beer for Ben, the cheese grease making his lips shine. Then I went home to my apartment and he went home to his. At nine-thirty, I tried to sleep. I was hoping not to feel gummy and wretched when the alarm went off at 5:07 A.M. Shing would pick me up in his van. I lifted the blind and looked out at Beacon Street in the gauzy streetlamp light; the streets were clear, and the snow had become gray slush.

Friday had been a workday, and at four o'clock my boss assigned me a new project: signage and a long specialized bar for a very upscale perfume boutique on Newbury Street. All they planned to sell at The Scent Bar were perfumes with names like Trash and Dumb Blonde and Stiletto and For the Money. She asked for preliminary sketches and ideas by

Monday. I almost said no, I couldn't. Saying no would mean more work, more uproar, than simply suffering through. I watched her bristly red hair as she turned to go; the gleam looked artificial, and her slim man-cut suit seemed pretentious and absurd. I stuck out my tongue, quickly. She didn't see me, but it felt good. I'd have to get up very early on Monday to finish, because there was no way I was missing this trip. Shing and I had planned pasta primavera to go with the tropical fruit salad, and we bought romaine instead of iceberg for the tossed salad, and jicama and baby carrots, even though they were heavy, and instant flan.

I lay in my bed again, listening to cars crunch through the refreezing slush. I missed Ben: his hogging the bed space, having one last thing to talk about before sleep. Two horns blatted; a car alarm wailed in the wind. The radiators clunked and moaned. The phone rang once. It could be Ben. Twice, it could be Shing. It could be important, I thought, at three, and I'm not sleeping anyway, so I answered.

"Hey," said Ted.

"Hey." We'd talked twice since the big dinner; he'd told me more about his weed garden and he'd alluded to something serious going on with Abby, but he never said what. Just something serious. Marla had called twice, once to say she was furious at Mom and worried about Dad and once to say she was furious with Ted and didn't I just love Reed. When I said I really hadn't gotten to know him, Marla said, "Yet."

"Dad's smoking again," said Ted.

"It's just to make us try to stop him," I said.

"Do you think he's serious this time?" Ted's voice wobbled.

"Of course not," I said. "And you heard Mom."

Usually, Ted was the first to call Dad's bluff. I remembered one time Dad took us swimming at Crystal Lake—I was still in elementary school; Ted was in junior high. It was past the official Newton Recreation Department hours for the swim area, but Dad climbed the fence and urged us over, lifting me down on the other side, letting Ted drop himself to the gravelly path. Dad dove in at the children's end and swam under the dock in long otter-smooth strokes. We ran down the worn wood dock and followed him out into the deep end. I felt guilty for breaking the rules, and thrilled, and then concerned, as my father ducked the lines marking the swim area and went out toward the center of the lake. We swam out to the barrier, then waited. The T rumbled past and the sun seemed to sweat a little more green out of the maples along the shore. I watched my father's head moving toward the middle of the lake. Then it disappeared.

"Ted?" I called to my brother.

"He's okay," he said, and I knew he was watching, too, though he pretended to be floating on his back, relaxed.

"He's not coming up," I said.

It felt like we'd been treading water for a month. I hadn't yet passed the test for the deep end, and here I was, out where only adults were allowed.

"He's okay," Ted said again.

Another train passed and evening threatened to succumb to night. Then something tugged my ankle. I screamed, but of course it was my father.

He didn't come up but swam over to Ted. I wondered how he could still be alive after all that time underwater, but Ted just kicked at him, refusing delight.

"Did I scare you?" he asked, when he surfaced. Ted swam for the shore, slogged up the sand, and climbed the fence. I kept treading water, but my father started swimming in without waiting for an answer.

"I'm thinking of using bladder weed," Ted paused on the phone. *"Silene cucubalus."*

All I could do was sigh.

I was ahead of Noah and Shing. On the drive up, in Shing's van, he and Noah had spent most of the time talking about all the peaks they'd bagged. It had an odd locker-room quality, and I'd felt excluded.

"Camel's Hump hardly counts," Noah had said.

"Except in the *mud*." Shing chuckled.

I'd sat in the back, playing with the cords on my pack and executing faltering attempts to join in the conversation. Six pairs of skis clattered up and down the aisle when Shing accelerated or hit the brakes.

The parking lot at the trailhead was a mess of snowdrifts and refrozen snow, so we made a wobbly start. We tried not to topple as we put our packs on first, then clipped into our skis. The pack balanced despite my slippery center of gravity.

"Why?" Camilla cried, leaning on Linda as she tried to get her binding to grip her boot. "Why do I ever submit to these trips? Nicky was smart to say he was sick."

"Because of the hut," said Linda. "And I think he has strep throat."

"We do it for the company!" Shing's binding snapped shut as he leaned over it, and he lost his balance, slipped, and fell over into a slushy puddle by the van.

"Shit!" said Camilla.

Shing bounced up fast, looking irked. "Got it!" he yelled, as his binding took. There was a slick of gray on the back of his bright red Gore-Tex jacket.

Once we glided onto the trail, though, I felt a tenuous strength. It was like a game, shifting the possible fall from leg to leg, gliding the weight along the trail at constant risk of toppling. But I wasn't falling; I was moving along: glide, shift, glide.

Then the uphill started, and I began to share Camilla's doubts. It felt as though I were trying to swim through frozen pudding. It was gorgeous, nonetheless—we were on a white track in a tunnel of green. Piney woods, a delicious scent.

We had hauled all sorts of junk along with us; the packs were ridiculously heavy. I leaned into the herringbone, stepping V tracks up a steep hill. My face glowed with heat, and I could feel a languid river of sweat seeping down my thigh. Then I hit a tree root and wobbled. My other ski crunched against a rock, and I fell over on my side and then backward, toppling Alan, who was right behind me.

"Sorry sorry!" I said.

"Mmph," said Alan. He lay face down in the snow; his pole, still strapped to his wrist, was pinned under one leg. His pack shifted up so it squashed his shoulders. My legs were twisted and one binding snapped loose. My ski slid back down the hill I'd been climbing.

I couldn't help it; I laughed.

"That'll teach me to follow your tracks," Alan grumbled, wrestling the gear and the slope to get up again.

Linda, looking down from the top of the incline, was laughing too.

Shing and Noah still hadn't caught up.

"Do you think we should wait?" I asked Linda, once I'd retrieved my ski and made it back up the inescapable hill.

"Nope," she said. "They'll whistle if they need help. That's why the whistle's on the list," she said, looking at me as if this were a lesson.

I still didn't have a whistle. I hadn't realized it was a mandatory item. Then again, on that first trip, I'd worn cotton socks.

"At the break," she said.

But at the break, I started to get too cold to stay still. The sweat congealed, despite my layers. All the warmth generated by effort evaporated, but the dampness stayed. Camilla was bouncing as she sat on a rock. Snowflakes fell, huge and soft and quiet, muting our conversation, our breathing, even our chewing.

"I think I got my shoulder back there," said Alan.

"Poor honey," said Linda. She rubbed his back. "Bad, or just the whiny kind of injury?"

Alan pouted. "Not sure yet," he said.

"Hey, I'm freezing," said Camilla. "Can we go, Hannah and I?" She looked at Linda.

"Hey, I'm not the boss," said Linda. "Shing's trip leader this time."

"No, Shing's food leader. And so is Hannah." Camilla smiled at me.

"So who's trip leader?"

"We've got to get more organized about this," said Alan. "Safety is no joke." He gazed down the quiet trail.

I wondered what that meant—more teacherly comment, perhaps. Things seemed awfully organized to me. And I thought I remembered, at the meeting, that he'd said, "I'll do the ski trip." I didn't say anything.

"Go," said Linda. "We'll wait for them."

Camilla looked at me and we stumped through the work of reassembling packs, skis, poles, and mittens.

"You first," said Camilla.

"But I don't know the way," I said.

"There's only one trail," she said.

———

At first, Camilla was right behind me, telling me about last winter's ski trips, how Shing was amazing at downhill skiing but always fell a lot on these trips. Then we started climbing again, and all I could hear was labored breathing and the clatter of poles and skis. Then I started to move ahead, not really far but far enough that I couldn't hear anything but the *shush* of my own skis packing down the snow, my own open-mouth breathing, and my own heart, working hard.

Just when I thought I was at the peak and the hut should appear soon, the trail stopped climbing and started a narrow wind through low evergreen woods. Then the trail opened onto a field, a wide cheek of snow. I felt as if I'd been led to something important, and the sudden change of landscape made me pause. But I didn't stop, even though it wasn't clear where the trail went.

If I can only stay in motion, I thought, no one can see who I am: a very ordinary designer, a worker bee constructing plans of pure function. Even my small whimsies—dingbats, copper corners—were stripped away by budgets. I cut across the field, my ski marks the only prints on the clean canvas of snow. A lake winked from far below; more mountains hunched across the landscape, green animals wearing white blankets. A rabbit zagged from shrub to shrub. It knew where it was going, and suddenly it mattered that I didn't. I stopped in the quiet. A stream gashed the white at the far end of the field. The light leaned, from bright to almost evening. It would be dark soon. I realized I didn't know where I was, and it filled me with a plain kind of pleasure, almost fear. But I knew the rest of the club was right behind me, and after a few minutes, Camilla, Linda, and Shing came gliding up, their poles creaking and skis clacking, followed by Alan and Noah.

"Hey, girl," said Shing. "You are *fast*."

"The hut's there." Camilla pointed northeast, though I couldn't see into the woods. "At the bottom of the field. And I'm ready for that dinner."

"It's only four," said Alan.

"Me too," said Linda, and she took the lead. I felt as if I was losing something concealed and significant, but the feeling slipped through me like a quick shudder.

The trail curved down and then wound up another hundred yards or so into the trees. The Hell's Gates hut rested there, in the woods' arms, waiting for us.

"Instant flan?" Camilla held up the box, laughing. Our fruit salad and pasta primavera had been delicious.

We were just outside the hut at the fire circle. The stoves hissed their blue flame halos and Linda had made a miniature pyramid of fire after she cleared the snow out from beneath the stones. The woods creaked with snow and ice and wind. The sky was all gray swirl, with a smear of moonlight behind the clouds. It was bitterly cold.

Camilla had brought her pad and sleeping bag out with her cup, and Noah was sitting on his chair. I put a plastic bag over a rock. My bottom felt like it was becoming ice, but the food was good and warm and necessary.

"Wait until you have this chocolate." Shing took out the imported Swiss stuff he'd picked out as we'd rung up the rest of our purchases. He'd paid for it separately, in cash, and I'd assumed it was for his private stash.

"You can't have kept to the budget," said Alan, popping two squares in his mouth.

"Ghirardelli mocha?" Noah pulled the cocoa packets out of the food sack he'd carried.

"Not a penny over." Shing beamed.

"More!" Camilla reached for the chocolate.

"More!" Noah reached for Camilla's hand.

"Piggy!" said Camilla.

"Pig pile!" Shing dropped the flan package and climbed on top of Noah, who'd started to burrow into Camilla's bag. I watched for a minute. I didn't feel ready to join in, even though I craved the warmth, the mass of limbs. I picked at the salad freezing to my cup.

"Get Hannah," said Noah, as if he'd heard me thinking.

The three of them rolled over to my rock, and Noah started to tickle me. I dropped my cup in the snow.

"Kids!" said Alan. He didn't join in. He and Linda sat, holding hands and watching.

Noah kept tickling me, and Camilla's knee was in my side. Then Shing picked up first Camilla, then me, swinging us around like kids. Snow slid into my socks as we all rolled. Shing gathered an armful of snow and pretended to bury us. It was silly and wet and delightful. It was sexual, all the closeness, and it wasn't. It was a kind of play I'd forgotten I knew.

In the bunks, we didn't have the warm cocoon of tent-sleeping. I was cold despite the down bag and socks and hat. Noah had explained that sleeping with fewer clothes on usually was warmer, so I no longer took my coat to bed. But my hands were cold and my thigh was wet from our snow play.

I could hear Alan's slow breathing below me, and Camilla, across, but Noah and Shing were still awake.

"You are the ski queen, Hannah," whispered Shing.

"Hm?" I said.

"Don't make me say it again."

"Shing's not very good with compliments," said Noah. "Especially because he's the ski dunce."

I heard a dull thunk.

"Missed," said Noah. "But I'll bet Hannah can't pee her name in the snow as well as you can."

"Yeah," said Shing.

"I have no idea," I said. "I'll have to try."

"Girls can't do it." Noah had stopped whispering.

"With a fud we can," said Camilla. "You guys are too loud."

"What the hell's a fud?" asked Noah.

"Feminine urinary director," said Camilla. "My grand-mother sent me one for the trip to Peru. I never used it, but I'll bet it works."

"We'll have to give it a try," I said.

"Go to sleep," moaned Alan.

I woke up a lot, too cold to sleep steadily. I listened to the others' breathing and the creaking of frozen trees outside. I thought about the mass cuddle by the fire and found myself longing for those bodies wrapped around mine. It wouldn't mean anything other than heat and sleep.

Sunday was dark; it was still snowing. The Irish oatmeal we'd bought took too long to cook and then tasted exactly like the instant variety.

"Just a little too fancy," said Noah.

"If it were up to you we'd eat pine needles," said Shing.

"Wintergreen tea," said Noah. "Or something called Life-of-Man. Pickings are pretty slim in the winter woods for wild edibles." He spooned the gloppy oatmeal into his mouth and chased it with a handful of half-frozen raisins.

"You'd eat Life-of-Man?" Camilla slid her hands into her sleeves. "Man-eater."

I tried to maintain my speedy pace on the way back down. Less than a mile from the cars, Linda was just behind me, and Alan and Camilla were ahead. As we crossed a stream, I tried an elegant move, stepping as I glided, lifting one ski to make the crossing without stopping. But I fell sideways, crashing into some low bushes and into the stream. Linda didn't have enough warning, so she fell on top of me. The ice crust rubbed against my waist where my coat had pulled away. The water was so cold it stung, and I was stuck, but since we were going home, somehow it was funny.

Five / "What are *those*?" Ben was looking at my feet. We were in my bed; the comforter felt as soft as skin. My pack had been sitting by the door all week, and I knew I ought to take out my cup and clothes and wash them, but I couldn't bear to face the mess after all the catch-up hours at work. And the marinating pack reminded me of where I'd been, and that I'd just returned. That I'd go again soon.

"Blisters," I said, proudly. They were disgusting. Oozing. I waved my feet outside the blankets.

"Very pretty. Wish I had some." Ben reached for me. He smelled flannelly and clean. "Where was this cabin in the woods, anyway?"

"Hut," I said. "Vermont. Thirteen miles to Hell's Gates and back."

"Mmm, such a cozy-sounding place."

"Oddly enough," I said, adding *"ouch!"* as his leg brushed a bruise on my thigh, "it *was* kind of cozy."

February slogged on, the horrible fat center of winter, with no trips scheduled. I wore leather boots to work, and the slush sank in and left salt circles around my ankles. Everything stayed cold—my hands, my toes, my insides—as I stood waiting for the T, stamping my feet to convince my blood to circulate. Even when I sat in the hot dry air of the office, under the heating vent, I felt frozen inside my skin.

My boss wasn't happy with my work for the perfume project.

"It's not that it doesn't *work*, Hannah," she'd said, leaning against the fragile wall of my cubicle. "It's just not *interesting*. There needs to be an *energy* in the minimalism, a *shock*, because this boutique is all about *place*. I mean, the clientele is going to pay three hundred dollars for a quarter ounce of Emergency." She sniffed the air, as if she smelled Emergency. I'd smelled a sample—it reminded me of the dentist.

"Maybe you should try thinking younger."

As she spoke, I watched her painted mouth move, the lipstick liner slightly too dark for the filled-in lips. *Thinking younger*. She was in her late thirties; she'd made a meteoric butt-kissing ascendance to partner, and it looked as if she'd aged a lot in the process. As always, she had a cup of fancy coffee in her hand: her pacifier, ringed with lipstick. I imagined her falling into a snowbank and laughed quietly.

She barked, "I'm glad you think it's funny. But I need a whole new concept by tomorrow."

It wasn't so bad, working late, when I didn't have a trip or plans with Ben. I looked out the office window; the sky was a chalky orange. My boss waved to me as she went out to get dinner to eat at her desk. My feet were still damp inside their useless dress boots. I swiveled in my chair and looked at the tepid light casting the shadow of the Prudential building

along the green carpeting. Inside the office, the light was captured. I remembered sitting in the dark hall during art history slide lectures, looking at the light captured in paintings:
chiaroscuro, a tiny lively piece inside stillness. When I took
studio art, I'd tried to contain light inside my own work. I
thought of that field at Hell's Gates, about how the office
was containment and Newbury Street was its own containment, and only that field was truly *without*.

Ben and I were in the kitchen, leaning on the counter and
looking through delivery menus, when the doorbell buzzed.

"Chinese," said Ben. "I think I can stand to have Chinese
again. How about you?"

"Hello?" I said into my entry intercom.

"Ted," said Ted.

"Okay," I said, pressing the buzzer button.

"I hope he brought food," Ben joked.

This was it; I would finally find out what was going on.
Ted always liked to say the important things in person.
When he and Abby got engaged, I was in college. He waited
a week to tell me, until he could arrange a flight to Min-
nesota. I met him at the airport, and he hugged me hard,
delivered his news, and then told me he had to catch a plane
home in two hours. We had flaccid linguine at the airport
restaurant. I'd toasted him with a soda.

"Hey, I know what," said Ben, generous as always. "I'll
pick something up. I'll surprise you." He pulled on his boots
and started lacing them.

"You don't have to," I said, but I wanted him to go.

Ted walked into the room, looking more threadbare than my
ancient brown velvet chair, one I'd inherited after Mom's

third living room redecoration. I'd never seen him move so liquidly. I imagined him in his condo, oozing from chair to bed. Oozing out the door.

"Drink?" I asked.

"Drink," said Ted. He took the beer I offered and sucked slowly at the bottle.

When they moved back from New York, Ted and Abby had bought a two-bedroom in an old converted church in Brookline. It had ancient stained glass and new walls with wainscoting to match the old. It was a marvel of modern design, a huge church split into seven living spaces, with mostly Jewish tenants living in sections of the nave and balconies, kitchens in the space of torn-out pews. Sometimes I thought the space was beautiful, and sometimes it seemed dark and hideous. But Ted and Abby liked it, decorating with foundling furniture and hundreds of houseplants. Oddly enough, Ted was unable to keep plants alive in his own house, but Abby nurtured them, watering and trimming and repotting and fertilizing. She grew purple and moth orchids and never neglected spider plant babies. She propagated jewel plants from corms.

"I'm the gardener of our interior," she used to say. "And Ted's responsible for all outside."

"Okay," I said, looking at Ted sitting in my chair. His hair was too long; curls covered his ears. "Are you ready to tell me what's going on?"

"I finished the weed garden. They love it. The president thinks he wants one for his own house now. And I've got my San Diego trim trip coming up."

"Uh-huh," I said, sitting on the chair's arm.

"And Abby's pregnant. I mean, that's not why she moved

out, but it kind of is. I think, I mean—we didn't plan on kids."

I breathed, slowly. I remembered what my mother said when we'd arrived for dinner: *I hope she's not pregnant.* I'd assumed she'd meant Marla. Maybe she had.

"Oh. She—I mean, did you change your mind? Did she change her mind?"

"It was an accident. I mean, unplanned. Except maybe it wasn't. I mean. She's staying with her sister. I can't talk about this now." He pulled the label from his beer.

"Okay." It was torture not to ask a thousand questions, but Ted would clam up entirely if I did. When he was able to tell me, he would.

"Okay," said Ted. He swirled the beer in his bottle, and I got up from the chair to sit on the couch. He had the entire label in bits in his hand. I turned away, to let his face be private for a minute.

"She's keeping the baby," he said. "And I said the wrong thing."

"The wrong thing?"

"I mean, when she told me, I said—I mean, I just assumed we wouldn't keep it. That's what we'd—well, we'd never discussed this exactly, but we weren't going to—"

The buzzer cut him off. Too fast for Ben, I thought, getting up.

"Hello?"

"Marla," said Marla.

"Oh," I said. "You're here."

"And you're going to let me up now, I hope, because it's freezing."

I let her in.

"How much of this does she know?" I asked Ted, whose

head was now resting so deep in the back of the chair he looked like he'd become one with the upholstery.

"Nothing. She wants to marry *Reed Scrum*," said Ted, and a fleeting smile lifted his lips.

Marla was wearing a white fluffy coat, her face was bright and her eyes their tragic blue, and I loved her, even though I was enormously annoyed with her for coming to my apartment then, with no warning. When she was a baby, I thought all that beauty belonged to me. She was my baby doll, even though Mom wouldn't let me dress her in doll's clothes or leave her inside my Little Dollie Kitchen Set, to nap in the full-sized frying pan. She let me give her bottles and change her when it was just pee. I pretended she was mine and renamed her Victoria, Jessica, Queen Eve. I licked her pacifiers to see whether they were yummy. They tasted of milk and rubber.

"I'll have one," she said, gesturing toward Ted's beer bottle.

"Of course," I said.

"Where's Ben?"

"Hi, Marla," said Ted, sitting up.

"Out for food."

"Good." Marla threw her coat down on my couch and went to the kitchen to get her own beer. It still surprised me that she treated my food and clothes as if they were her own. As if my home was an extension of our mother's suburban castle. At college, she'd come to visit, and when I returned from class she'd be wearing my shoes, my favorite cream silk blouse, my pearl barrettes in her long hair. Of course, everything looked better on her. A bit baggy and short, but better.

"So. Here's the thing," she said, her cute behind swaying to her own private music as she pulled off the bottle cap.

She'd tossed a whisk, a spatula, and a pasta fork on the counter in her search for the opener, which was already out.

"I'm worried about Dad," she started. Marla never worried about Dad, I thought. She worried about herself. She continued, as if to prove me right, "You need to marry Ben—it would do so much for your *moods*. And you—"

She swung a long-fingered hand toward Ted as she gulped her beer. I could hear her noisy swallow from across the room. It was just like Mom. We joked that Mom could make pudding crunch and water sound like a running toilet in her throat.

"You should just get over it. Abby will be the most incredible mom, and even you can keep up as a father."

Ted sank back down into the chair and closed his eyes. "How did you know?" he asked.

"I'm not stupid," said Marla. She swigged and flushed a mouthful again. "The thing is, I want to get married, but the two of you need to get your lives organized first, so Mom and Dad can *deal*."

I couldn't stand her. Her completely undeserved beauty, her selfish rant, the way she seemed unruffled by our father, her noisy mouth on my last bottle of beer.

"We're not stopping you," I said. "Though Dad might kill you if you marry Reed Scrum."

"Oh, Dad—what's wrong with Reed?" She pouted.

"You're only twenty-one," said Ted. "Please think a little, first."

"You two are making this all about me."

"No," I said. "You are."

"Dad might really be sick this time," she said. "We might want to get our ducks in a row."

Ducks in a row. I tried not to laugh at my sister.

The key scrabbled in the lock as Ben came in bearing two enormous bags. His hair looked freshly trimmed.

"Chinese," Ben said. He looked sane and calm and I adored him.

"Think about it," said Marla. "When you're not so busy being an outdoors woman."

"What?" said Ben. The sesame oil scent made me very, very hungry.

"I'm not really an outdoors woman," I said. "I'm just kind of a woman who goes outdoors."

"Whatever," said Marla. She picked up her coat, kissed Ben's cheek, and went right back out the door with her beer.

I missed the March trip because I had to work on the perfume boutique. My boss wanted me at the installation, so I spent a Saturday when I could've been caving—sliding around in the mud, as Linda described it—watching a carpenter in saw-shredded pants trying to fit the square crystal Filthy perfume spritzer into the counter. The good part was, the project was finished. The bad part was, even my boss was happy with it, so I was assigned another new boutique, if it could be called that: an oxygen bar.

"It's kind of a *spa*," she said, as I stood outside the towering glass office doors with her, watching cars redistribute the mud on Massachusetts Avenue. She was sucking on a skinny cigarette and blowing the smoke sideways, as if to save her face. As if to save me. I'd reek from proximity, but I didn't really have a choice.

"It's complicated, because the machinery must meet some hospital code regulations or something. You'll look into it." She waved her cigarette. "I can't wait to go, though. I went to one out in LA once. So *purifying*."

Shing called and left a message on the machine. "You're avoiding us, aren't you? Or are you scared of caving?"

I was too weary to call him back. I waited until the next meeting to tell him I'd gotten his message. I'd make the next trip, and no oxygen or perfume boutique, or whatever was next—a *foie gras* bar or sandal showroom or plastic raincoat factory—was going to keep me away. I wondered where all the Children's Museum projects had gone.

Ben agreed to come along on the club's next trip. He'd watched me mooning over my pack as I finally unloaded and cleaned my gear. It was the Sunday after the installation, and I couldn't believe I'd have to wait another month.

"You really love it, don't you?" He was stirring a fork in cold coffee.

"Yes," I said. "It makes me feel sane. It's like a magic trick." I looked up from my sleeping bag stuff sack and smiled at him. The scent of woods emerged from the bag along with some loose down and a few pine needles. A dirty silk sock liner slipped onto the floor.

"So, am I invited next time?"

"Yes, Ben, yes, please. It's rock climbing. We don't even have to backpack to base camp. It'll be easy."

"Like, ropes and cliffs and stuff?"

I gazed up at him. His face looked fleshy over the pink coffee cup. It was only winter pallor, I thought. It would wear off. "I haven't done it either. So I can be a beginner with you," I said.

"Do I need a rope?"

"Only a harness, my space explorer. Maybe you can borrow one from Noah."

"Who's Noah?"

I felt the heat in my face, envisioning Noah's blue-green eyes, remembering his warm chest under my hands at Mount

Isolation. "He's a guy in the club. A serious climber. He has lots of gear. I'm borrowing an extra harness from Linda—"

"Okay," he said. He sighed, long and hard. "I'm coming on your Adventurers' Club trip. And it was space *engineer*. I just designed the settlers' domes, I didn't wagon-train across Mars."

Mostly, I was glad, but a small part of me was nervous. That he wouldn't like it. That I'd be different with Ben there. That maybe they wouldn't like him.

At meetings, we'd started to talk about the summer trip, and I'd started to worry, privately, that I wouldn't be in good enough shape to keep up. The ski trip had been a fluke. So when I wasn't measuring out the area for oxygen tanks and serene coffinlike bed spaces in the storefront on Newbury Street—across the street from a floundering rare bookshop and a shiny new cigar store; WALK-IN HUMIDOR read the banner out front—I was planning my fitness program.

I calculated on scraps of paper: the weeks remaining before August, the cost of gym memberships, times I could exercise before, during, after work—if I ever dragged myself to the gym. I didn't mind the bikes or the rowing machines, but I hated aerobics classes, which made me bounce all over and feel foolish and petty. I took a class once in college and found I was watching other women's bodies with a kind of scrutiny, a kind of comparative lust for shapes, that I thought I'd banished in high school.

Reviewing my calculations, I determined not to join a gym and not to let myself obsess about eating. I decided the best approach to summer-trip training was to save the gym membership money for gear and start jogging instead.

Every early morning I could manage to rouse myself, I went—on weekends, starting out at the late hour of eight. It was grueling to leave the luxury of sleep. After a few weeks, I invested in a good pair of running shoes. They felt so light on my feet I wanted to wear them all the time, but I saved them as a reward for facing the pavement. I started with a route down the median of Commonwealth Avenue and soon was making it the four miles to Newton, along the carriage path. There was a whole culture of jogging—the passers and the followers, the men with too-tight tights and the women who wore shorts regardless of the temperature. I'd started to let the initial resistance pass into an aching gratification of motion, of winning the fight, of cutting through space with some grudging speed. I was up to six miles a day, sometimes even eight, four days a week. When I couldn't go, I got cranky.

Ben watched me stretching one Sunday morning. He was lying in bed, his arms behind his head, as if sunbathing. I'd brought him the paper and a cup of coffee and asked him, twice, if he didn't want to come. He looked pallid and thick and slow, and I felt slightly superficial for thinking it, but he could've been in better shape.

Me, only a month ago, I reminded myself.

"Are you sure? I could jog slowly. Or we could walk," I said.

"No way," said Ben, reaching for his coffee on the bed stand. "Not on Sunday. I'm too worn out."

"It'll revive you."

"That's okay."

"And when we come back all grungy we can take a shower together."

"That's okay," he said again. He scratched his chest. "I like you sweaty."

The climbing trip was the next weekend. He'd get sweaty

enough then. As I was unlocking the door to go, he called out, "Want to pick up some bagels on your way home?"

I pretended I didn't hear him.

It was early spring, and the crust of winter was starting to flake off the streets. There were still salt stains around the storm drains, and resistant wads of cruddy snow around the bases of trees, where the sun never got strong enough to penetrate the shellac of carbon emissions.

I started out unhurried, because it was a weekend and because I was thinking of Ben in bed, his dark hair on the rose-colored pillowcase. He hadn't asked me to stay, which was good, because it meant he was letting me do my own thing. He hadn't begged me to stay and spend the morning with him, with three pillows and the newspaper and coffee in bed, which was annoying, because it meant he didn't mind lounging without me.

I sped up as I rounded the reservoir. I ran a half moon, passing morning speed-walkers, mothers with carriages, dog owners who matched their pets (an Afghan hound and a shaggy, skinny man; a short squat woman with a Boston terrier). I took Beacon Street up past Boston College, remembering weekends in my own dorms at Carleton, sleeping until eleven, days spent in the library, trying to study the Renaissance period but really looking for whichever man most recently interested me, wandering the stacks, hoping accidentally to happen upon him, a conversation, a distraction.

The dorm rooms all had their shades drawn. The day grew warm, late March asserting its spring potential. I paused and peeled off my windbreaker, tying it around my waist and, though it looked goofy, pushed my sweatpants up to my knees. I felt the heat and evaporating sweat as I resumed my pace, cutting through some side streets and back to Commonwealth. There were hardly any cars out, and the joggers made a steady stream along the carriage path. A skinny fair man with a yarmulke and a rabbi's white beard followed the sprints of a greyhound, her long legs incongruous around a bearish belly. A woman with wild thick hair was pulled in different forward vectors by two orange chows on their leashes.

I was in the middle of the stream, slower than the dailies but faster than the weekend-only crowd. Every fifth jogger pushed an all-terrain stroller, half of which were doubles. A baby wailed from within one, such a small sound, and the mother in motion squinted against the grievance and kept going.

I heard someone coming up behind me as I approached Center Street and the poodle-grooming shop that had been there since my childhood. Maybe they groomed other dogs too, but I thought of it as the poodle shop, because the sign depicted a black poodle and a set of shears. The someone behind me decelerated. My sweatpants slipped back down my calves. I needed to get some good jogging shorts. Some leggings. I really didn't like Lycra, though; it made me feel naked in public.

Now the breathing was so close it sounded as if the other jogger were about to hitch a ride on my back. I reduced my speed, hoping he or she would simply pass. I didn't turn, because that might invite conversation. Twice, going around the reservoir, I'd been asked out. Before I'd met Ben, I went four months without a date; I'd never known jogging was a meat market. I had imagined my sweatpants were a sure signal that I wasn't out on that market, but they obviously weren't working.

"Hey, lady, what's a nice girl like you doing in a town like this?"

Oy, I thought. I stopped entirely, and a body slammed into mine. I fell, and he fell, and I thought, I'm being mugged in Newton, on Commonwealth Avenue, in front of a hundred joggers and their dogs and babies.

"Hey," said Noah. "What was that for?"

"Oh, no." I looked at him. His hair had gotten shaggy in the month or so since I'd seen him. Shorts bared his long legs, and his thigh was bleeding where he'd scraped it against the pavement.

"I didn't see you. I mean—"

"It's okay, Hannah, my fault." He stood up, bouncing slightly, and reached down to help me up.

"What are you doing out here?"

"My mom lives in Newton," he said.

"Mine too. Did you grow up here too, and did you know me in high school, and is my memory shot from all those wild college days?"

"Nope. Used to live in Southie. And I went to a boarding school. Mom moved here after the divorce."

"Oh. I'm sorry."

"Me too. She married the second viola. Let's not talk about it; I hate family stuff."

I couldn't tell how serious he was. Or what he meant by second viola. He was looking straight ahead. We had stopped in the stream of runners; we parted them like rocks in the water. I thought of Ben in bed and was annoyed at myself for noticing Noah's good square jaw, the sun in his hair. So I was quiet.

"Okay. Dad was a cellist in the BSO, and they divorced fourteen years ago—he moved to Cleveland—and she got married too soon for my puritan tastes. And now let's talk about you."

Noah started jogging, very slowly.

"I didn't know you were a runner." He held my shoulder for a second, as if it were a steering wheel for the conversation. His fingertips marked my skin through the cotton shirt with a pleasant heat.

"Just started a few weeks ago. For the summer trip." I could tell he was trying to run slowly, but even so, two of my strides matched one of his.

Noah ran with me all the way back to Brookline, his scraped leg flashing bright blood as we went. He told me all about the other summer trips—he'd gone four years in a row—and I listened, too breathless from trying to keep up to say much. And I was afraid I'd ask the wrong thing. I wanted to know more about his family; questions hung on my tongue. What was it like to have a musician father? Which instruments did Noah play? Which private school had he attended? And, more importantly, was Noah still seeing Jenni?

Linda had told me, driving me home from a meeting in Cambridge, that Noah taught music at a junior high in Revere, he wasn't close to his parents, and he never stayed with one woman for long. Now I tried to imagine him stomping a beat for the junior high orchestra, wielding a baton in the sour-smelling school air. His students, especially the girls, must sit eagerly in their chairs, waiting for him to demonstrate how to bow, his hands on theirs.

There were green shoots elongating the forsythia alongside the Boston College dorms; soon there would be fat green buds. Noah stopped to show me some edible lichen attached like a blister to a boulder.

"Rock tripe," he said.

It looked horrible, but I could imagine tasting it on a trip. Noah said good-bye at the reservoir and I ran on, faster for having had his company.

When I came home, Ben was sitting on the couch, a strange look on his face. Ben's face revealed everything. If he didn't like someone, I could tell by looking at his eyebrows. They knitted; his whole brow strained with the effort to appear civil. When he was happy, his eyes were more open, and his mouth took on a sweetness around the corners, as if he were holding a smile in, letting it live inside his mouth. And desire dazzled his eyes, deepened the blue, made his lips plump, and set his jaw so he looked ready to bite.

Now his expression was enigmatic. His cheeks were slightly flushed. I noticed how short his hair was—freshly trimmed.

"Your father called," he said.

"Oh, okay. He called here?" My father almost never called. I gave my calves a perfunctory stretch.

"He wants to take us out to dinner."

"He said he'd take us out? That's rare. Usually we go Dutch." I peeled off my clothes on the way to the shower. I felt minutely unfaithful; I needed to wash off right away.

"No. Oh, well, I assumed that part. He said, 'Let's meet for dinner on Thursday.' He wants to go to some great place all the way out in Wellesley. Asian-fusion cuisine."

"Okay," I said, yelling from the bathroom. "Do you want to? Are you free?" The whole thing made my throat constrict.

"Of course," said Ben, coming to the door as I stepped into the water.

The water was even hotter than my sweaty body. My legs tickled with slowing circulation.

"And he wants to know what my intentions are."

I was glad I was in the shower. That way I couldn't see his face, and Ben couldn't see mine.

"Hm?" I said. "Can't hear you in here."

Six / "I'm glad he called," said Ben. He was leaning against me on the T, holding on to the pole as I sat in the little plastic seat.

"I suppose," I said. Ben looked down at me, and I saw too much chin, his nose hairs, and not enough of his eyes. "I don't really feel like talking about Ted right now. He always expects me to have some secret information to share."

"Well, you do have a secret."

"But it's Ted's business to share it. Or not."

"He probably knows. Besides, he said he wanted to know about *us*."

"That's even worse." The seat was hard and cold. I slid back and forth, hoping to warm up.

"Is it?"

"Yes," I said. Ben was running on some fantasy of family togetherness.

"But he did ask—"

"I think he was teasing." My stockings irritated my skin, but I didn't scratch for fear of starting a run that my short skirt wouldn't hide. It was purple silk, and Ben loved it.

"About that? Really?"

I looked around me, at men in gray overcoats hanging on the poles like sleeping pigeons, at a mom with a baby asleep in a sling on her chest. The mom was asleep too, her eyes incompletely closed, so I could see the darting blue of her dreaming eyes.

"He's never that direct," I said. "Can we not talk about it?"

"Okay, okay, I'll stop. So, tell me more about this trip next week," said Ben. "Should I be watching *Spider-Man* for tips? Should I borrow a sleeping bag from Fish?"

For once, my father wasn't late. We took a taxi from the T and walked into the restaurant's entrance, a plant-filled atrium that smelled like mango.

I'd expected to wait at the bar, but the maître d' led us to a banquette near the front. Dad was drinking something in a martini glass. He let his hand rise in a casual wave and ordered a bottle of wine as a woman in a velvet cap took our coats. I held on to my purse, thinking about the things inside, objects that would never save me in an emergency: three lipsticks, a comb I never used, cinnamon gum, matches from Clio, slightly linty mints, receipts, a little notebook, and two New York subway tokens. Stuff. I supposed the mints and gum could keep me from starving while I lit a receipt fire with the matches.

"Don't I get a kiss from my favorite daughter?" Dad leaned in and kissed my cheek. He smelled of cigarettes.

"Favorite, eh?" He sat down too fast for me to kiss him back.

"And you." He grunted at Ben. He reached out his hand for an awkward shake.

"Thanks for inviting us," said Ben. He glowed, his face open with enjoyment. Family, his favorite place, I thought. I couldn't believe, after the scene at my mother's, that he was willing to assume my father was a sane and ordinarily kind person.

"Yes." My father tasted the wine and then gestured for the sommelier to pour. I peeked at the menu. This was going to be an expensive Dutch dinner.

"I want to tell you what I think," Dad said.

"Have you been here before?" I ran my finger down the ribbon on the menu.

"Don't change the subject."

"Are you smoking again, Dad?"

"Your brother," he said, wrapping his wine stem in his fingers, "is making an idiotic mistake. And in that light"—he turned and gave Ben a crooked little grin—"I don't want anyone else getting married soon."

Ben's face didn't change. He inhaled slightly and sipped his wine, looking into the claret belly of the glass.

"And yes"—he turned to me—"the food here is great. I came with a *date*. And yes, I'm smoking again. It doesn't matter anyway."

He held up his hands in mock surrender. I knew he wanted me to ask what he meant. And I wondered, Was he simply referring to his usual fatalistic outlook, that he'd die someday anyway, his old excuse, or was there something more immediate going on? My father liked to hint. And usually I was game for a guess. But I was tired of the whole thing. I drank more wine and looked around the room and let the silence sit on my shoulders like a gargoyle.

My father cleared his throat. "Do you like cigars, Ben?"

Ben took my hand under the table. He exhaled, a long measured sound. His voice didn't even wobble as he said, "Actually, I don't."

Then he and my father started talking about the menu, about Long Island duckling and duck from New Jersey and organic milk and French cheese. I wondered whether I could fit into my purse, if I squeezed really hard.

The food was exquisite. I had duck, and the rich meat, flavored with red and black peppercorns and apricots, seemed to dissolve on my tongue. My salad tasted of lemon—field greens. I imagined a great field of radicchio, the spiky green lettuces and silky baby reds sloping down to the sea. It didn't dislodge the gargoyle, though.

When my parents separated and my father left, somehow he seemed better, more wanted, because he was the one who was missing. Before, he'd always been around, making things in his studio, starting and never finishing his home improvement projects: a partially installed sprinkler system lived out on the grass like a nest of plastic snakes; six sets of refurbished brass bathroom faucet fixtures rested, along with their screws and sleeves and some mysterious rubber bladders, on a windowsill in the mudroom. He'd left one of the ponds half dug for a French drain. Later, Marla finished it. She'd been able to watch him, to study and improve on his methods. I couldn't stand to sit with him when he was puttering, but it was important to me just the same, like background music that, once switched off, left a room entirely too silent. Now, though, he was all dangers, all kinds of things I didn't want to hear. I realized I'd been hungry for him to adore Ben. But my father was too wrapped up in his own useless family puppet strings to notice. He was busy trying to keep things from moving along without his direction.

I thought of what Marla had said and examined him for signs of sickness.

"So, did you start some kind of treatment for the lupus?" I asked, succumbing at last.

My father looked at his wine and then swatted my question away like a gnat. He must be over it already, I thought. Mom had said it was treatable, eminently treatable. Maybe he didn't even have the disease. I wouldn't fall into the sticky trap of concern.

"Now *that* was a meal." My father sighed as the waiter slid the leatherette folder of evidence between the salt and pepper.

My father and Ben split the bill, and Dad seemed happy about Ben's credit card, a platinum one with a wildlife logo.

"You a naturalist?" Dad asked Ben.

"Not really," said Ben. "But I would like to keep the great outdoors around, you know, for diversity's sake. And medical potential. And for your daughter here." He put his arm around me. Proprietary. I let him be a buffer. I would probably be annoyed in retrospect, but for the moment I didn't mind a little safety.

"Damn doctors." My father scowled. "She did always like trees," he said, smiling a little in my direction. Then, as we walked out of the green atrium, he lit a cigarette. The smoke clouded our faces as my father and I kissed good-bye.

On the T on the way home, I noticed I'd gotten a run in my stocking after all. It had laddered up from my calf and was wide on my thigh beneath the silk skirt. Ben still glowed. I was amazed that he was happy. He found a seat and pulled me onto his lap.

"That wasn't so bad," he said.

I didn't answer.

"I was wondering, actually," he said. He pulled my hair back in his hands and made a ponytail in his fingers. "I was wondering if you thought maybe we should live together."

"Oh," I said.

"Oh? Well, just think about it. Don't answer now."

"Oh." For some reason I imagined Fish and Mark sitting on my couch, all four of us in my bed. Guitars would fill my living room; the kitchen mold would come too.

"I can't believe my father said all that," I said. "I mean, first of all, I don't see what Ted's *mishegoss* has to do with Marla or with us—" Ben's fingers were tugging a very fine temple hair, and it hurt. I shook my head free and sat on my own seat beside him.

"And second of all, it's absurd, worrying about us getting married now."

Ben looked at me, that movable face instantly full of hurt. "It isn't absurd."

"No more absurd than Marla and Reed Scrum, I guess," I said. Then I felt bad. "I mean right now," I added.

But it was too late. His face closed. It went from wounded to hard, his lips a line, his gaze averted. He was staring at our reflection in the pole. Us, elongated. Tall and so skinny we could squeeze through the crack between the closed train doors and out into the damp suburban night.

I looked out the window of the rattling subway car. "Are you going to be ready for the trip?"

Ben was quiet, and I didn't look over. The bland gray lines of houses blurred. We stopped near the hospitals, and two nurses walked out into the evening.

Ben had parked his car at my stop.

"I'll walk you home," he said, after stepping down to the street. "Or I can drive you."

"That's okay, it's just two blocks. I'm a big girl," I said.

"Fine," said Ben. "Fine," he said again, as he unlocked his car.

It had been a long time since we'd parted without kissing. I blamed my father for the whole thing, for making us tense, for making Ben leap into all sorts of premature discussions.

But I also blamed Ben for not staying his steady self, for making me think about us when I was busy thinking about *them*. It wasn't his family, after all, his perfect family. I jogged home from the T stop in my square-heeled dress shoes, the silk of my purple skirt slipping across my thighs. I unlocked my apartment door, thinking, Mine, mine, mine, like a two-year-old, happy for the quiet but guilty for not wanting him there. I threw my stockings in the trash and took a long shower.

I didn't hear from Ben all Friday morning. I ate lunch at my desk: a chicken burrito. Rice spilled onto the floor. I had to call him. It was my fault. I was being small. I wouldn't bring up moving in; I'd stick to more immediate plans, the trip. Maybe once he came along with the club he'd see me as capable and fresh. Maybe I'd see him anew too, in the flattering light of the outdoors.

I had to go through his secretary. When he first got a secretary, Ben used to joke that I'd have to say I was his wife or she'd never let me through. She'd been trained in evasion and forced-messaging. She thought she was doing him a favor.

I said, "It's Hannah Blue," and she put me right through. Ben's *hello* sounded miserable.

"So, ready for tomorrow?" I tried to be perky.

"I'm sorry," he said. "But I can't go. I'm sick."

"Jesus," I said. "You do sound crummy."

"Yeah. I don't expect you to stay home, of course."

"Of course," I said.

I looked at my date book, where I'd written CLIMBING in big letters. I'd drawn a box around it, and stars.

"But I'll stay home. Don't be silly. I'll bring you soup."

"You don't have to." He sounded almost bored.

"But I want to," I said. I crossed out CLIMBING and tried very hard not to cry into the remains of my burrito.

On Saturday morning I woke up early, not quite the 5 A.M. I'd have seen for the trip, but at 6:45 the light was bright and I was awake and alone and no amount of counting or thinking about sex would send me back to the dream zone. My apartment was quiet and my pack sat half packed by the door, accusing me of something. I wasn't sure of what. If I had gone, I might have been able to forget it all. Of course, if I'd gone, it was quite possible Ben would be very angry with me. I wondered how angry he got. I'd only seen Ben sulking, hurt, and frustrated. I'd never actually seen him *mad*.

I put on my jogging clothes and went out into the tender green of April. The trees on Commonwealth Avenue were heavy with leaf buds, and there were birds everywhere, sparrows bathing in puddles and crows claiming the grass. I jogged across Brookline, over the river, into Somerville, and past Ben's apartment. His neighborhood was grungy, a wasteland of dead cars and eroded pavement and buildings sagging under their own dreary weight. I thought about stopping by, about how maybe he would forgive me if I climbed into bed with him.

Then I wasn't sure I was ready to be forgiven. I turned back toward Cambridge and Mass Avenue. Jogging along the bike path, I watched rowers out on the Charles, giant water bugs. Even the air smelled green, ready to burst into leaf and flower. And I felt trapped. I needed more than running through the city; I needed woods and a broad sky. I needed to be taken away from my own small circles around my own limited territory.

By the time I got home I was sore from running hard, and I had decided I did want to be forgiven. Once, when I had an awful flu that kept me in bed and in the bathroom for three days, Ben took a day off to care for me. He brought incongruous Happy New Year party hats, videos, two movies he thought I'd like (though he probably wouldn't), and a new novel I'd wanted, which he read aloud to me while I snuffled and moaned. He held my head while I was sick. He changed the sheets on my bed and rubbed my feet. No one in my family had ever been so generous when I was sick; as far as I remembered, no one had ever been so intent on helping me forget my discomforts.

I went to the Chinese market and bought tofu, cloud ears, ginger, chicken stock, and golden needles. I took the recipe Abby had written out for me, because Abby, among her other talents, was an excellent cook, and tried to make hot-and-sour soup. I did something wrong with the cornstarch, so there were cloud ear and golden needle lumps stuck to the pot bottom, but it tasted good. Healing. I duct-taped the lid to the pot to avoid leaks and drove Lemon back to Somerville to see Ben.

Fish, who was rarely home, answered the door in chili-pepper-printed boxer shorts. His skin was ashen and almost glinted in the dark apartment, and I wondered if that was how he got his name.

"Hey, *Ben*," he yelled, facing me, so I bore the brunt of his volume. "Gorgeous girl here for you."

I walked through the apartment living room, where sheets and socks crowded the floor, congregating with empty cereal boxes and a splintery wooden oar. Purple and tortoiseshell guitar picks were cast like tiny flowers on the gray carpeting. The room smelled of tuna.

"Laundry day." Fish smirked at me. Then he tapped my ass. I swung around, my soup in hand, and would've slugged him if I'd had a free fist.

"Don't do that," I said through my teeth. I parked my soup on the stove and waded through the debris toward the oasis of Ben's room.

"Sorry." Fish looked pathetic.

Ben, on the other hand, didn't look so bad. He was sitting up on his bed, dressed in jeans and a sweatshirt. He looked too good for someone sick; he didn't look like he needed to be read to. And he was on the phone, his voice cheerful and clear.

"Oh," he said, looking up. "Guess who's here."

Hi, I mouthed. "I brought soup," I said out loud.

"Uh-huh," Ben said into the phone. "If you think so. . . . I'll try. . . . Me too. 'Bye."

For the briefest second, I was jealous of whoever was on the other end of the phone, privy to our mutual world and to Ben's other private worlds. I felt invaded, and also as if I'd caught him doing something untoward.

"My sister."

I looked at Ben's face for clues. I didn't see hurt, but I did detect a little weariness. "Are you feeling better? I made soup."

"Thank you." He didn't kiss me. "I *am* feeling much better, actually," he said. He looked as if he were waiting for something.

"I'm sorry," I said. I sighed, trying to figure out what, exactly, I was sorry for.

"Did you think about it?"

"About what?" I felt a plum-sized tight spot in my throat.

Ben smiled sadly. "I guess about the *absurd* idea of living together. But if you haven't, don't say anything now. I don't want to talk about it until you're ready."

I smoothed his worn flannel sheet. I didn't know what to say.

"So thank you for the soup," he said. "And I was thinking, since we didn't get to go on your crazy adventure trip, we could go for a walk in the arboretum or something. Tomorrow, I mean. I've got a little work to do today."

An olive branch, I thought. Then I wondered if he'd even been ill. Could he have been playing sick, like an employee with tissue up his nose, calling in to the boss? I looked at those clear blue eyes and tried, very hard, to trust him. He reached forward and touched my leg.

"I'm sorry we didn't get to go."

This lovely man did not seem capable of so much deception. Unless he'd convinced himself he was sick at the time. It was too much to think about, so I said, "Yes, let's go for a walk in the arboretum. Tomorrow. Now I want you to try my soup. It has many ingredients."

On Sunday, the arboretum was full of families. The lilacs were about to explode into purple, and the first rhododendrons had split their heavy buds into red and white and amethyst grins of bloom. The grass was soggy with rain, and chickadees declared their great food finds. Ben and I were quiet together, but we held hands the whole time. We'd eaten breakfast in silence, both pretending to read the Sunday paper as we sat in a café that smelled so strongly of coffee it was almost like smoke.

We walked along the pavement, and I tried to let the cultivated green overtake me the way the wild did. Mockingbirds sang their copycat songs in the maples. I steered Ben off the paved path and toward my favorite tree, an old corky thing whose branches rested on the ground. I told him how it was my family's tree, how when we were kids my parents had taken the whole family here. I remembered bright skinny-limbed Marla being carried because she was too tired. But when we got to the tree, she monkeyed up and down the branches with Ted and me, wildly energetic. We'd come here at least half a dozen times, on the weekends, after bagels or diner French toast in Jamaica Plain. I remembered believing I was in a jungle, in this single tree. The branches dragged along the ground and sprang back up again; the thinner branches were a tangle of new stick growth around the old gray.

When Ben and I reached the cork tree, a sign that read PLEASE DON'T CLIMB greeted us. I must have looked stricken, because Ben said, "I don't think they mean don't *lean*." He led me to a branch.

It wasn't the same, but at least it was still alive. The limbs were propped up with stakes and rubber slings. A little wire fence circled the original trunk. I leaned lightly against the trunk, worried that I was crushing the whole sprawl of ancient tree, that I could ruin all that history. Ben let his lips press mine, gently. Besides imagining jungles, I'd imagined having a boyfriend back then, I'd imagined being the mommy of the group, with my own husband and my very own babies entertaining themselves. I hadn't thought about that in ages. Of course, back then being the mommy meant having nice clothes, and kissing, and being in charge of all the cookies. As Ben kissed me, I let the naïveté of that memory come back. It didn't seem impossible.

"I like your idea," I said to him. "I need to think about it for a little longer. I think we could make it work," I said. "I'm just not sure I'm ready to give up all my space."

"Okay." Ben kissed me again. "You think. But think, along with that, about how maybe we could get a new place, so you could still have your own space. Maybe a two-bedroom."

"One bedroom just for hiking gear." I smiled. *Not yet*, I thought. My keyhole-shaped apartment. I wasn't ready to leave it.

Ben was buoyant for the rest of the day. He didn't seem one bit sick as we went out for Korean food in Coolidge Corner, stirring up hot stone pots of *bi bim bop*. He ate the egg right off the top and kept creeping his hand along my thigh under the table.

If I couldn't have adventure this weekend, I thought, at least there would be delicious sex, ignited by conflict and reunion. We ran up the flights of stairs to my apartment, giddy with anticipation. As I tried to get the key into the lock, Ben took off my jacket and started unbuttoning my sweater from behind. His fingers were fast.

The phone was ringing as I finally got the door open and fell inside, my T-shirt up around my shoulders; I was pulling at Ben's belt. I didn't answer it, but as the voice started speaking into the answering machine, Ben stopped his mouth, which was busy moving up my bare back, and reached for the phone. It was his sister, her voice with the same rounded edges filling up my living room.

Ben was jumping, literally, his pants sagging down to his knees, as he talked on the phone. I sat on the couch, hugging my T-shirt, feeling naked. When he put down the phone his face was pink and he flung his arms around like an excited conductor.

"The baby! She's born, she's early, she's fine! Her name's Hannah, actually. Kate always liked your name." He beamed, as if he'd somehow made the baby happen. "She was born three hours ago."

I tried to imagine a baby from Ben's family, a baby with my name, red and new and wrapped in hospital blankets. I had never seen Ben so entirely full of glee. I'd seen him happy, I'd seen him satisfied, I'd seen his soft collapse into pleasure, but this was bigger than any of that.

"How did she know to call you here?"

"Well, I gave them the number, because I'm here so much. Baby Hannah. It's incredible when you see them, so new—" He kissed me, very hard, and I felt strange, as though his family were watching us and as if he'd already moved in, even though I hadn't decided.

"Well." He kissed me again.

"You look silly," I said, pointing to his pants. But he was sexy, sexier than before, luminous with delight, his cheeks rosy and his mouth wet with kisses.

"Do we have to go somewhere, or do we still get to have sex?" I asked.

"Oh," said Ben, pulling his pants off the rest of the way and turning that sweet, ecstatic face to really look at me. "Definitely sex."

Seven / By the end of May, Ben and I had visited five apartments, and they all felt murky and cold, despite the warm weather. I had waited so long for an Adventurers' trip, I was beginning to doubt whether the club really existed, whether I would ever go again. Deposits for the summer trip were due at the next meeting; Nicky collected, and I wrote out my check, trying to envision the redwoods, the glaciers.

Ted called almost every night. He and Abby were in couples therapy, but while she seemed to be thriving, he was wilting. Even his voice on the phone was diminished. I listened. I didn't say what I thought, every time, Marla's phrase: *You should just get over it.* That wasn't my decision to make. Parenthood loomed like an invisible horizon. I wondered how my parents would behave as grandparents. Probably my mother would buy all the gear; probably my father would get down on the floor to play. If he ever ceased his criticism of Ted. And assuming that he wasn't really sick—he couldn't be, he never was—*and* that this baby stayed in our lives.

Marla called, too, because she was shopping for rings. Reed hadn't asked her yet, she explained, but he was about to; she knew he was orchestrating something, so she wanted to pick out a ring before he chose the wrong one.

When she asked me if I'd be a bridesmaid, I laughed. I couldn't help it. I told her I'd let her know as soon as she had picked out the ring. Selfish little me, kicking the edge of my couch as we talked, I kind of hoped Reed would simply vanish. For Marla, but also for me.

On the Friday evening before the May trip, I drove Ben to Logan airport. We left three hours early and he still had to run up the departures ramp while I sat in his Volkswagen in the stagnant stream of traffic. Then I had time to fume: four hours of return traffic.

He had meant to come caving with me. The trip didn't involve any hiking, just camping and spelunking, which I had never done, so we'd be wandering around like lost miners together. I'd even borrowed a headlamp for him and dug through his closet for appropriate layers. I was determined that he wouldn't be ill prepared on his first club trip. But then he'd had a New York work trip—there was a touring butterfly exhibit at the Museum of Natural History he needed to consider for booking, and he hadn't realized it was the last weekend he could go—and he decided to go see the new baby too. I was disappointed that he hadn't made earlier arrangements. He was disappointed that I wouldn't accompany him.

So I suppose it was a little bit of revenge, taking his car on the caving trip. I knew we'd be muddy on the way home. I didn't realize how incredibly muddy, that in order to clean the upholstery I'd have to take it to the fancy leather-cleaning shop in Harvard Square and pay more than our dinner out with my father had cost.

I had considered driving Lemon, but my car was getting less and less reliable. Instead I'd taken it in to Holy Motors, where the guys called me Patch-Up Suzy and did their best to keep the bills low. This took creative accounting, they explained, and waiting for parts, if what I brought from my junkyard reserve, or duct tape, didn't solve the problem. Leaving the car there, at least, I didn't have to worry about moving it on street-cleaning days.

Ben had been talking about the great "if" of moving in together as though it were an immediate plan. He told me I didn't need to keep my car; I could use his. He calculated how much I'd save on rent, assuming we found something in our price range. I didn't say I wasn't sure. I just told him which apartments I hated. All of them.

When I drove the VW up to Newton city hall on Saturday morning, Shing and Noah were playing Frisbee by the duck pond. The grass had a new summer look, as if it had been freshly painted. The enormous city hall flag cracked lazy whipping sounds in the early morning wind. Ours were the only cars parked in the ring around the fountain. Shing and Noah waved; Shing caught the Frisbee backhanded, and Nicky sprinted up to my car.

"Hey," he said, as I got out. "New wheels! You're driving us on every trip."

"Not enough room," said Shing, leaving the game.

"And anyway, it isn't mine," I said. "It's my boyfriend's."

"Ah, the mythical boyfriend," said Shing. "Your excuse to miss two trips in a row."

"If we've never seen him," added Nicky, "he must not be real."

Nicky, I'd learned, had a girlfriend, a climbing instructor who had already gone out to Colorado for the summer. Shing never said anything about girlfriends of his own, and Noah had stopped talking about Jenni, so I assumed they were both bachelors.

We packed up the cars. I took Nicky and a whole lot of gear and the sheet of directions Alan handed to each driver.

"After you're done with these," he said, shading his eyes, "you have to give them back. Or destroy them."

"Eat the evidence," said Shing.

"Why?" I held the paper in front of me, its hand-drawn map faint on the copy.

"Because the National Speleological Society doesn't want everyone knowing where the caves are. Have to protect them."

"Long live the bats," said Nicky.

"Right," said Linda. "See you in New York State."

I can't remember my own birth, but I'm sure it was something like caving. After getting lost twice on the drive, trying to follow Alan's crabbed little map, Nicky and I found the other cars parked behind a red octagonal barn that had half collapsed into a field of timothy grass and clover. We layered ourselves in long underwear, old T-shirts, and army surplus jumpsuits. I put on the construction helmet I'd bought, taping the headlamp on with Shing's help. Finally, I struggled into one of Noah's extra climbing harnesses, then lumped along behind Shing and Alan and their ropes.

I followed them through the birches to a subtle slit in the earth. I would never have stopped there on a casual walk through the woods. I would never have noticed the crack, the cool breath of the earth emerging, sweet and silty. Shing and Alan set up the ropes, and in a few minutes Shing belayed right down into the opening. His voice echoed up to the group of us, standing around, steamy in all our gear.

"You're next, Ms. Hannah," said Noah. He helped me clip into the rope, and I walked backward, down into a cave.

It was like a hidden cliff, like a whole world hiding beneath the woods. Tree roots hung down like badly groomed hair. I knew Shing was below me, but still I could feel a fast heartbeat pulsing in my legs and hands as I lowered myself on the rope. If I fell, if a rock crumbled from the edge and hit my head, what would happen? Would they fish me out and call the paramedics? The chill issued up from below like steam. The voices above—Alan, coaching and holding the rope—were muffled by the drip and the rock. I was inside a cold soil-scented mouth, lowering myself down the throat. Water landed on my face and hands like cold coins. The stillness was not quite complete; it was almost as if someone were breathing gently.

"Welcome to Caboose Cave," said Shing, helping me land on a pebbly floor. In my short descent, I'd temporarily lost my ground legs, and I wobbled up to standing.

After we'd all belayed down into the cave entrance, we followed Alan down a corridor, crunching along a pebble floor.

"Which are stalactites and which are stalagmites?" I asked, between shuffles.

"Mites are mighty, because they stick *up*," said Alan, happy to explain. "And tites look like legs—you know, in tights—hanging *down*."

"Not my legs," said Linda.

The ceiling got lower and the floor got higher, and the pebbles gave way to smooth soft silt. No one spoke as we labored along. The breathing sound was still there, louder than our own, which was amplified in the tube.

Eventually, we crouched, Noah first, because of his height, and then we crawled. I felt as if the cave was a manifestation of some childhood fantasy—that a whole other world existed beneath the grass and trees and blacktop, that the earth hid secret passages. Of course, in that vein of fantasy, I wasn't entirely sure there weren't any dragons or treasures or talking rabbits up ahead. I couldn't believe everyone else was so nonchalant, though they had some idea of what came next, whereas I had none. I followed Linda's behind as she followed Noah's. Our headlamps cast circles of light in front of us, illuminating scraps of blue sock or green army surplus jumpsuit among the browns and grays.

"Here we go," said Linda, turning slightly in the limited space. She flattened out: paper Linda, practically two-dimensional.

The ceiling and floor had almost met, and suddenly we were in a narrow fold, flat on our bellies, worms in the mud. I stopped.

"Um, this is kind of tight," I said to Linda.

She grunted. "This, believe it or not, is nothing." She could no longer turn around. My headlamp shone on the bottoms of her boots. I wondered which way we were headed, toward the center of the earth or back up. I was cramped; my chest felt tight, but I started to inch, pulling myself along with my fingers and feet, waiting for Linda to get far enough ahead to keep her boots from hitting my head.

Nicky was behind me. At first, that seemed comforting, but then I realized it meant I couldn't back up. I tried to turn and look at him, but I couldn't move my head that far in the space; my helmet struck the ceiling and stuck.

"Hannah," said Nicky. "Don't kick."

"Sorry," I said. "I just felt a little—well, trapped."

"You okay, honey?" His voice changed. The honey was comforting. I felt crushed, immobile, unable to breathe.

"Don't think about it," Nicky continued, when I didn't answer. "We're almost into a room. This is the hardest part."

"Okay," I said, inching some more. I tried not to think about what Linda had said: *This is nothing.* A room, I thought, a place to sit up; there will be more space and air. Linda's feet had moved ahead of my light spot, so all I could see was more gray silt, an occasional stone, and what looked like a bit of black plastic bag.

"What else?" I wanted Nicky to keep talking. His voice seemed far away, though I knew he was right behind me.

"You're in Mother Earth's intestines," he said. "But soon you'll reach the stomach."

"Great," I said. "Stomach acid. Can't wait." I inched some more, and the black plastic bag squeaked.

"Oh, shit," I said. "A bat."

"Careful," said Nicky. "Try not to wake it up."

"Right," I said.

"Are you scared of bats?"

I considered this, as my face was almost pressed against the black lump. It stretched slightly and refolded a wing. Up close, it was exquisite, the skin stretched between the tiny wing bones, the black almost translucent in my headlamp light. It was the size of an apple.

"No, I guess I'm not," I said. I inched past and strained to keep my legs pressed on the wall away from the bat. I felt a surge of victory. I'd passed the bat. I didn't wake it. It didn't scream or bite me. Of course, now Nicky had to pass it, and Camilla, who was behind him.

My fingers hit a rim. It felt strange. I'd started to get used to the inching, and suddenly there was something to pull. I pulled, hard, and whacked my head against the ceiling.

"Trying to get somewhere?" I saw Noah's face ahead of me, his head and hands as free as a normal person's in normal space. I wondered whether I was hallucinating. Then I pulled up to the rim, and I was in a room as big as the stadium lecture hall at Carleton. Linda, Noah, Shing, and Alan were points of light.

"Not too loud," whispered Linda. "The bats are sleeping."

I slid out onto the new floor, feeling nimble and weightless in the open space, and cast my light around the room. Thousands of bodies huddled together on the ceiling: small living spots. Here and there, something fidgeted; a wing or a foot emerged from the folded bat and readjusted. A squeak. A flutter. We were in their bedroom, sitting on sloped silt and occasional stone. Our breathing echoed.

After Nicky and Camilla oomphed their way out of the crack, we ate gorp in the dark. We switched off our lamps and whispered, to keep from waking the bats. In all this space, I started to think about the darkness. We'd entered the cave at around eleven-thirty, so now it was probably around one o'clock or so, though I wasn't sure. I realized how, in the world of ordinary days, I relied on light to tell the time. Even in my apartment, even in the office, some light cast time across the rooms. Now, underneath the earth, I had no idea. I liked it; it was a strange small freedom.

After the squeeze and the room, I thought I was a caving expert. For a while, we crouched down a long corridor with a skinny stream running along the bottom.

"Okay." Linda's voice interrupted our shuffle. "Just to

prepare you a little." She stopped. I could hear the others moving on ahead, and Nicky, crouched right up behind me.

"The next pass isn't really long, but it's really really tight. It's called a lemon squeeze, and it gets narrower and narrower, but you pop out at the end."

"Into a room?" I asked, trying to prepare myself for that little repeat birth.

"This time, just into a small chamber, but it'll feel great. Relax in the squeeze, if you can, and if you get stuck, try something new, hands instead of legs—"

"Teeth," said Camilla, from the back. "Or step on Nicky," she added.

Camilla's addition turned out to be helpful. As the squeeze got narrower, it felt as if my shoulders were being compressed by rock. My legs were stuck, and my arms were wedged, one up, one down. The only free body parts were my tongue and my feet. Even my helmet felt immovable.

I couldn't hear Linda ahead of me, so I knew she must have moved through. Linda was taller than me, I thought— okay, so she was skinnier—but how could she have passed through this opening? I felt like frosting mashed into a bag. The only way out was a tip, and I wasn't that narrow. My skin was hot with the tension, and inside I was cold.

"Hey," I said. "What do I do now?" My voice stayed in the small stuck spot with me. I wiggled the fingers wedged up ahead. Silt. I tried to walk them ahead of me in the space. Stretching, one finger found a hole. I had no idea how big it was, but I needed to get to that hole. I was sure I was starting to run out of breath.

I tried the toes. I tried again, and suddenly they had purchase on something hard. Behind me, Nicky made a muffled noise.

I shifted forward less than an inch. I wiggled my toes again, and then I could bend my knee slightly, so I shoved my foot down hard, bringing my face up about six inches to the hole my hand had discovered. It grew as I approached. The hole was the size of the little round windows in the closets in the eaves at my mother's house, miniature portholes, maybe a foot in diameter.

"You found us." Linda's voice came from the other side of the hole.

I shoved again and grabbed on with my fingers; then Linda pulled my arms and I was born into a space the size of a rowboat, with Shing sitting in it. Noah and Alan had already gone ahead, because there wasn't enough room.

As I sat panting on the floor, I looked into the hole, lit by Linda's beam. Nicky's helmet emerged, an unmistakable muddy boot print marking the yellow plastic.

"Oh," I said to him, once he was out. "Does it count if you have to step on someone to make it out of a lemon squeeze?"

Nicky smiled weakly. "Everything counts," he said.

When we reached the last passage, a weak glow diluted the darkness. I could hear the outside before I could see it: the birds, the drip of the water around the exit. It sounded artificial. I watched Nicky crouch, then stand, as the corridor grew taller, and the ceiling filled with traditional stalactites, icicles of stone. Then we were walking, upright and evolved. The birds got louder, and the light cast a grainy gray over everything. I could see in front of and behind me, and the dim circle from my headlamp was a moot yellow moon.

The exit was wider than the entrance; there was no climbing; we strolled right out. We passed through an unlocked gate, which Alan locked behind us, and then we were out in the bright of the sun and the dazzling greens of foliage. I was slick with mud and felt heavy. My boots were full of pebbles, so I took them off and sat beside Linda, letting the sun warm my pale pickled feet.

That night, we had a big campfire in a circle of stones. We cooked chicken and peppers on skewers in the fire. Linda, in charge of food, had packed a cooler, since we didn't have to carry everything in. Shing drove his minivan to the nearest local market and brought back ice cream, which we passed in a circle around the fire. The creamy texture filled me. That night, sleeping between Shing and Camilla in a tent, I dreamed of eating the silt in the cave. It tasted like chocolate.

The next day, we drove through birch woods along a dirt road that grew rougher and narrower as it progressed. Camilla rode with me in the VW.

"Not so great for the suspension," she said, tapping the dash.

For a second, I thought of Ben. He could have been here. He was missing all this. He probably was holding baby Hannah, thinking the same of me.

"No big deal," I said. "She can take it."

The road telescoped further, and then it ended. No opening into an unexpected room. I parked behind Shing's minivan and noticed the smear of mud across the seat where Camilla had been sitting in her caving clothes. I took a tissue from the glove box and tried to wipe it off, but my efforts embedded the mud more deeply in the leather.

The entrance to Spider Cave was a wide-open mouth with a tongue of stream. There was no clear path, which Alan said was purposeful; unfenced, marked caves were subject to the wiles of the unprepared, the drunk, and the stupid, who harassed the wildlife and left broken bottles and sometimes got lost and injured and required emergency rescue. So Alan used a map from a little spiral-bound notebook and a compass. He led us like a shepherd through the birches.

Noah, walking stiffly in all his layers, pointed out a miniature field of what looked like clover and informed us that it was wood sorrel and good to eat. He grabbed a handful and illustrated, smacking his lips. Then he pointed again, this time toward a plant about a half a foot high with little white flowers.

"Ooh, chickweeds," he said. "The leaves and stems are good, and even better cooked." He popped a leaf into his mouth.

Camilla picked one of the white flowers and tucked it behind her ear. I noticed there was mud from yesterday in her pale hair.

"And wild lettuces, too," said Noah, pointing. "We'll make a salad. And sassafras tea." His hand brushed the low branch of a tree I recognized, with three leaf shapes: mitten, two-fingered glove, and the traditional one-lobed leaf.

"You've been waiting all winter to poison us," said Camilla.

"You gave me the book." He chucked her shoulder and she stumbled before leaping onto his back. He carried her a few feet before they both fell in the sorrel.

It was morning when we entered Spider Cave, still June cool; the sun cast thin beams through the trees as we trudged, helmets in hand. Nicky and Alan were wearing wetsuits under their jumpsuits, so they walked like tin men. Nicky lugged his new toy, an inflatable boat. Alan explained that inside the cave lay the largest underground lake in the east; he and Nicky were going rafting. The rest of us would take a drier route once we reached the lake.

It was an easy stroll in, and it wasn't until we started crouching down a narrow passage that my body remembered all the previous day's affronts. The stream was only a trickle, but it had already soaked my knees. Alan and Nicky were at the back, shoving and dragging their unwieldy boat. I could hear water, a drip and a low running sound from the stream. I wondered what lived in the lake—blind fish, maybe, or dragons. The group was quiet; I imagined everyone was considering their day-old bruises or trying to digest the hefty granola-and-fruit breakfast. Linda, behind me, emitted an occasional grumble. I had never seen her really cranky. Only Camilla, when she fell a lot skiing, and Shing, when someone scratched his van with a metal pack ring, had ever snapped at the group. Alan could be fussy and bossy, and Noah was usually aloof, but I hadn't seen any real fights or great complaint.

The lake was at the end of a narrow squeeze. Not a lemon, not anything that required treading on a friend's head, but I was tired and cold already. The lake seemed impossible: a long arch of water in our lights. Alan and Nicky were already rustling with their boat and a foot pump, and Noah and I sat and looked out, our headlamps revealing the whims of our vision. And the limits. The ceiling was about ten feet above the water. I tried to believe it was real, that there was a lake encapsulated inside the body of the earth.

Nicky waded in partway. "Cold!" he said, with a gleeful squeal.

"Caving must be awful in the winter," I said to Noah.

"Cave temperatures stay constant; this one's fifty-eight degrees," he said. "It's the same in here, winter and summer. Makes it all that much better when you come out. Like the time of year is a surprise."

"Hey, kids," said Shing, sliding down between us on the bank. I could feel the moisture seeping through the long underwear on my thighs as I scooted down from crouch to sit. That's why we were crouching, I thought. I stretched my legs, since I was already wet.

"Nicky and Alan are sailing on out," Shing said. "And Linda and I are going back out the way we came in. Neither of us is really up for exploring many Spider legs today. I think"—he started to whisper—"that Linda's not feeling so well."

Linda was up to her ankles in the lake, helping Alan and Nicky shove off from the dark shore. They were sailing, I thought, into the belly of the earth, into the liver, the spleen, and the circulatory system. I envied them their wetsuits as I shivered. I envied their boat and paddles.

"But you guys can come out the Head Path or Balls." Shing reported this straight, as if there was nothing the least bit amusing about the names.

"Head or Balls," said Camilla. "Sounds awfully masculine." She shook her head, and her headlamp zigged on the lake's surface.

"There's that path out we haven't done," said Noah. "Falls."

"Right," said Camilla. "You follow the stream and it gets wider and wider, and then there's a little squeeze and the falls and you're out."

"Let's," said Noah.

"You and me and Hannah," said Camilla.

"You guys be careful," said Shing.

I was so happy they were choosing me—like being first draft on the school softball team, something I never was, being buried in the athletic middle by height and early development—that I didn't say what I was thinking: that I'd really just like to go back out again.

After Shing and Linda crouched their way out of sight, their voices fading into the tunnel, and after we could no longer hear the diminishing splashes of Nicky and Alan paddling away, Noah and Camilla and I looked at the little sheet Alan had given Noah, a map of the underground, as reported by someone in the National Speleological Society, who'd come and later sketched it from memory.

"That way," said Noah, pointing at the map, then into the dark. We followed him around the lake's bank, searching for an opening. Finally, we found a loaf-sized heap of pebbles, an underground cairn. Noah walked beyond it, into the invisibility past our lights, and yelled out, "No wall here!" We joined him and lit the landscape; a stream flowed through a wide corridor and Noah stood square in the middle, like a pillar.

We followed a walking path, then crouched; then the way compressed until we were in an envelope of space: a wide crack with no side walls, ceiling and floor about two or three feet apart. The stream followed, too, growing shallow and hushed in the envelope. But soon we couldn't crouch and had to lie in the water. Constant temperature or not, it felt cold to me.

We crept into a big room, divided diagonally by the stream. It was a relief to stretch and stand. There was a dim glow in the room and the thinnest seam of light along the ceiling, letting in the green. No bats, just smooth visible rock, and plants and roots hanging down, about twenty feet up from where we stood, where the world was outside the cave. I gazed at the hairline of radiance and thought I felt its warmth, all the way down below. It was like looking through a pinhole camera, all the dark surrounds, the picture through the tiniest opening. Inside, we were mostly ruled by touch. Outside, sight was king.

We crossed the room and shuffled along a new corridor. Soon, we were flat on the slippery silt, crawling through the stream. And then the descent started. It was like a hill, only the ceiling sank parallel to the floor.

"Roll!" Camilla called. She turned her body, and started rolling, fast. I followed. I closed my eyes to stop the bizarre vertigo effect caused by my headlamp's spinning, floor-ceiling-floor. The silt was slick and the floor felt spongy. My body warmed with exertion. Noah laughed. We were kids, rolling down a hill, only we were deep under the earth, and, apparently, going even deeper.

"Are we still following the stream?" asked Camilla, at the bottom.

We'd rolled into a puddle; it was shallow, and about a dozen feet across. My light revealed Noah's face, bright with exertion.

"That way." Noah shifted his lamp and, sure enough, the puddle flowed off at one end.

After a while, I grew cold again. We were slogging through the water, having long since abandoned any hope of keeping our suits dry. The ceiling rose and dipped, and we'd had a few brief squeezes, but mostly it seemed endless. The stream was about three feet deep, and there was two feet of air space above, then one, then three. I wondered if we were going the right way, but I didn't want to say anything. I wasn't leading, and Noah, of all people, would know what he was doing. Camilla, in front of me, whistled a tentative tune.

Then we came to a dip. The stream traveled under a wall of rock, and the only way forward was face down in the stream, kicking through. It looked like about a foot and a half of space.

"Okay," said Camilla, her voice unexpectedly hard. "I'm freezing and this looks bad. Let's go back up."

"Up?" said Noah. "I don't think that's the way out."

"I mean back the way we came." I didn't light her face with my glance. "I'm freezing, and I'll bet Hannah's freezing, and just because you're made of asbestos doesn't mean we want to dive in there."

"I'm going," said Noah. "I think this is the right way. I think the waterfall exit is here, or very soon." He didn't sound convinced, but he did sound irritable.

He didn't wait for discussion, he ducked. His kicking was loud, for a second or two, and then he was gone. All I heard was the stream, the incessant cave drip, and Camilla, breathing hard. A minute of breathing, two or three.

"*Hey, Noah!*" screamed Camilla.

Just the drip and breath.

"*Noah Baum!*" she yelled.

"Um," I said, after a long minute. "What now?"

"Fuck," said Camilla. Then she turned toward me, her lamp dazzling my eyes. "Well, we have three choices. We say fuck Noah, and go back and don't die. Or I go, and if Noah is dead then I probably die too, and you're left to make the next choice. Or if it was the waterfall exit then we sit in the sun and warm up and he says I told you so, of course." She paused. I looked at her and she smiled in the beam of my headlamp. The light was going yellow, and I wondered whether my batteries were dying. I had an extra set in my very wet daypack. I also had an emergency blanket. I was thinking of wrapping myself in it and taking a nap.

"Or you can go first," she said.

"I want a nap."

"No naps," said Camilla. "I'll go."

She looked at me again. Her light temporarily blinded me. "If that's okay?"

"Okay." I watched as Camilla dove into the shallow river. She splashed and kicked, and her feet disappeared under the rock. A shard of sound followed the splashing. A scream, I thought, my heart speeding up and then slowing with fear. Something floated through the hole, something black and spindly. I climbed against the side wall, afraid to let my light reveal what it was, what animal had killed them both and left me stranded underground, knee deep in a cold stream and about to vomit from fear. I swallowed and looked.

Camilla's backpack.

Now it was my choice. I could try to go back. Or I could find out what precipitated that scream. Maybe there was something I could do, even; maybe I could help them. Or at least, if I was going to die, I wouldn't have to be alone.

I put Camilla's pack on over my own, loosening the waist strap so I could secure it. Camilla, I thought, was very slender. And very brave. And on the other side of the barrier. Then I took a deep breath and ducked. I kicked. My helmet scraped rock. I dug my boot into the floor and shoved. I kicked more. Then I came loose on the other side and tried to stand up for a breath. The floor had slipped away, and I couldn't find the ceiling; I couldn't find any air.

I remembered swimming lessons at Crystal Lake. How Dad walked us out in the cold mornings, his supposedly secret cigarette clouding him on the bench by the baby area. Ted, skinny in his suit, running out along the dock to the advanced group, the sharks. I was a minnow. I was supposed to be able to swim one length between the docks by the end of the summer, but when the test came around, I panicked. I had to touch something, and when my feet couldn't find the sand and leaves at the bottom, I grabbed onto the buoy between lanes, embracing it as if I'd been drowning.

I had to repeat minnow, and I was the oldest girl in my group, and at a birthday party at the lake, I was the only one who wasn't allowed to play Marco Polo in the L of the deep dock. I sat on shore with my friend's mother and talked about school; my mouth tasted of algae and disappointment.

I didn't think there were algae in the cave river. The water tasted clean and cold as I took some in my mouth. I let the last bubbles out of my nose and kicked hard toward the surface.

Something grabbed me roughly, dragged me forward and up.

"Hey," said Noah. "Welcome to the Other Side." He pulled me onto a sort of shore past the deep spot where I'd been floundering.

Camilla and Noah and I sat on a pile of silt, saying nothing. The stream continued into what distance we could see, the ceiling dropping, the space narrower still. It was too small to be a lemon squeeze, too small for much more than a snake to pass through.

"We're lost," said Camilla.

"I think you were right," said Noah. "We should probably go back."

The duck-under was a lot easier on the way back. Knowing where we were going made the whole underworld seem less dangerous. But going back up the slope we'd rolled down was protracted, grueling work. We slithered up, using fingers, knees, pack buckles—anything for purchase. Noah, slightly chagrined, followed us, and sometimes I felt his hand bracing my foot as I slipped on the silt. I said thank you the first three times, but after that I stepped into his palm, saying nothing.

Camilla was silent. I wondered whether she was still angry. She was shivering and her hair was dripping. She looked so cold I felt warm and brave beside her. Now she was climbing up the slope, and our breathing and the shuffle of our packs against the ceiling were the loudest sounds.

We made it through the room with the ceiling crack, the light casting only a tepid yellow glow. I didn't look up; I followed Camilla as she walked, fast, determined, her day pack dripping a stream behind her.

When we arrived at the lake, I almost laughed, thankful for the familiar, for knowing we were nearly out. Noah sat down, and I realized it was the first time I'd ever seen him tired.

He reached for Camilla's hands as if to warm them, but she pulled away.

"Hannah," he said. "Can I help you get warm?"

"That's okay," I said, sitting, relishing the space around my head, around my limbs. I was cold, but we were almost out.

Camilla moved to a further boulder.

"Camilla?" he said.

"I'm mad," she said.

Noah sighed and there was the sound of water dripping, the cave scent I couldn't get out of my nose, silt and damp.

Their silence made me uneasy. In my family, there would be yelling, but here we were in an irritable standoff.

"We're almost out," I said, to have a voice ring against the walls.

Camilla said nothing. I wondered if I could find my way out alone, how long they'd sit here in the cold and spite.

"I didn't mean to get us stuck like that," whispered Noah.

"Let's get the hell out of here," said Camilla.

The entrance, when we returned, wasn't bright. I wondered whether we'd made some mistake. The air grew drier and slightly warmer, but no sunlight flooded the passage.

We stumbled the last few feet, then up the slope to the outside. There were stars, and the moon was fat and silver. It was night. I felt disoriented, more lost than I'd been inside.

"*We're out!*" Camilla shouted, as she started to strip off her wet clothes.

We ran toward the cars in our long underwear. Shing was by his van, and he let out a loud "*Christ!*" as we reached him. He grabbed us hard. His hug hurt my neck and ribs. He wouldn't let go of Noah. He was whispering as he squeezed, his voice uneven and loud beneath the rasp. "You bastard, you jerk, you idiot. . . ."

Noah let himself be crushed for a second longer and then shook out of Shing's grasp. Mud clots tangled his blond hair. He didn't say anything.

Shing's face was vivid with anger. "You're okay? You're okay?" he repeated. The flush of anger cooled and he looked sad, relieved, exhausted.

Camilla didn't look at them as she pulled dry clothes from her pack in the Volkswagen, which I'd forgotten to lock.

Linda was talking into a cell phone. "I'm calling off the search," she said. "We had Search and Rescue out already."

"What time is it?" Noah asked.

"I was afraid I'd have to inherit that nice leather jacket of yours," Nicky said.

"Not funny," said Camilla.

"Calm down, guys," said Linda. "Everyone's okay, right?" She cast her gaze on me, on Camilla, her eyes glossy.

"Everyone's okay," I said. I layered myself with a sweater,

sweatpants, coat, and hat. I jiggled to alert my body to the possibility of heat.

I felt as if I'd lost something. Maybe it was because the day had vanished while we were inside the cave, maybe because so many hours had disappeared while we were trying to find our way. But I moved through the wobbly feeling. Shing insisted on driving Ben's car, with Camilla and me under sleeping bags in the back. He kept saying we were experiencing shock, that no one who'd spent the day lost in a cave was up for a five-hour drive. We didn't stop for dinner, we went to a drive-through, and Camilla and I ate French fries in the backseat under the sleeping bags, sleepy as winter bears.

It tingled, the strangeness, that we were holding all this adventure under our skin, and that we were okay, the fear dulled, eating French fries and Filet O-Fish, our lips slick with the grease. I thought about Noah, his whispered apology, the length of his limbs and his irritating, fascinating pride. He was riding with Linda as she drove Shing's van, somewhere else along the time tunnel of the turnpike.

"So, Hannah," said Shing. "You are now officially initiated into Club Crazy. I hope you won't hold it against us." His words had a bitter coating.

"It wasn't your fault," I said.

"But maybe we can find some way to blame you," said Camilla, her mouth full.

"Not a joke," Shing mumbled. "Still want to go on the summer trip?" he asked, with a forced lift in his voice.

"Of course," I said. I hadn't been thinking about it.

"You okay, girl?" Camilla bundled the down bag under my chin.

"Yes," I said. I wanted to talk about Noah, about romance in the club, I wanted to ask about the man in the climbing trip photo—Vijay, his browned-butter skin and mouth open with laughter—but being lost had made me too exhausted to converse. I pulled two sleeping bags over myself, shivering despite the car heater and warm surrounds of June, and fell asleep against Camilla's shoulder. I dreamed of lying on the cool cheek of a cave, the dark just as deep with my eyes opened or closed.

Eight / The cave stayed with me, silt too far under my nails to brush out, the shiver of that stream running through my skin, the duck-under in my dreams. I kept the memory of fear to myself, like hidden sour candy. I didn't tell Ben we'd been lost. I told him about the lemon squeeze and the bats, about stepping on Nicky's head. It didn't feel like deception, exactly.

All week, Marla kept coming to my apartment unannounced. She rang the buzzer at dinnertime, she rang when Ben and I were getting ready for bed, mouths foaming with our respective toothpastes. Ben liked cinnamon gel, and I bought whatever was on sale. I was tempted to tell him, when he brought over a full-sized cinnamon ("so I can always feel clean"; "You aren't clean, my dirty man," I'd said, smiling), that Noah, Camilla, and Nicky used Dr. Bronner's Peppermint Soap for everything—washing, tooth brushing, dishes—when we were on a trip. It tasted kind of nasty, but it was biodegradable.

Each time Marla rang, I let her in, and she camped on my couch or at the table, unfolding wedding ideas from her purse like found treasures. First, she had pictures of rings, then brochures from estates that rented themselves out for ceremonies and receptions, then an article from a glossy women's magazine about mixed marriages.

"What do you think, Hannah, would you go with a rabbi and a justice? Or a rabbi and a priest?"

"It isn't relevant," I'd hissed. Ben was in the shower. We'd already determined that Reed didn't care what kind of wedding he had, but his mother would be disappointed that Marla wasn't Catholic. He hadn't told his mother yet. He hadn't asked Marla to marry him yet, either. He had quit his job to take a modeling course, and an acting class too.

"It could be," she said. "Do you consider yourself Jewish?"

"Do you think you can come back some other time to talk about this? It's eleven and I've got work tomorrow morning." I felt petty. I couldn't do what she wanted; I couldn't simper and exclaim. Maybe if she were really getting married, I could muster some enthusiasm for details. Maybe if it didn't seem like an elaborate excuse to make me talk about marriage for myself.

"Mom thinks Dad's mother was a hidden Jew. That would make us real Jews. Which we are anyway, if you go the maternal route. I'm worried about Dad," she added; it was like a cough she couldn't shake. This was odd. I was always the one who worried about Dad. Maybe we were trading places; maybe she'd taken over in my hour of neglect.

"God," I said, "I don't know. But he's getting that treatment, Mom said—and Marla, I really am tired."

On Saturday, the buzzer woke me at eight. I didn't believe it could really be someone at the door, so I ignored it and rolled over in bed. I looked at Ben, asleep with a stripe of sunlight across his cheek. One arm was flung up, his fingers around the headboard dowel, as if he were climbing the bed. His tuft of armpit hair, his cheeks as pink as a child's. I looked at the lines around his eyes. Smile lines, tiny creases in the skin from that repeated gesture. Smiles for me, smiles for work. Smiles for his nieces and nephews. I'd said I would go with him on his next visit to New Jersey. What if they didn't like me? We'd searched our calendars for a free weekend and finally found one in early fall. It was a long way away, beyond the bright horizon of my summer trip. But saying I'd go seemed to land him on a solid square of content.

If I could manage to put off all decisions until after the summer, I would know what to do. After the trip. If Ben and I moved in together, would there be any summer trips in my future? He had stopped asking about my big decision, and we'd settled into a new comfortable pattern, with him sleeping over most nights, cinnamon toothpaste and half a drawer in my old pine bureau, a few shirts hanging like giant pale moths in my closet, his sleep-warm body in my bed in the morning, his dark hair and the surprise of his eyes when they opened, star sapphires.

He kept finding open houses for us. Now he was pushing for us to buy a condo instead of renting.

The buzzer sounded again. Twice. The third time, someone leaned hard and let it drone on for over a minute.

I got up. The sun-drenched living room floor was warm on my soles.

"Hello?"

"Me," said Marla.

"Too early," I said. I wished I'd kept ignoring the buzz. Why did she think she could keep coming over?

I stood by the buzzer, knowing she'd press it again. I wondered if anyone ever told Marla *no*.

When she buzzed, I let her in.

"Hey," said Ben, exiting the bedroom in only his boxer shorts as I opened the door for Marla. He was golden in the light; I wanted to touch his skin.

"Don't you have anything better to do than harass us?" I felt gummy, standing in my apartment in the midmorning sun, with an unwanted guest on a delicious rare Saturday with Ben.

"It's important," said Marla. "And I brought these." She put a bag of bagels from my favorite place, Rosenfeld's in Newton, on my table.

"Yum," said Ben. He took the top one out, Everything flavor, and started eating. "Shower," he said, taking his bagel with him as he ducked into the bedroom.

Marla went into the kitchen and started digging around in the fridge.

"Got coffee?" she asked.

I sighed. "I'll make it."

"He's so yummy," she said, when I joined her in the kitchen. She nodded her head toward the bedroom.

"He's not food." I was really cranky. If I'd wanted to get up early, I would have; I would have pulled on my running clothes and escaped into the day before the early summer heat started to swell the sidewalks. I'd wanted sleep, luscious erasure, the gentle arms of dreams.

"Han, I can fix this. Do you have a wrench?" She tapped my drippy faucet. At night the sound reminded me of the caves.

"What is so important?"

"He asked."

"He? Asked?"

"Reed asked me to marry him. He bought the ring on his own."

I looked at her hands, which still only sported the band of emeralds and diamonds my mother gave her for high school graduation. My graduation was at the very beginning of the money. I'd gotten a nice Cross pen and pencil set.

"Where is it?" Suddenly it was real. I wanted to be happy for her. I reached for happiness, but I just found queasiness.

"I told him I'd say yes as soon as I had everything sorted out."

"What do you have to sort?" The queasiness was spreading, growing like a mold from my center out.

"I want to make sure Daddy's okay. And Ted and Abby too."

"You're waiting for everyone else? Getting married isn't about everyone else." *Daddy*, I thought, bristling. I wondered why I was defending her right to marry Reed.

Marla dug in her purse and brought out an adjustable wrench. I wondered what was really holding her back. I hoped it was something else. Even when she annoyed me, I still thought Reed Scrum was barely a crumb compared to the great chocolate cake of Marla.

"They won't live forever, you know. We should make them happy while we can."

Ben came out of the shower as the coffee began spluttering through the filter and Marla finished reassembling the faucet.

"I'm going running," I said, glaring at Marla.

"I've got some wedding stuff to show Ben." She smiled, beautifully.

"I don't think Ben has time—" I said.

"Oh, it's okay," said Ben. He smelled of my apple shampoo.

He tore a chunk out of an egg bagel and wadded it into his mouth with a smile.

When I came back from my jog, they were sitting close together on the couch, examining a catering brochure.

"Hey," said Marla. "Ben's amazing with this stuff." She held up a piece of paper with columns designated for food and music, numbers written out in his neat hand. "He should sideline as a wedding planner."

If she wanted to get married so desperately, I thought, and she wanted to convince Ben so desperately, and Ben was so interested, maybe she and Ben should just have a big old wedding themselves.

"Great," I said. The sweat wasn't cooling me. Dense summer heat filled the room. I switched on a ceiling fan, and the papers in their laps fluttered. The columns spilled onto the rug.

"Hey," said Marla.

"Hey yourself." I tapped an invisible watch on my wrist. "I think it's time for you to go."

"Honey," said Ben. "She told you her news, didn't she?"

I sighed and went over to the window. I opened it, and stepped out onto the fire escape. My shirt was heavy and wet. The metal stairs rang as I held tight to the rail and climbed to the landing at the top.

The sky was syrupy with humidity, the air thick with the scents of tar and drowning worms, and it started to rain as I sat down.

From my perch at the top of the fire escape, the new green leaves and the buds unfurling like hands obscured the streets. The roofs were growing slick, the air was struck clean by fresh rain.

My muscles began to feel stiff as I cooled down from my

jog. I was soaked and chilly. I couldn't go back into my own apartment. It was too crowded. Maybe I'd move. Maybe when I went on the summer trip I would fall in love with Seattle, and I'd stay there with my backpack and camp stove. I could find a new job and an apartment with a view of the mountains or Puget Sound. Ben could come if he wanted to; he could get a job as a wedding planner, but Marla would have to stay in Boston.

The rain intensified. It was like a delicious cool shower. I could move outside, anyway. I wasn't planning on coming down until she was gone.

"Hey." Ben's voice was cautious.

I didn't move from my perch. A vent sighed with fried-egg-scented oven exhaust.

"Hey. Hannah my love?"

Ben's head was dripping. His arms shone with rain. His jeans were wet too, splatters darkening the denim. He started to climb the stairs. He looked nervous.

"Are you coming down?" He sat down one step below me, looking childlike with his legs folded up.

"Is she there?"

"I told her to go."

"Big of you," I said.

"I didn't realize—"

"She is just so *insistent*," I said.

"Kind of reminds me of you."

"Hah," I said. "I'm much less blond."

I felt mean. This wasn't supposed to be about petty jealousy. My jealousy was bigger, more warranted. It was because she was robbing me of privacy, privacy with Ben, privacy over the issue of marriage. It was because she had our father all wrapped up and manageable, not to mention dressed in a tux. She didn't care if he approved—how could she not care? She

was leaping into my future and waving her arms for me to follow. Maybe I had different directions in mind.

"Oh, Hannah." Ben didn't get up. "I don't have the
slightest interest in your sister, not *that* way. I've already got
my girl."

"You don't have to," I said to Ben. I was at my desk, picking
at a plastic overlay. The O_2 Spa project was full of complica-
tions. Permits and technical details. I thought of Marla,
grudgingly, wishing she could fix the mechanical parts for
me. I just wanted to work on designs. Actually, I didn't even
want to work on these designs. I thought the whole idea was
ludicrous.

"It's okay, I didn't want to go to this reception anyway.
I'll duck out early and take a cab to Newton. Upper Lower
Side Falls Centre."

"Ha-ha. But really," I said.

"But really," said Ben. He made a kiss noise into the
phone.

I couldn't decide what to wear. It really didn't matter, but for
some reason I changed out of my fish-print sundress and
into shorts, then into another dress, a dark-blue crepe that
looked like it needed pearls. I put on pearls. My father was
coming again, though Marty was out of town. Ted and Abby
would be there, and Marla and Reed Scrum, and I'd asked
Ben. I would meet him there in his car.

I sat on my bed in my crepe dress, slipping sandals on and
off my feet to feel the smooth slide. Maybe I'd forget to go.
Maybe Ben could be my representative. He could tell them
whatever they needed to know about me.

There was no caterer, and no Marty, so we were having
plain roast chicken and rice. The salad was iceberg and the rice

was dry, but my mother had opened a delicious Sauvignon Blanc, so I sipped lots of that. My father was late. Ben was late. My mother decided we wouldn't wait, since the food was hot and, she said, since Abby was probably starving.

Abby, five months pregnant, was gently swelled. Her skin was winter white despite its being June, and she rivaled Marla's beauty. Ted held her hand.

"We'll eat without your father," my mother announced, for the second time. "You did say we were expecting Benjamin?" she looked at me as Marla served chicken.

"He's a little late. It's not the end of the world. He had a reception."

Ben would be here; I had no doubt about him. I tried not to wonder what was keeping my father.

"Well," said my mother, after five minutes of quiet eating. "I have to check something." She disappeared into the kitchen.

"Sorry," said Ben. He'd come in without ringing or knocking. He sat down beside me, looking dramatic and older than everyone but my mother in his dark sharp suit. I'd never seen his tie before, a deep red with an almost metallic glow.

"You didn't wait?" said my father, arriving behind Ben. Once again, he toted a large bag of birdseed, which he plopped on the Persian rug in the living room. Millet and thistle trailed him as he sat down at the head of the table.

"Well." My mother came in with an apron and a baked potato in each oven-mitted hand. "Glad you decided to join us, Wolf. We were about to start dessert."

"I've got to go," said Reed.

"The bathroom's in—" said Marla.

"No, I mean I have an appointment," he said.

"No," said Marla, "you can't. We have to, you know, tell them. . . ."

"Now, really?" asked Reed. He put his napkin on top of his plate, and chicken *jus* spread across the linen.

"After dessert," said my mother.

After dessert, which was an extravagant, bakery-ordered, three-layer lemon cake—"not as good as Marty's," said my father—my mother had us retire to the living room, where she passed around a box of chocolates and sat in the biggest chair, looking like a diminutive queen, her apron still on.

"Well," said Marla. "We wanted to talk about something—"

My mother interrupted. "I hope you've thought this over."

"Wait," said my father, patting the bag of seed. The striped sunflower seeds slipped out through the burlap holes and into his hand. He nibbled, cracking a shell and eating the meat. He held up the empty shell to the lamp as if reading it. "I'm dying."

He wasn't smiling. I should have worried, I thought.

My mother was coughing, choking on the chocolate in her mouth. She started to gag and I looked at her, wondering whether she was going to vomit. I was unable to move, mired in couch cushions. Finally she stopped and moved to the love seat, sitting next to my father.

"Well," said my father. "The drugs aren't enough—the lupus—I have kidney damage. Have had for a while." He dropped the seed husk on the floor and gazed around the room at us.

The lawn was sharply green and the sun was still hanging on to the horizon, even though it was almost nine o'clock.

"But your kidneys—can't you treat them?" Ben took my hand. I hadn't expected the next words to come from him.

"Not really," said my father. "I don't want to—it's really too late, and too nasty."

"Now, Wolf," said my mother. Her knees almost touched his as they sat together on the love seat. "We should talk about this."

"Okay," said my father. "But not in front of the children."

He gave her a brief smile, and the picture of them, sitting together on the love seat, sent a quick shot of pain and memory through my nerves. It tingled and ached out to my fingers.

"So, who else has news?" My father looked at Reed and then at Ted, as if daring them. He didn't look at Ben and me.

"We're having a baby," said Ted. Everyone except Abby laughed. She excused herself to go to the bathroom.

"Excuse me," I said. I cleared the cake plates from the dining room table; then I slipped up the back stairs to the third floor. The ballroom door was open, and the sun, finally setting, spilled its light across the floor like a great handful of gold.

I went up two more flights of stairs and out to the widow's walk on the roof. I could see my father and mother, walking together in the yard. I hated him for using her like this. I knew she still loved him. He was impossible to turn away from, a demanding, irresistible toddler of a man. I'd known she still loved him all along, but it wasn't fair. He still loved her, too. They were horrible to do it. If they'd just learned to erase their history, we'd all be better off.

My father was always late, we always worried, but he was not supposed to have a real disease.

A pair of cardinals chased each other from oak to maple. When we were little, my father and mother had helped us tap two of the sugar maples in the yard. We'd collected the blood of trees, as Ted called it, and boiled it for hours on the stove to make maple syrup. After two weeks of collecting and twelve hours of simmering, we had a thin syrup, about a quarter cup. My father had eaten an entire tablespoonful plain. "Testing," he'd said.

Testing everything. Testing us. I hated him for having lupus, for waiting too long to start treating it. That was what he'd meant when he said the smoking didn't matter. I hated him for all his faults and for the fact that I loved him anyway. I hated him for threatening to die when I hadn't done anything yet. When I might still need him. My mother touched his back. The air smelled of sap. They walked around the pond, circling three times. My father held back the pussy willows with his arm so my mother could pass. The bright green shoots tipped with little cat paws of softness. I wondered whether pussy willows were edible, the roots or shoots or flowers. I couldn't bear to watch my parents anymore, so I watched the moon casually cutting a white curve into the sky.

"I wish you'd stop climbing out of buildings," said Ben. I had forgotten that I had left him downstairs. My parents' house made me forget. Not my parents' house, my mother's house.

"Why? You don't have to follow. I like it outside." I bit a fingernail and kept looking at the sky.

"But I want to follow, it's just—"

"What? I'm not begging for attention, I'm only trying to get some *air*, to see a little, to get out." I shouldn't have left him, I thought. I shouldn't have made him come with me in the first place.

"Like your club."

"What's wrong with my club?" Quietly, I realized I was picking a fight. He didn't deserve this.

"Oh, Hannah, nothing. It's me."

"What's wrong with you?" I asked Ben. I hadn't thought about Ben at all. He was here with me, he'd come, and I had put off meeting his happy sister for so long. I shared fighting and death with him, and I wouldn't let him share glee and babies.

"I'm a little bit afraid of heights." I looked at his pale face. He was smiling slightly, sweetly, leaning against the doorway as if the contact kept him safe. I took his hand, then put my arms around his waist. In the suit, he looked like he was dressed for a wedding. Or a funeral.

"I had no idea," I said. I let him go first down the stairs.

Nine / All week I had been trying not to think about my father, and all week I'd been talking about him: with my mother, who came to meet me for lunch; with Marla, who called me every day; with Ted, who needed me to help him move, at Abby's request, out of the condo the next weekend. It was the weekend before the summer trip, before I'd leave for two weeks and hope no one got married or died while I was gone. Or maybe I hoped they would. Settle themselves. Stop needing me to be inside the tempest with them. The only person I hadn't talked with was my father himself.

On Friday morning, Ben was sitting at my kitchen counter, spinning on a stool. I was scrambling eggs. We were both a little late for work, and his black-and-white checked tie was open around his neck like a scarf. I could tell Ben was being evasive, because he kept his eyes trained on the basket of paper napkins between twirls. His lashes looked long as a child's, and the blue between them was dark in the grainy light of the kitchen.

"I wonder if this is the best time for you to go away," he said, sighing as he released the thought from containment. He quit spinning.

"Hey," I said. I stopped worrying the eggs and turned to face him fully. "What do you mean?"

"Hannah." He sighed and started to twirl the napkin basket, still looking down. "Don't you think you should be around for your family?"

"My family. *Mine*. Not that I haven't shared them with you. But Ben, I thought you could tell by now that my family is always having a crisis. One trip won't make any difference." I didn't say, *I have to go, I have to escape; I'll sizzle into dust if I don't.*

"It is your family," he mumbled. "Your sick dad. And there will be other trips."

"Hey," I said, almost mute with frustration. I dumped all the eggs onto his plate and picked up my bag. I couldn't think of anything else to say, so I left for work.

Later I apologized, and he apologized, and we went out for ice cream after dinner, walking through the Public Gardens with the remnants of our cones dripping down our fingers. Evening looked like afternoon; everything was elongated. Ben was silent, and at first I left him in his own parentheses, but then I licked the chocolate mint off his knuckles because I felt slightly contrite. Contrite enough to flirt, but not enough to let him tell me what to do about my father, even if he was trying to help. The swan boats were full of after-work couples and tourists with bright hats: pink, orange, yellow. Children swung their feet in the empty spaces below their seats as the boat captains made mighty efforts with their thighs, backs, calves, some even standing to pedal their heavy crafts. The ponds were slick and green with algae bloom. I walked to the water's edge but couldn't see my reflection.

On Saturday, I sat on the floor of Ted's condo, packing up books in the red-and-blue radiance of a stained-glass rose window. All over the apartment, plants had wilted or burned brown. Even the spider plants had let their babies die and drop, and the edges of the leaves were lined with a reddish brown that looked like dried blood. The dark living room smelled of dust and decay. Ted sat on the couch, watching me, his hands working through a *Field Guide to the Fishes*.

"She says she needs the space for the baby," he said, still meandering through his explanation. I didn't really understand why he was moving. I didn't understand why they, the couple I most admired, couldn't get past what he'd said when he first found out. "I guess she does. But I thought we might be doing better; I thought we might make it."

"You should get rid of those, Ted," I pointed to a pruney jade and a withered lump that used to be an African violet in a shimmering ceramic flowerpot. The biology and geology books quickly filled the box.

"It's more than the baby," he said. "I mean, it wouldn't have come up if it weren't for the baby, but—"

"What?" I suddenly thought of all sorts of horrible secrets. Abby had been married before. They'd had affairs. It must be something terrible to wedge apart such a seamless pair.

"I assumed she'd want to go back to work, but she doesn't. And she wants to buy a house. She likes Newton. We can't afford Newton. And there's all this awful little stuff, I guess it's stuff about me. About what I don't give her. About my closed emotional state. The therapist helps, but it still seems like it's all about me, what I haven't managed to be."

"You *are* going to the therapy," I said, shivering slightly with the memory of our own family therapy. "You're doing your best. She can't ask you to be someone else."

"I know," said Ted. "I don't know if I can change, just like that." He started to pick the withered leaves off a potted tree. "Sweet bay," he said. "She used to cook with it."

"It's not totally dead," I said. "Maybe it needs water."

"Sun, it needs sun," said Ted. "*Laurus nobilis.* Do you think you ought to stay home this summer? I mean, because of Dad? Mom says she's going to get him into treatment, but she might need our help. And if you're away—"

"Oh, no." I groaned. A shoot of pain unfurled in my stomach. "Not you too."

"It's kind of a long time," he said, looking down at the crumbled leaves in his hand.

"Two weeks, Ted, just two weeks." I felt as if I was in the office again; the same angry flush marked my cheeks with heat. The O_2 Spa was running into some permit delays, and even though my designs were ready, even though I wasn't the project manager or the engineer or the builder or the partner, like my boss, she wanted me to forsake my trip to see the project through its rough patch. I told her I couldn't cancel. She said I could always cancel and that I should think things over before I left next Friday. I said the permits probably wouldn't be resolved in the two weeks I'd be gone and I couldn't do anything about it, and she turned and glared at me and repeated, "Just think." I was tired of being told to think.

"I know," Ted said. "Mom just thinks—"

"Everyone thinks too much," I said. "Mom and Dad are not married. Dad is going to play this out as long as he can, getting her to hold his hand through tests. He's known for *months*, Ted, *months*, and he's kept it secret until now. Don't you think that's a little bit manipulative?"

After I dumped all the books in the box, I started pulling leaves off the bay plant myself now, glaring at Ted, who sank, defeated, into the couch cushions. His fingers were pastel green in the light, and his plain gray T-shirt hung loose around his arms like a shed skin.

"He told us he was sick before."

"He's said it for years, if you think about it." I sighed. "And usually I believed him."

"This time it's true," he said.

I felt nauseated. If I'd believed him at first, would it have been less dire? Would it have been treatable, as Mom had said?

Ted sighed. "I guess everyone needs you," he said.

"For what?"

"To be the calm one," said Ted, sounding very calm himself.

"That's ridiculous," I said. "I am not one bit calm."

"But you fool us all," he said. "I'm sorry."

"Me too."

Bay scent filled the room, covering the dust, as if someone were cooking something delicious.

After packing all the books, while Ted finished wadding his clothes into suitcases and laundry bags, I walked to the Brookline Booksmith to read about Seattle in the travel section. I was leafing through *Thirty Hikes in the Northern Cascades* when someone came up behind me and put a hand on my shoulder.

"Hannah," said Marla. "What are you doing here?"

Abby stood beside her, wearing a red cotton dress that

draped her rounded belly and made her look glossy and bright. I wanted to touch her. I'd never wanted to touch pregnant women before; it had always struck me as invasive, the idea that somehow procreation was a public act and therefore rendered the body public property. But she looked so full, so luminous, that I understood the impulse, if not the act—to share all that life, to warm yourself as if holding your hands above a fire. And at the same time, knowing she wanted my brother to change, I didn't adore her as purely anymore.

"Hey," I said, shaking my shoulder loose. "Know how to startle a body, don't you."

"Thanks for helping him pack," said Abby. "I was afraid if I went in there with him I might relent." She held both hands over her belly, shifting them slightly, like mice resettling in their nest.

"You shouldn't be doing that anyway," said Marla. She was wearing pink lipstick that diminished her mouth.

"What are you doing here?" I asked.

"Talking things over with Abby." She had a private smile. Then she nodded slightly. "Abby's been through the cancer thing with her mom, and it's kind of like this," she said.

"I know." I didn't appreciate Marla's making me a stranger to my own family's history.

"I hear you're going on an expedition," said Abby, her hands settling, resettling. The nails were perfectly highlighted with clear polish. She wasn't wearing any makeup. "I hope it's wonderful." She leaned in and kissed me on my cheek. I found it annoying that she even smelled good, like strawberries.

The night before the trip, I worked until midnight. I had packed, mostly, on Wednesday night—my new gaiters and borrowed ice ax, glacier goggles with their goofy-looking leather side blinders, stuff sacks filled and strapped to the pack, and a duffel of additional things: wool sweaters, chocolate bars, a tiny photo-booth snapshot of me and Ben, extra film, an empty journal Marla had given me for my twenty-third birthday. Everything was piled in the hall, waiting for me to go home and finish.

But as I was shutting down my computer at 4:52 on Thursday, my boss bounced into my cube, her heels shushing against the carpet.

"You've decided, then," she said. She wore a lopsided smirk, as if her face was waging an expression battle.

"Um, I put in for this vacation months ago. I decided *then.*"

"Just checking." She shifted her black rayon hip onto my desk. "I've got a few details you *must* wrap up before you go. These little lockers for the clientele are *horrible*. Fix them. And we've decided we need a little kitchen. Nothing special, but a full-sized fridge, and at least two burners, and if you don't do it before you go, unless you want to come in tomorrow, the whole thing might simply go down the toilet, and we can't have that. Oh, speaking of toilets, there are only two on your specs. We need three, even if the *facilitays* are unisex. Unisex! As if there could be a single sex! Ha!"

She arranged her face into that horrible smile again, flopped the whole fat file onto my desk, and slithered out.

I stood looking at the rug, my bag still riding my shoulder. It slipped down to my wrist as I sagged back into my chair. I cleaned my fingernail with the edge of the file and weighed quitting against compliance. It wouldn't be perfect, but did it really matter? The toilets did matter, the plumbers were already at work. The contractor had already ordered the lockers. I chewed on the inside of my cheek, which hurt, and sent a quick slick of blood onto my tongue.

I stayed.

At ten, I was almost done. My boss was lingering in the office. She didn't come to see me, but I heard her heels as she passed by and checked. She was winning and she loved it; I could feel it in the air.

I took a break for some cold coffee and a package of orange peanut-butter cheese crackers from the vending machine, and I checked my messages at home.

None. Not even Ben calling to say good-bye. He was going to spend the night with me before I left, but when I called him to tell him I was staying late, he'd said, "Well, I should probably stay home anyway. I mean my place, that is."

"Hey," I said, when Ben answered the phone. "I think everything's going to be fine here while I'm gone. Did I tell you my mother knows the guy who's managing Dad's treatment, and that Marty's doing all the chauffeuring? It's a pretty funny picture, actually."

"Funny? Well, okay. It's kind of late."

"I'm not missing anything except dialysis."

"Hannah, we've talked about all this. It's your life."

"I know, but I don't want you to disapprove."

"Okay. I don't." He sounded flat. I tried to conjure him, his mouth right beside the receiver. He would be running his hand through his hair, the way he always did when he was on the phone.

"Not like that."

"Hannah. I've got to go to bed. I'll see you in two weeks."

It was so aloof, I was temporarily silenced.

"Okay?" He relented the tiniest bit. "Have an amazing time. Watch out for grizzly bears."

"Um. Okay."

He'd already hung up. I listened to the silence for a few seconds before getting back to the toilet redesign.

I printed out all the instructions and put them into a neat stack, clipped to the outside of the folder. Everything my boss had asked for. Nothing I was particularly proud of. I wondered how long the O$_2$ Spa could possibly last. Maybe Marla would go, Marla would take Abby, and Ted and I would sit sadly across the street in the last non-chain coffee shop left on Newbury Street, like rejected children.

At eleven-forty-five, I called my father.

The phone rang seventeen times, and I hung up. I took the folder to my boss's desk; I'd heard her ring for the elevator about an hour ago, and the dim office seemed to buzz with quiet. It was spooky to be alone with the cubes and the moth-colored fluorescent bars of light.

I looked around my office. Then I picked up the phone again, and let it ring twenty-two times, until he picked up.

"What, already?" snarled my father.

"I didn't mean to wake you up; it's Hannah."

"I know," he said. "And you didn't. I was working."

I tried to imagine what work he could do in his tiny apartment. Piles of clay on the floor, hand building on the cold concrete slab he kept in his living room, the slip spilling puddles onto the owl-patterned carpet from my childhood playroom.

"Okay. Anyway. I wanted to make sure it's okay for me to go away. I mean—everyone says my leaving is a bad idea, and I wanted to know what *you* think." My shoulders ached. My back itched.

"When's your plane?"

"Um, in about seven hours."

"And you're calling now? I think you've already made up

your mind." He coughed, a gravelly sound. I cringed. Before, when he coughed, I hadn't noticed. Before, his smoking had mostly annoyed me because of the stink and because I knew he wanted me to try to stop him. When we were little, Ted and I used to hide his cigarettes in the refrigerator coils or between pans in the pantry. He would bellow at us, but I could tell he kind of liked the game of us protecting him.

"Minds can be changed," I said, feeling very, very small.

"Don't be silly. I'm going to die, but I promise, not in the next month or so. You have time to go on vacation, and to finish whatever business you've got with me. Besides, if your mother has her way"—he paused to cough again, only this time it sounded slightly forced—"I won't get to die for some time yet."

"You're sure?"

"What, you want a contract? I won't die while you're gone. I can do that. Go in peace. Go with my blessing. All that crap. And, sweetheart." He never called me sweetheart. I hugged my bag hard against my side. "I meant what I said about my daughters not rushing to the altar. It's a big mistake."

"Okay," I said. He was the very same man. He thought he had a say in what I did. Unfortunately, he was right.

Outside in the dark, summer heat leaked from the sidewalks as I waited for my taxi.

At six-thirty in the morning, before boarding my plane—also Nicky, Linda, and Alan's plane, though I hadn't seen them in the waiting area yet—blinded by extreme exhaustion, I wandered to the bank of pay phones and called Ben.

"Hey," I said, when he answered.

"Hey, Hannah," said Ben. "I think I miss you already. Have you left? Where are you?"

"Airport," I said. "I miss you too." His voice, his gentle words, full of sleep, sounded sexy. And I was sorry for whatever it was we were fighting about. Of course he should move in. I'd tell him as soon as I came home.

"You're definitely going?" He didn't sound judgmental, just slightly sad.

"Yes," I said. "It's only two weeks." *Dad promised not to die*, I thought.

"Two and a half," he said. "Have a good time and send postcards and don't worry."

I fell asleep on the plane, leaning against the cold window shade. The man beside me woke me with his elbow when the pretzels came, but otherwise I pretended the thick hum of airplane noise was the sea, and the sour stench was no worse than my office. Finally, I was going, and if I didn't sleep I'd never survive the first day of backpacking. We had five miles to go once we finally got there.

Ten / I woke to the unmistakable scent of fish. I was

squashed against the rental van's ripped vinyl seat. I wondered what I was doing, why I'd left my comfortable apartment, my sick father, my reasonable boyfriend, to weave my way groggily through the airport, hoist countless packs and boxes and gear onto the shuttle, then pull them all off again to cram them into a stinky van with macho peak-bagging hikers. What kind of daughter packed up and left when her dad was dying? What kind of dad waited so long to tell the truth? I gritted my teeth. My head pounded, but then I looked out the window.

Trees, stripes of green, and peaks pressing the sky like great iced wedding cakes. The sky was the shocking bright blue of late summer afternoon; the light outlined the mountains so they looked surreal, like woodcut prints inked onto the horizon.

"Hey, sleeping beauty," said Camilla. She tapped my shoe from her sleeping spot on the van's floor.

"She's up!" Shing turned to me from the front seat and pointed a video camera in my face.

"No," I said. "Don't."

"This is our little Hannah on her first summer trip," said Shing. The record button on his camera glowed red. "She had a wee nap, but now she's joined us."

"Hey," said Camilla. "Linda's waking up too."

Shing turned to tape her, but Linda reached across the seat and swatted at the camera.

"Hey, this is expensive," Shing snapped.

"So are my consent fees," said Linda. She cleared her throat.

"We're there," said Noah. He turned the van onto a dirt road, and the floor rumbled. Our packs squeaked against each other and Shing stowed his camera. I watched as the trees engulfed us. We were driving along the hip of a mountain, into the thick of the woods. I hoped the rattly van would make it, and I opened the window to let in the clean green scent.

We stopped at a ranger station, and Noah went inside to pick up our permit. Stretching against the van, I felt as sore as if I'd already been hiking for hours. I wondered what Ben was doing this afternoon—evening already, at home—what my father was doing in his apartment.

"Most people don't go for summit attempts from this side," the ranger said. Short and round, with a face like a pink moon, he'd accompanied Noah out of the station. His skin was a map of wrinkles. He squinted to inspect us.

"You-all look okay, though. I hope you've got enough food and emergency gear." He inspected Alan, the oldest, the father of the group. I wondered whether Alan minded.

"All the gear," said Noah. He was holding the permit two-handed, like a hard-won blue ribbon. "Thanks, sir," he said to the ranger.

"You've got to watch for new crevasses. Sometimes you get ice quakes in August. Don't want to have to call in the S and R. Too many helicopters out these days—and last year we lost three in avalanche. You all sign in now."

He passed around a clipboard and we wrote our names. In case of emergency. Ice quakes and avalanches made me think of my family; if they heard I had an emergency, would they fly out or would they sit warming their hands on disbelief like a cup of tea? Hannah doesn't have emergencies. I had never broken a bone. I had never insisted they come to a school play or wrecked the car, as Marla did. I had never undergone quiet trauma that demanded unwanted attention, the way Ted did. Poor Ted. Part of me could imagine how trapped he must feel, forced to change when he wasn't ready to change, even though Abby wasn't really doing the forcing. Sex had possible consequences, all the time. Every time I slept with Ben, our bodies were doing their best to procreate, despite our chemical and mechanical methods of prevention. I shivered and got back into the van.

The road wound around and we turned off onto an overgrown path, still climbing. The van started to shake, as if every bearing and strut and hose were about to give way and leave us with a hissing mass of useless machinery. I thought of Lemon, still at Holy Motors. She might have been more reliable than this beast.

Then we stopped. Noah jumped out and started pulling packs from the van. Camilla groaned and got up to help. I peeled myself from the seat and climbed out into the fresh world.

I took three silvery packets of food for my pack, stuffing them in beside the wool layers and sleeping bag.

"Got room for some tent poles?" Linda handed me a long yellow stuff sack.

"Climbing gear?" Camilla passed me a heavy pile of metal and webbing wrapped together. I crammed it in as best I could and strapped the poles on top inside my foam pad.

"Wait," said Noah. "Can you fit another food pack? Did you get five?"

"Three," I said, sheepish. "Oh, okay. I thought it was three."

"Five," said Noah. "One isn't a whole meal, easy mistake. But Shing has to take seven, because he ordered desserts for lunch *and* dinner."

"Mars food," said Nicky, picking up his freeze-dried packets. I took two more, hoping my seams wouldn't explode on the trail. Shing sat on the ground and held his pack in two fists, shoving things in with his feet.

"Let's go," said Alan. "Five miles, and only three hours until dark."

"Easy-cheesy," said Nicky.

"Uphill," said Alan.

And it was—uphill, not easy. At first we walked along a flat pebbly road, but soon we were plodding along a steep rocky incline. We were already high up, and the trees were giants with gnarly toe roots. They were breathtakingly tall and wide and looked like the photos in the guidebooks. I had to keep marching, glancing up only for a second at a time. The light reddened the trunks, but my pack was so heavy I could hardly look past the trail in front of me. My back and hips burned with the weight. The air was delicious, but I couldn't possibly stand weeks of this. It was torture. Forced march. I watched Camilla's feet in front of me, her boots sinking into the dark soil between the stones. The forest whirred with wind and birds hooting and calling. And our feet punctuated their conversation: shuffle, land. My chest hurt with effort. I wondered what it would cost to change my ticket, whether I could ever face the club again if I gave up now. Was this what had happened to Vijay? Had he simply quit?

The trail leveled out and we came to a suspension bridge, which swayed over the wide arm of river as Camilla crossed. I wondered why no one talked about him. Nicky and Shing were already on the other side. They looked minuscule beneath their colossal packs. I watched Camilla stepping from plank to plank, gripping the ropes on the sides. She faltered, and I thought of insects, how their many legs balance the body; she needed more legs. I needed more legs. Standing felt all right, leaning on a trail sign, my finger tracing the letters of BAKER SUMMIT: 17. Seventeen. I didn't think I'd make the three more to that night's campsite.

Then it was my turn to balance on the planks, looking down at the singing river, water planing the stones and curling off into eddies and narrow rebellious streams that wandered the forest until they sunk below the soil. The planks rocked beneath me as I crossed, and I watched one foot step in front of the next and promised myself I'd make it through this one day without the embarrassment of quitting.

A mile before base camp, we crossed a boulder field and moved into a pink and blue bliss of wildflowers. The sky was heavy, almost purple at the horizon. Our pace slowed. I could count the whole group out across the field, paced twenty or thirty feet apart. Alan strode first, off the curve of color and into a forest, then Noah, then Linda, then Nicky, and then Shing, in the field's middle. Camilla was in front of me, parting the flowers.

The colors: brilliant orange poppies with dazzling black seed faces; blue windflowers; fireweed, which Noah had pointed out at the trailhead; and other flowers I didn't know, purples and whites, a field of liquid color. As I passed through them, I forgot the weight on my shoulders; I forgot the new hot spots where my ankles had begun to blister. The air spread clean and cool across my face. Thoughts of my father and Ben passed across the horizon like the gauzy clouds backlit by the gradually sinking sun.

Then we were in a low, foggy forest. The slender birches and pines were shorter than the giants we'd passed by earlier, twelve feet at the tallest. The wind swept through and the air was dense with fog. Five miles of change, I thought, as the fog condensed and rain dripped down my forehead and cheeks. I shivered. It seemed we'd risen above the sun in the field of flowers; we'd sped up night's arrival by climbing. I couldn't see Camilla in front of me, but I could hear her boots thud on the thick ground. The earth was wet, and the prints before mine in the mud reminded me I was last. Still, we kept climbing.

"This old stove, she won't work," sang Nicky, as he primed the pump again. I sat on the floor of the tent I'd just finished erecting, too tired to take off my boots and examine my painful feet. I wondered how anyone would know this damp little site was where we'd chosen to camp, since we sat inside a woolly sock of fog. I couldn't see the tree, about eight feet away, where I'd tied the tent fly.

"Tired," said Camilla, shuffling out of her own tent in sneakers to help Nicky make dinner.

"Hannah's not tired," said Shing. I sighed and pulled off my boots. The white liners were spotted with blood. My feet looked like hideous pizzas.

"Well, we'll toughen those up," said Shing, leaning in and looking.

"Goddamn stove!" Nicky flung the pump against a rock.

"Hey," said Shing. "Watch that temper." He sounded so sharp I held my breath for a second.

"You do it," said Nicky. He walked off into the fog.

Shing leaned over the stove and reassembled the pump. I put on my sneakers, and by the time I limped out to the circle of stones where Camilla was slicing open the freeze-dried food packets, the stove was working and the pot of water was almost at a boil.

"Sneak attack," yelled Nicky. He poked Shing in the back with a plantain. Shing turned and laughed. Then he stood up and grabbed Nicky, slinging him over his shoulder and carrying him around the campsite.

"How do you *cook* plantain?" Nicky asked Noah, who had started another stove and was cleaning his knife.

"Sauté, I think," said Noah. He sliced one with a chef's flourish.

The freeze-dried food was a bad approximation of chicken curry. I wondered how we'd survive on a week of it before we emerged from the Baker wilderness and bought some fresh stuff. For now, there were only a few oranges, one last lettuce, and the plantains, which Noah served us with a grand gesture.

"Ooh, yummy," said Camilla, biting into hers. "It tastes like glue!"

I tasted mine and agreed. Then I started laughing, which felt good. It was only in my sleeping bag, my toes cold and damp and my ankles sore to touch no matter which way I turned, that I almost felt like crying.

In the morning, my back hurt so much, a pounding center of pain, I thought I couldn't move at first. I looked up at the anemic green light coming through the tent and willed myself home. Birds were chortling outside, and Noah snored softly.

A loud bird started in on something that sounded like Mozart.

"Ugh," moaned Noah. "Here we go." He rolled over and Camilla woke too, sighing as she sat up, a caterpillar in its sleeping bag cocoon. Her jacket-pillow's zipper had indented her cheek.

The bird was Alan, whistling loud and almost rhythmically. I stirred slightly around the pain and realized the lump under my back was a tree root. Sitting up, I felt much better, though I still ached.

Outside, everything was fog. The field of flowers had been like a *Wizard of Oz* dream, and I wondered whether our next march would lead us to a grand and glorious view of more fog. I shuffled out into the forest and found a place to pee. My mouth was sticky with last night's curry, and I felt coated in old sweat and dust. One week, I thought, and we'll be at a campground with showers. I found Linda by a stream, scrubbing her face with a bandanna. She smiled at me.

"I love this," she said. "Isn't it bliss?"

"Mmm," I said. She handed me a clean bandanna and I dipped it into the water. It was shocking, icy, but I scrubbed until I could muster a smile.

"Heaven. No one here but us crazies and the birds." She sipped water from her cupped hands.

I thought about the warnings in my trail books, about giardiasis and other water-borne illnesses. Worms. Parasites that set up camp inside your body the way we set up camp on the saddle of the mountain.

"Glacier water," said Linda, as if divining my thoughts.

"But we still treat the stuff we cook with?" Noah had already started filtering the morning water when I'd left camp. Our half-gallon for dinner had taken about an hour.

"Well, it's kind of a personal decision. This stuff isn't far from the source. Unless there are parasites from the ice ages." She rubbed my shoulder companionably. "But then, I still remember when it was okay to drink straight from the White Mountains' rivers."

"Okay," I said. But I didn't drink.

"Guess what?" I said, spooning oatmeal into my mouth.

"Okay," said Camilla, yawning. "I'll bite." Everyone looked so sleepy. I was the only one chattering. I wanted to fill the quiet. I wanted to talk so I wouldn't have to think about the hike to our base at the edge of the glacier. It would be an eight-mile day—Noah had said it twice the night before—and the hike would be steeper than yesterday, and my pack sat like a lumpy gorilla against the closest tree. The tent poles were loose in the foam pad, and somehow, despite the packet we'd used for dinner, it looked fuller and heavier than it had yesterday.

"Okay, so my boss said, before I left—well, actually, before *she* left—that I needed to leave a contact number, somewhere she could reach me."

Shing smiled across the stoves. He dug in his pack and pulled out a cell phone.

"Oh, no." Noah groaned. "Not again. I hope you don't get service here."

"I don't know," said Shing. "I only turn it on for emergencies."

There was a slight pause; no one spoke.

Then Noah said, "Right, like ordering pizza in the Wind Rivers."

"Hey, it was a car campground," said Shing. "And as I recall, you had seven slices of pepperoni."

"I gave my boyfriend the park service number, though," I said.

"Ah, yes, your imaginary boyfriend!" Shing said.

"He—oh, never mind," I said. I'd given the number to

Ted, too. He needed it in case something happened. It wouldn't.

"Hey." Alan was emptying a second oatmeal packet into his cup. "It's time to start taking turns being in charge of map work. Linda and I can't be the parents all the time."

"Oh, Daddy," said Camilla, hugging his side. She still had the zipper impression in her cheek.

"I mean it," said Alan, his jaw working in a most paternal way. I couldn't help thinking of my own father. What would dialysis be like? What else would they do to him? He hated blood. Needles were no problem for him, but blood sometimes made him faint. In second grade, I cut my chin on my best friend's bike fender when we fell racing down the driveway. My friend watched me, a puzzled look on her face, as I wiped my chin and my hand came away covered in blood. I found Dad in his studio in the basement, scoring a seam; he gripped the wire-cutting tool with intensity and precision, like a composer about to mark the final tonic on a score. Sometimes he snapped the wood stems of his tools as he worked, expecting them to take too much force, the demands of his intention.

"Daddy," I said. "I think I need a Band-Aid."

"Always," he'd grumbled, before turning around. When he saw me, his face changed color. It was like watching the TV signal fade and the characters on the box go grainy. He swallowed and I watched his thick neck working.

"I'm okay," I said.

"I'm not," he said. He put his head down, almost on his knees. After a long minute, during which I wondered if he was having a heart attack, whether I should call someone, forgetting all about my chin, he looked up.

"Okay." He stared straight ahead as he marched up the stairs. "Band-Aid coming up."

I had needed stitches, but the only part that hurt was the doctor's bony fingers pressing into my jaw as he sewed.

Alan stirred his oatmeal. "Hey, I'll do the route today." I said it quickly, before I could think about it too much. I had very little confidence, but as I said it, it made perfect sense. Alan smiled and handed me the map. I'd make my surrogate daddy proud.

Two miles later I wasn't so sure. I got out the map and compass whenever the trail turned. The fog made it hard to determine if the trail was really the trail, if we'd missed a possible turn. And sometimes the compass needle continued swinging after I'd read it.

"You do know how?" whispered Nicky, who was behind me. He pointed to the compass and kicked a stone. We were inching along because of me. I didn't realize it would work that way, that navigator was also leader. And Question-Answerer General. Everyone was right behind me, a clot of restlessness. At least the trail wasn't too steep. Though according to the tight pack of lines on the topographical map, it should've been steeper.

"Leave her alone," said Noah. He wore his walking-slow grimace and almost stood on Nicky's heel.

"You could try triangulation," said Nicky.

"With what?" I asked. My mouth was dry again, but every time I stopped to drink, everyone else stopped too. Alan cleared his throat and Linda gazed off into the trees as if she were indulging in a leisurely bird walk.

I started again, the map a poorly folded wad in my hand.

We wound around, and slightly upward. The trees grew shorter and shorter, so at least we were definitely going up. Alan whistled. I felt as if they were all hanging onto my absurdly heavy pack, dragging me backward down the mountain. I stepped faster, starting to sweat hard. I wanted to lead; I'd said I would lead. Leaders were in front. I tripped on a root and grabbed a rough little sapling so I wouldn't fall. My hand was sticky and scraped. It bled. Faster, I thought; keep going.

"About how far have we gone?" Camilla's voice, for the first time since we'd started our ascent. I wouldn't look back.

"How can she know that?" Noah was my champion, but he sounded impatient too.

Suddenly the fog peeled off the mountain, like a woman lifting her sweater over her head.

"Hey!" Alan's voice sang out.

"Triangulation points!" said Noah. And I'd thought he was trying to trust me.

"Okay," said Alan, crowding in beside me. "Let me just show you—" He pointed out two peaks. The view was glorious: snow-sided slopes and bright fields of flowers and dark smears of green forest. My heart slowed as we stood. The sweat congealed. I focused on Alan's instruction. Here and here on the map. Here and here with the compass. Two points, and your location is the third. Like geometry. Make a triangle with the compass degree readings.

"Here's Baker Lake, and here's Table Mountain, so we are—oops."

"Oops?" Nicky crowded in. The others were sitting on flat rocks, looking out at the view, drinking and eating gorp.

"Relax, Nicky." Alan put his hand on Nicky's arm, and Nicky shrugged away. He walked over to the edge of the rock where we stood, inches away from the cliff.

"Move in a little, okay?" Alan said, but quietly. I looked at his finger on the map. We were on a trail, but the loop trail, not the one to our base camp. He stretched his other finger to the camp. We'd have to go another mile out of the way before we'd come to an intersection. I approximated with my finger as a ruler. An eleven-mile day. Not an eight-mile day, which would've been hard enough. A little less uphill at first, but come late afternoon, we'd face the tightest cluster of altitude lines on the map so far. Steep steep scree. And it was all my fault.

"So, we've changed our plan a little," announced Alan. He put his hand on my shoulder. I thought I might topple over. I could roll twice and fall over the cliff. Then they'd have to use Shing's cell phone to call a helicopter. Probably I'd break something, but I'd get a ride out. And I could go home. It might be worth it.

"Jeez, Hannah," said Camilla. She sat with her head resting on her arms.

"Hey," said Alan. "Everyone makes mistakes."

"What's the damage?" asked Noah.

All eyes on me. The cliff was just two rolls away. My pack kept me off balance. The eyes didn't help. Alan sat down, still studying the map.

"Um, a few extra miles," I said.

"Like, how many?" Camilla didn't look at me. Nicky was still standing away from the rest of us.

"Well, three," I said. "I'm sorry."

"It's okay, Hannah," said Noah. "We could use a little extra training."

"Right," said Linda. But no one smiled.

Alan started on ahead. We would keep the breaks short. We would walk fast to beat the sunset. There were always other campgrounds, Alan said, other places to stop. It was all part of the adventure.

I wondered whether the awful feeling that spread in my chest was part of the adventure. Whether my feet would survive the adventure. I could feel the blisters getting blisters. And now I'd lost the right to complain.

I was still officially leading, but as we crossed another field of flowers, descending in the direct gold light of early afternoon, Alan and Shing and Nicky were in front of me. Noah and Linda were following behind me, with Camilla bringing up the rear. Every now and then I turned to look at her, her pack bobbing along. She seemed to limp slightly. It felt like everything, everyone's every pain, was all my fault. And I was carrying it in my pack along with tent poles and flashlights and Gore-Tex rain pants.

After a very quiet lunch, I conferred with Alan again. We were making decent time and had only five miles to go. Five miles and two thousand feet, in steep bouts. The tiny space on the map seemed just too far.

"Should we pick out an alternate campsite?" Alan studied my face as I considered. A pink glob of strawberry jam rested on his square front tooth like a jellyfish on the beach.

"Okay. We could stop here." I pointed, unsure.

"No water," said Alan, with a little sigh.

"I'm new at this." I hadn't meant to blurt it out, but the scrutiny was too much. I didn't want to be the enemy or the child. And my back and feet and legs hurt, a wobbly, heated pain.

"It's okay, Hannah," said Alan. "This is how you learn."

I wanted to bite him. To pull the map away and chomp right down on his sanctimonious hairy hand. If I was truly the leader, I could have us camp right where we were. They could set up the tents and I could climb a tree and dine on lichen and live there.

"How about here?" I pointed. Three miles and we'd be there. There was a stream, and a relatively flat spot directly off the trail. I couldn't tell anything about the trees or exposure, but it looked okay otherwise.

"Good," said Alan. "Saddle up, everyone," he said.

We made it to the alternate campsite with daylight to spare. It was on a ridge and the wind pushed against us, making passage along the trail precarious. Alan stopped as I caught up. Camilla was getting farther behind, and her limp had grown pronounced. But she didn't say anything when she stopped, and I didn't ask. What I didn't know couldn't make this day any worse.

Alan nodded at me as if we'd made a decision together.

"So, guys, everyone okay for a few more miles? We'll be at base camp then, the bottom of the glacier. We can take a day to practice self-arrest tomorrow, and rope skills."

"And map work," said Nicky.

"Hey," I said. "Cut it out. I'm not perfect, but I didn't see you leading today." I leaned forward toward him. I wanted to shove him. Instead I tapped his shoulder lightly.

"Yeah," said Nicky. "I'm sorry. I guess I'm being impatient. I want that peak!" He managed a weak smile.

"Okay," I said. I waved my hand, not minding the responsibility so much this time, and we started marching again.

By the time we reached the bottom of the glacier, the sun had set. There was an orange sunset below us, but at this altitude—almost eight thousand feet—it was just dark. The glacier was a white field, a strange slope with scree and flowers around the edges, and it flowed over the mountain out of our vision. The air smelled clean, like stones. My body hurt so much I thought, If I were to lie down, I could go right to sleep for a few days and let the cells go nuts repairing themselves, and I'd still wake up feeling and looking like one gigantic bruise. Instead, I got industrious, setting up both tents and trying to start the stove, which wouldn't cooperate. I put it down and pretended I'd only been unpacking. I collected icy water from the stream and started pumping it through the filter. The sweat had chilled and I was sticky and cold.

Camilla and Noah straggled into camp a full half hour after the rest of us. She was leaning against his bumblebee pack and laughing, and I envied their ease. But then, when we sat down to eat dinner, it seemed as if everyone had forgotten I'd been the one to make them suffer. It was like a language I didn't know, the way the group worked, the forgiveness, the assumptions.

We did our dishes in the glacial stream and didn't even bother with a bear bag. I slid into my sleeping bag in the tent with Shing and Camilla and fell asleep so quickly I forgot to get out a stuff sack and sweater to make myself a pillow.

Eleven /

"Just step, Hannah," said Noah. "Like climbing stairs."

"Stairs don't have loops," I said. My mouth filled with icy air as I spoke; my legs, burning inside with effort, felt dipped in cold like bananas in chocolate. We'd found a crevasse, and I was practicing the climb out, sliding webbing steps up the rope as I ascended. The crevasse felt cavelike, only it was much colder than a cave, and it was the glacier's split slit, not the earth's. Such an old enormous piece of living ice. And I was stuck inside it, hanging like fish bait, trying to rise on loops of rope.

I could fall, I realized; it wasn't just theoretical. I remembered Spider Cave—how I'd longed to stop and sleep. A place at the end of trying. Even with all the tools of safety around me, attaching me to the outside of the crevasse, to Noah, I felt that same sensation just under my skin. Resistance, fear. I was still safe, but I wished I didn't remember how that desperation felt.

Slide and step.

"Good, good," Noah coached.

I'd watched Nicky struggle out, and Alan, who was measured and methodical as he slid the steps up the rope.

"I think I'm okay now." I wanted Noah to stop coaching. It was well intentioned, but his eyes and the stream of sound were distracting. I could think it now: slide and step. Falling would be easy.

I was strapped in, wearing a harness with an extra Prusik sling attached at my waist. My body was linked to Noah's, and Noah's linked to Nicky's. The other four were roped together, practicing self-arrest with ice axes. Each time I slid one step, my foot was secured in the other, but I couldn't shake visions of clipping out, falling into the cold, and hitting the ice walls, hit and slide, bump and scrape, until I found the blue-white bottom, where I could bleed or freeze to death with whatever woolly mammoth was preserved there in the great natural refrigerator.

I stepped. Slid the loop, with effort, as the knot held. Stepped again. I could almost reach the lip of the crack with my fingers.

"Hey, look at you go," said Noah. The edge of the glacier was a new white horizon. Camilla and Shing and Alan skimmed along and then stopped themselves with their axes in a sudden pitch-and-turn against the ice.

"Oops." Noah reached his hand down as I bumped my chin on an icy protrusion. The sun shone into my cave, an arrow of light. I took Noah's hand and pulled out. He was less secure than the rope and hardware but somehow more helpful.

"My turn," said Noah, as I lay on the ice, breathing hard and letting the sun defrost my cold exterior.

He checked the "dead men," gear buried in ice and snow, alternate holds in case he fell or my hands slipped. Then he ran the rope around my boot, handed me the end, and slipped right down into the crack. I lay at the edge and watched his ease as he rappelled. This was where he became the most natural animal, outside, with his climbing gear and the impossible ups and downs. I could see his arm muscles working; he wore only a T-shirt above his rain pants. The glacier goggles obscured his eyes, but his moving mouth revealed his concentration. And his pleasure. Noah was beautiful: strong, lean, fully lit by the theater of the climb, the blue and white ice, the dimming layers of light.

This job was easier than practicing: watch, coach, secure. Nicky, roped to my other side, was lying ten feet down the glacier like a basking cat, an emergency blanket spread out beneath him, reflecting the sun's intense glare. His arms were white birch branches. Linda and Alan kept telling him to put on sunscreen, but Nicky seemed determined to absorb as much solar energy as possible. In the morning, when Shing had smeared zinc oxide on our noses, Nicky wiped his off and onto his wool sock.

"Hi," said Noah, already back up at the edge. He reached for my hand, and I felt as if he were lifting me, instead of helping himself out with the grip.

Self-arrest was more fun than Prusiking, and exhausting, and a little like playing with knives. We slid on our backs down the glacier's incline until the speed was too much to stop with crampon tips; then we turned and slammed our axes into the ice, graceful as dancers. Lumberjack ballerinas tied together with ropes. When Noah demonstrated, he stopped right away, his ropy arm muscles fighting weight and momentum. Shing was a little less elegant in his approach, but his ax dug so far into the ice that spiderweb cracks radiated from the ax's assault. And he stopped fast. Shing must've won musical chairs as a child, every time. I laughed out loud, imagining Shing as a shiny-headed five-year-old.

"Okay, let's go as a rope," said Noah.

Nicky and Noah and I spiked our crampon-tipped shoes up a hundred feet and started our slide down, axes gripped against our chests.

"Ready, *now!*" was Noah's muffled command, muted by the slippery sound of our gear sliding along the slick snowy surface.

I turned and slammed my ax in. The impact tugged the muscles of my arm and back, and for a second I thought I wouldn't stop; I'd keep sliding, my ax making an ineffectual scratch across the face of the glacier. I pressed my arms forward and felt the sharp jerk of arrest. I was hanging from the ax's point. Exhilaration hummed through my body. I'd stopped myself from sliding. And so had Nicky and Noah, independently, so my arms didn't have to hold them too.

I pulled my ax out of the dent, exhilarated.

"Again," said Noah. "Let's go!"

We started to slide, the snow layer lifting off the ice and dazzling the air as we went.

"Ready, now!" yelled Noah, and it worked again. Only this time Nicky, a little too close below me as we turned to embrace the cold surface, pinned my pant leg with the point of his ax. Another inch, I thought, looking down at my specimen self.

"God, Nicky, be careful!" I yelled.

"Sorry, Hannah." He was, as always, all sunshine and accident. I wanted to believe it had nothing to do with yesterday's extra miles.

We started our slide again. Slush slipped up my leg and burned my skin where the ax had left a gash.

At dinner, I was too tired to eat more than a few crackers. I lay on my foam pad, watching fog obscure the stars, listening to Linda and Alan as they debated the next day's possible summit attempt. The weather was key; if it was very foggy, we'd have more time before the ice melted and new crevasses formed at the top of the glacier, but there might not be any view from the summit. We'd have to leave at 4:30 A.M. either way, and we wouldn't know until midday what we were up against.

"Well, if it's no good, we'll come back down and make it the next day." Linda sighed.

"I don't think we've got two consecutive attempts in us," said Alan. "Not at this altitude. Two dawns in a row." He tapped his spoon in his emptied cup.

"If we come back and rest," said Linda.

"Don't think so," said Alan, his teacher voice set on high: *tap, tap, tap.*

"*You* don't think so." Her pants and parka crinkled as she stood up and walked two steps away.

"Fine," said Alan. "Let's vote. What do you say, Noah?"

"Oh, no," said Noah. "Keep me out of the marital bliss."

"This has nothing to do with us," said Alan. Now his spoon was scraping in the cup. A trapped mouse, digging for escape.

"Okay, then, all eyes closed except Linda's," said Noah. "She can count."

I closed my eyes against the stars.

"Hands up for a summit attempt tomorrow," said Linda.

"That's eight hours from now," said Alan.

"Fine." Linda paused.

I put up my hand. What I really wanted was to take a bath, to sit in the wet heat, and then to get into a warm thick towel and clean sheets. But we were going to climb the mountain—at least, we were going to try—and I wanted to do it sooner rather than later. I didn't think my body could take another day of glacier practice. My lungs were tired from the extra work of breathing at this high altitude. Maybe after we saw the whole top of the world we could take a day off, sit in the tents, and let the blood in our wounds stop for long enough to clot and scab over.

"And against?" Linda asked. She barely paused. "We're going."

"Fine," said Alan. He put down cup and spoon. "But you're navigating."

"Noah?" said Linda. "You'll help, right?"

Noah murmured his assent. I was glad I would be roped to him.

Four o'clock was as dark as the night's middle. I had slept thickly for an hour or two, and then I'd woken and kept wondering when we'd have to get up for real. Shing and Nicky snored. They had a rhythm going, their breaths over-lapping slightly. It made them seem vulnerable. I lay with my bag over my head to mute the sound, envisioning us, three tents staked to the ground at the edge of a glacier, seven bod-ies melting the earth's ice hat, surrounded by fields and forests and stars. Then I started to worry. I'd be roped between two men who were strong and show-offs, fast and determined. I would probably keep us from making it. What if we fell through faulty snow bridges over the lips and deep into a crevasse? I'd already done it, I reminded myself; I'd climbed out in yesterday's practice. But it had been planned, the edges had been firm, and I'd had all the time in the world. Still, I noticed that no one other than the park ranger had ever mentioned avalanches.

Nicky's breath, in and out. Why did I doubt my body? It had been perfectly cooperative so far. All that running made it stronger. And I wouldn't have to navigate; all I had to do was follow.

I liked navigating, really. Despite the foggy mistake, which was only a mistake—anyone could've missed the turnoff in the cloud we'd traversed—I could take charge. I liked making decisions. At least, I liked making decisions about which way to walk.

Shing's snoring stopped. Then I heard the beeping of his watch, exclamations in the frosty air.

"Up," he said, his voice a flat sound from his tent.

"No way." Camilla groaned. "I'm still asleep."

"Up," said Shing again. And then we were moving in the night, headlamps on as we grabbed bags of gorp and extra dried fruit. I slid my clothes on before shedding my sleeping bag, took my day pack and headlamp, and joined the shuffle of preparation and departure.

There were cat-sized ghosts darting around the campsites, and they chirped.

"Raccoons?" I asked Shing, hoping for the familiar. In Brookline we had mobs of marauding raccoons that emerged from the woods in Chestnut Hill the night before garbage day. They walked side by side down the narrow streets, blocking late-night traffic like thugs. They made me laugh, a gang of raccoons, come to rough up the chicken bones and take-out scraps. But I steered clear, the same warning in my blood as I felt at fifteen when I saw the bad boys cutting through the woods in a pack.

"Huh?" Shing patted my back. "No raccoons at this altitude. Marmots."

The ghosts squeaked, a high strange song. As we walked out of the campsite they skittered away, but I imagined the cat-sized forms settling into our sleeping bags like furry Goldilocks while we were gone.

"Nicky," said Noah, "you have got to stop eating skunk." Nicky was first in our group as we climbed, crampon tips biting the ice. The sky was still dark, but light painted the horizon a dark blue. Nicky was barely keeping up with Linda, Alan, Shing, and Camilla on the rope ahead.

Being strung together reminded me of school, of being part of a team, us against them. In elementary school, I was short, short, short, and then briefly tall. My growth spurt pushed me, at eleven, to five feet, and the only one taller in my sixth-grade class was Greg Ward, who at five foot four was the classroom giant. For once, I was chosen in the first group for teams. Then I grew breasts, which slowed me down in the minds of the other kids, even if I could still run faster than most of them. The whole thing was embarrassing. But I remembered wanting to win, that buzz of being ahead in a race or game. I found myself wishing our group was in front, but Linda was leading. Noah took concise, even steps.

Suddenly, daylight beamed across our path. I looked back at our two hours' worth of tracks: faint cuts in the glacier, then a barely visible path across the field of rocks and snow, then the snowy pass we were crossing, leaving pebbles from the rock field like eraser crumbs on the white page of the ground.

Waiting for Nicky to make progress up a steep pass, I watched the knotted string of the other group advance above us. They looked like a geometry problem, dots connected to make a curve over the snowfield; we were on top of the whole ice-cream sundae of the world, advancing on the cherry. For a minute I understood the urge to get to the top, strong enough to get up at 4 A.M., strong enough to keep walking through blisters, to lug gear through fog and rain, to eat reconstituted food and sleep on the ground. All for the glory of the top, the unobscured light, a unique possession of the world. An ownership streets could never afford, and so much space and sky, fields that didn't belong to anyone, naked of human forms.

Then I looked down and started pushing forward again. The clink of gear, the rope weight against my waist, the shush of steps, our boots crunching snow and ice.

"Gotta rest," said Nicky. His expression was hard to read behind his goggles, but his mouth looked tight. His face was patched with oozing sunburn; his nose and cheeks were white and red. It looked painful, the nose especially, where I imagined the white spots were visible bone beneath the burn.

"Let's catch the other group first, okay, Nick?" Noah's voice lilted indulgently. I knew that sound. It was usually for me, when I was last.

"Nope." Nicky sat down. "I think I need to rope out for a second."

He sat on the snow, pulling at his harness.

"Nicky." Noah spoke slowly and loudly. Coach. Train conductor. Parent. "We need to stay together right here. It isn't safe to go alone."

"For a minute." Nicky spun the lock and snapped open the carabiner at his waist.

"No." Noah took six quick strides past me to get to Nicky. "It's really not safe."

"Jeez. If Hannah weren't here, I'd just dig a hole." Nicky's voice was thin.

"Hannah's not here." Noah looked at me. "Right? Can you please just look at the view for a little while?"

"Oh, okay," I said.

"See," he said to Nicky. "She won't turn around."

"Don't listen either," said Nicky, a panicky five-year-old. I heard his gear clip back in.

"Done," I said.

I listened to the wind. It hissed against the cheek of snow. Nicky groaned. Then Noah started singing, words I thought I recognized from *The Hobbit*.

"Roads go ever ever on, over rock and under tree. . . ."

His voice was melodious; I could picture him in front of his choral students, mouthing the words, then unable to keep from singing along. Without turning, I let the comfort fill me. Noah kept singing, the sound dwarfed by the wind on the side of a mountain, but rich and good for Nicky and me. Like warming our hands on his chest. He had a particular kind of generosity. Sexy, I couldn't help thinking. I didn't know anyone else who would sing to a friend with a stomachache, roped together, ice ax strapped to his back. I wondered whether Ben understood more than I thought he did. More than I did. Maybe Ben wasn't only concerned about my father when he tried to convince me not to go on this trip. Maybe he was jealous. I felt a rush of annoyance. Then I looked out at the view. This was not a window in Brookline, this was the whole of the other world. Why I'd come.

Noah ran out of words and sang the tune with syllables, la and ma and dah and, at the end, a little riff of la-de-dahs that made Nicky laugh.

"Okay," said Nicky. "Now I'm okay."

We started again and caught up with the others by climbing fast. We reached another scree field, and this time Nicky roped out to go to the bathroom.

"Ain't no bathroom at ten thousand feet!" Alan yelled after him.

"Maybe I can catch an airplane," Nicky shouted back.

"I think we should stay away from the turkey tetrazzini," I said.

"Ew," said Camilla, passing me the bag of gorp.

The sun was high and intense by ten o'clock. When we stopped again, Noah and Linda huddled over the map, scanning the red lines the ranger had added for this year's new known warm spots, possible problems with the ice.

"Where are we?" Alan stepped over to them, crossing rope with Camilla.

"Don't," said Noah, pointing to the rope. "Cardinal rule."

"Okay, okay." Alan walked back and sat between Camilla and me.

"So, how's our Hannah?" He smiled at me, trying to distract himself from the charge he clearly wanted to take. I smiled back and nodded.

"How's our route?" Camilla asked.

"Well." Noah turned. "There are more cracks in this mountain than the map lets on. She's got some new wrinkles."

"Ugh." Camilla groaned. Her face was hard to read in the light, with goggles covering her eyes. So much sun, it felt like sandpaper on my skin.

"But we've got another few hours before we have to turn," said Linda. "It looks like we can cut around here, over this snow bridge." She pointed at the map, then looked up and pointed at the snow dunes in front of us. I couldn't see the bridges or cracks, and I was glad she was leading. Her arm made a curving motion.

"Whatever you say, boss." Alan's grin was awkward.

Nicky had to rope out again, so it took awhile before we managed to get going.

Ice ice ice ice, I thought, climbing. My legs felt as floppy as overcooked pasta. Each time we stopped, the other group traveled far ahead within minutes. We came to two unexpected stopping points, crevasses sneering at us, cracks wide enough to stop our unsteady progress and force Linda and Noah back into a huddle. The sun was high and the icy surfaces were melting.

Twice I'd thought we were on the last stretch, but then another point of mountain would poke the sky over our current horizon. I started thinking about our campsite and of my deliciously soft foam pad, thick as any mattress, and my parka pillow—a featherbed. The world spread out below us. Map in hand, Linda pointed out Cathedral Crag, the long blue eye of Baker Lake, the peculiar dark haystack of Cinder Cone.

"Remember, Baker's a volcano," she said. Then she pointed north and said, "All Canada is ours!"

I wouldn't have minded turning around; we'd been taking in the view from the mountain for hours, but looking at Nicky and Camilla and Shing and Alan I knew it wasn't enough for them; we were supposed to get to the very top.

"Another hour," said Noah, "and we should probably turn."

"No way," said Camilla. "I can see it."

"I don't know," said Alan. He sighed, a loud arc of sound. "This is pretty good."

No one said anything. We kept going.

For the next hour, we watched the sharp point of the true summit slide away and reappear as we circled the flank's parabola. It looked the same as our other view spots, just ever so slightly higher, with a signpost on top and a notch for our belts. My blisters burned, my arches ached, and my lower back was so sore I could easily imagine what it would feel like to be old. I took out my camera at each stop and clicked, thinking, This could pass for a summit photo. No one would ever know. Except Camilla, Nicky, and Shing.

Camilla's nose was burning to match Nicky's. The skin had split slightly, and a tiny creek of blood flowed over her lip. Shing, his nose white, passed his tube of zinc around again as Linda and Noah conferred once more.

"Sorry," Noah said, turning to us.

"No *way*." Camilla squashed the tube in her hand, and Shing reached to take it back.

"We made good progress, but if you look over there"—he pointed a pair of compact binoculars toward the peak—"you can see a bergschrund on this side. We'd have to descend almost a thousand feet and circle the cone—"

"It's no good," said Linda. "It isn't us, it's this side of the mountain."

"Okay," said Alan. He grinned. "This is as good as the summit for me. Let's get some shots before we turn around." He took out a camera and offered Camilla his hand to stand up.

"I can't believe it," she said. "Fucking bergschrund!"

"What's a bergschrund? Is it really such a big deal?" I knew as soon as it was out of my mouth that, of course, it was.

"Big crevasse at the top of the glacier," said Shing, scowling.

"If you stand over here, I can get the cone in the background." Alan seemed vaguely thrilled. I wondered whether I-told-you-so, even unspoken, gave him perverse satisfaction.

The view was no less extravagant on the way down. I was so happy to be headed for rest that I loved looking out even more than I had on the way up. The dark cone divided the sky, and the peaks purpled the air. I wanted Noah to sing again; I wanted to join in. Our group took the lead, and our steps had a rhythm. The rope stopped growing tight and slack and swung between us, perfect shallow curves of measured space.

But the slick surfaces were precarious, especially going down, and as we descended more sharply, Nicky kept speeding up, getting too far ahead of me, so the rope tugged. As afternoon kicked the ball of sun from its perch at the top of the sky, melted glacier soaked through the hole in my rain pants and through my long underwear, bathing my skin with each sliding step down. Nicky tugged again.

"Nicky," I said. "Can you slow down?" It was becoming a refrain. And for once, I wasn't sluggish; when I kept up with Nicky, the rope between Noah and me tugged taut.

Nicky was silent, sliding as he went, giant steps, too fast.

"Hey!" Noah yelled as Nicky pulled me forward and I pulled him forward. He slipped and started to slide down the ice, then dug his toe into a lump to stop.

"*Cut it out, Rambo!*" he yelled at Nicky.

Nicky stopped but didn't turn.

"Can you please be more careful," said Noah, regaining his balance. It wasn't a question.

We started again, and at first Nicky took tiny steps. My foot snagged on the ice and I slipped, then caught myself.

The surface resembled a half-melted skating rink—with occasional boulders and a 45-degree slant.

The other rope was advancing as we slowed, Linda out in front, her pants shushing along the surface. Nicky started his slide strides again, and the rope went taut at my waist. I watched him step and slide, with a slight jump, as if he were playing. At our last break, he'd refused any food or water; he'd stared up at the summit like a dog studying an empty bowl.

We started down a folded patch of ice, moving steadily, one at a time. The terrain was almost level for a few moments as we traversed at a horizontal. Nicky took chopping steps; I watched the ice chips spit where his crampons hit. Then he passed over the edge of the wrinkle and picked up his pace. I walked onto the flat spot too, pausing for Noah to finish his cross.

Nicky took a huge step, almost a jump, down the steep slope. A boulder field loomed at the bottom.

"Stop, c'mon," I said. I didn't want to talk about it; I just wanted to be roped to someone more reasonable.

Nicky didn't hear me, or he pretended not to, and then I watched as on his next jump step he slipped and started sliding down the mountain, one leg bent beneath him, the other out in front. I didn't think of our practice training, I didn't think of anything. I simply watched his oddly elegant fall while cold wicked up my body from my wet leg. Nicky was going too fast.

"Stop!" yelled Noah. I didn't know if he had seen the fall or just felt the tug, the enormous tug, of our rope.

There was a crack as Noah slipped off his step and started sliding too. I stood still, the highest point in the triangle, as Nicky and Noah fell below me. Then I was lifted off the ground by their momentum. Up off the ice, a quick flight.

The world was blue and there was wind. And then I slammed back down on the glacier and started sliding, grains of ice digging into my cheek. I tried to turn onto my back.

Self-arrest, I thought, wondering how I was supposed to extract my ice ax, which I'd stowed during our horizontal passage. It was on the back of my day pack, instead of in my arms, as it had been when we stepped down, sliding, in practice. Like I was now, sliding—only fast and face first.

Then stopping. A quick wrench. Someone yelling. Noah.

"You *idiot!*" he yelled. I thought, for a minute, he meant me.

"Sorry," said Nicky.

I turned around and sat up. My face burned from the friction. Noah had stopped us all; his ax and boots were still dug into the ice, secure as nails hammered into a wall. He was above me, and Nicky and I were a few feet from the boulders. The other rope, Camilla and Linda, Shing, and Alan, hovered above. I looked at Nicky. Lobster red in patches, stupid with disappointment. I'd hit my hips and butt on the ice when I landed. But nothing was bleeding, and Noah had saved us from the rocks. I counted my fingers to be sure the rope hadn't torn any of them off. I started laughing. It was my body's method of discharging the fright. My legs shook and my teeth felt loose. Then it was time to start our descent again; we unstrapped our crampons to walk across the rocks.

Somehow, we felt successful in spite of the failed summit attempt. Mostly because no one lost any limbs. Back at the base camp, after even Camilla and Nicky agreed it would be silly to make another summit attempt or to start again on the other side and forgo our trip to the Southern Cascades, Alan and Camilla built a fire and we basked: sore, exhausted. Full of ourselves despite the disappointment, because it was a hard climb and we'd almost made it. Watching Camilla as she ate her reconstituted lasagna, I wondered how much it mattered to her, if the peak sat in her throat. And what kept her going.

The food tasted exquisite, the too-salty noodles, fatty cheese on my tongue. Water was delicious, the chill making my lips ache. It was dark and the fog came back in, a blanket of damp. Nicky fell asleep on his foam pad as Alan was telling Noah how to cut joists for a theoretical cabin in the woods. I could feel my bones beneath my flesh, the muscles more worked than I ever remembered.

We celebrated with s'mores, spearing marshmallows on a spare tent pole because there were no trees tall enough to make sticks. As Noah passed me a gooey marshmallow, melted on one side, burnt on the other, I said, "Thank you," and smeared the marshmallow on my graham cracker with a chocolate square. But I'd meant for saving me. His fast body cutting our arrest against the ice. Saving me from falling, saving me from mistake. I was starting to learn what it was that made me come here, made me give up comfort and face the heavy steps of my own resistance. Not the summits, not the views, but the coming back down, arriving safely. It was one thing I could try to control. As long as my rope mates didn't kill me.

Twelve /

Camilla had entered a quiet sulk. As we drove along in the fish-scented van, I studied her, plugged into her portable CD player, nodding along to the music in her private cell of sound. The drumbeats squeezed out of her headphones and tapped tiny holes in the air. Our wet gear was spread over the ripped seats, my long underwear linking knees with Linda's, hats slipping onto the floor as we pulled off the highway into a campground at Cougar Flat, where we'd hit the trail at Goose Prairie in the Southern Cascades.

We'd camped, the night before, just a few miles from the van, so the morning's trek had been brief, though we kept dropping the sloppily packed gear as we neared the road. The van wouldn't start, at first, and Linda had bent under the hood poking at coils and wires and hoses while Alan kept trying the ignition. Noah and I sat on our packs and watched. As much as I'd wanted to be back in semi-civilization, as I stared at the road I felt the absence of the view, the green tunnel of the woods. And I started thinking about the hike ahead—Goose Prairie to the American Ridge—about navigating and not missing a turn or degree or a single bug on a redwood stump. Noah was slicing a stick with his knife.

"Stupid van!" yelled Linda. She jumped away from the hood, shaking her finger. Alan turned the key, and it spluttered to a start.

I couldn't remember exactly when Camilla had closed herself off, but it became obvious in the van. She kept her headphones on all day, even when we stopped at the supermarket. The packages of food looked bright and artificial—an embarrassment of food, all you can eat, cookies colossal in the pictures on their packages, cereal puffed with air in the pillows of plastic bags, seven kinds of milk.

Shing bought a watermelon, which he swore he would carry to our first campsite in the American Ridge. Alan picked out steaks for our car campground, though only half the group ate steak. I hadn't had red meat since college and chose turkey burgers instead, tapping Camilla to ask whether she ate them. She nodded, crinkling pretzel bags on an end-cap display until a seam breached and salt spilled out into the aisle.

I made a phone call from the parking lot booth; my hand felt oddly weak as I dialed Ted's number. I got his machine, which made me more worried—and relieved too—my mouth dry as I spoke Shing's cell phone number after the beep.

"Just in case," I said.

I felt sheepish; I hadn't asked Shing whether I could use it, I'd just copied it down from the label on the case.

We were ascending again. I'd all but forgotten last night's shower. It could have been hotter, with more spray, but I'd felt clean then, flip-flopping back to the tents in heel-squashed sneakers, wearing my last pair of clean shorts and a T-shirt.

Now we were climbing. The trail was socked in by fir and pine, and it smelled clean. It wasn't too steep, but my restocked pack felt ridiculously heavy. We were quiet, walking close together, the dapples measuring each of us as we passed the same spot on the trail.

Camilla was last. She'd made Noah and me go ahead as we stood waiting for her to start at the trailhead. She was a little bit behind. Noah followed me. I wanted to ask him about her but didn't feel qualified to express concern without sounding condescending.

Almost two miles into the trip, we started crossing streams as we traversed the ascension on switchbacks. It seemed like there were dozens of them, but then I realized the same two streams crossed and crossed again. We were weaving the ridge.

"Will these switchbacks never end?" Noah said, sounding very cheerful, behind me. I wondered whether the tone was for my benefit.

"They just started," said Shing, his bright red socks directly in front of me. "Two miles of this. And I've got the watermelon." I worried for that melon, that it might slip out at lunch break, that it might smash on the trail, a pink and seedy loss if Shing stumbled.

"Oy," said Noah. For a second, an image of my father flashed through my forest-green vision. My father shaking hands with Noah, assessing his height, approving. The image faded fast.

"We've got to make a game of it," said Shing. "Something to keep us from going mad."

"I know," Linda said, second in line. I hadn't realized she

was listening. "For each switchback, we'll say what we're going to be doing one year from now, then two, and so on."

Nicky groaned.

"Okay, then, you propose something," said Linda.

"Five years," he said. "One year's too real. Let's start five years from now."

"Then you go first." Linda started walking again. "And speak loudly, so we can all hear."

"Five years from now I'll be thirty—eek—and I'll own my own outdoors gear store in Harvard Square," said Nicky, almost shouting. He kicked a rock, which thumped down the ridge, cracking against the trunk of a fir. "And all the undergrads will buy my Gore-Tex coats and bicycle panniers with their parents' hard-earned dough."

"I didn't know you wanted to open a shop," Noah said.

"No commenting," said Nicky. "It's Hannah's turn."

"Oh," I said. "Five years from now." I put one foot in front of the other, breathing in the pine scent as my boots crushed needles. I had no idea. "I guess I'll have graduated from architecture school, and I'll be designing new State Park shelters and symphony halls and libraries and houses."

"So you'll really be specializing," said Linda, laughing.

Five years from now. If I really thought about it, I wouldn't keep following the trail's turns, step up, step up. My father would probably be dead.

"No commenting," said Nicky. "It's Noah's turn."

"Five years from now," said Noah, "I will have my own music school in a big old Victorian house in Back Bay, and my students will go to Juilliard and Oberlin and I will probably be married."

"What was that last bit?" Nicky asked.

"No commenting," said Noah. "Camilla's turn."

For a minute, I heard only the sound of our shuffling boots.

"Camilla?" Noah turned. She was a little way down the trail, but not too far to hear our loud talk.

"I don't want to play," she said.

"You have to," said Nicky.

Camilla sighed. "I'll have met the girl of my dreams," she said, "and I won't have any *cats*."

Noah laughed. I wanted to turn around, but I'd lose my momentum. How hadn't I known? I had obviously never paid much attention. I'd thought Camilla was interested in Nicky or Noah. My own bubble vision. Had she been involved all along? Had she recently broken up with a girl-friend? She lived in Jamaica Plain, and I'd seen the outside of her narrow apartment building on the way to a meeting, once, sitting in Shing's van. She worked at a public radio station, WGBH, doing something in production, and the face of her house was crumbly gray stucco. Her doorbell was shaped like a chili pepper, bright red amid a bank of dull yellow oblongs. I'd wondered whether she installed it herself, but I'd never asked.

We'd picked up the pace since we started Nicky's game, and I didn't mind as we turned the corner of the next switchback.

By the time we stopped for a lunch break, we could see the trail intersection up ahead. Linda had three children, and Alan had opened a cross-country ski center on two hundred acres in Vermont. Nicky opened and sold business after business and invented some kind of essential climbing gear and had me, the famous architect, design a mansion for him right in the middle of the Public Gardens. Camilla kept saying she'd met the girl of her dreams, but not much more. Shing had sixteen children. He named them A, B, C, and on, through P.

Since we'd increased the pace of the fantasy, I'd become famous, though never particularly rich. I'd traveled the world and been in space. Chef's school was a quick stop; fruit desserts were my specialty. Alan interrupted me because he said I was making him too hungry, conjuring towers of strawberries, chocolate, and cream. I said nothing about my family, decided nothing about Ben.

Noah never did say whom he planned to marry, but his wife appeared every few half-decades in the narrative, accompanying him on a South American rain-forest exploration, producing twins, opening an organic foods co-op. As he spoke, I could almost see the twins, boy and girl, their eyes his bright blue, their shiny brown hair, the girl tall and running, legs like a doe's, muscle and grace.

I didn't want to start hiking again after lunch. Only Shing and I were left sitting on a rock.

"C'mon, Hannah," said Shing, giving me a hand up. I took his hand but kept sitting.

"What happens if I quit?" I asked. Despite the pre-lunch revelry, I was suddenly too tired to go on. I knew I was being a baby, but part of me wanted to be convinced.

"You will be shunned forever," said Shing, pulling me up with more force than I could resist. "And we'll have more to eat at dinner."

"Is that what happened to Vijay?" I asked, considering sitting back down.

"Stop being so lazy," grumbled Shing. He strode ahead on the trail without answering my question.

———

We camped by a spring right below the base of the ridge. Our day hadn't been too long—under five miles—but we'd climbed out of the ordinary firs and pines and into Alaskan cedars, subalpine firs, and wind-bent pines, a low gnarl of green. Alan named the trees and asked Noah what we'd find to eat up here.

"For when we run out of this," he added, digging his spoon into the giant split watermelon. It had proved impossible to slice with our little Swiss Army knives, so Shing had cracked it on a sharp rock, then wedged it open. It had been a surprise that it wasn't pink, but yellow, and it had no seeds. It tasted like a soft perfume. Nothing had ever been so delectable.

"Or all get the runs," said Nicky. Camilla grimaced and ate a bite off his spoon. She seemed to be warming up a bit.

"Not much," said Noah. "Western blueberry."

"You've seen blueberries?" Camilla asked.

"No, but there is such a thing. And you can eat the shoots and stalks of fireweed, or make tea. And there's mountain sorrel, but that's a pretty minor mouthful." Noah looked around him as if expecting a roast chicken plant.

"So basically we'd starve," said Alan, licking his fingers.

"No," said Noah. "We'd camp down at the cirque at Big Basin and hunt elk."

The air turned cool and sharp and full of mosquitoes. Rather than swat and bleed, we went to bed early. Camilla and I were sharing a tent, and I reveled in the spaciousness of having just one other person in my nylon prism.

Camilla was inside her bag, holding a paperback in front of her headlamp spot. She wasn't reading; she never turned the pages, and she kept sighing. Dark crept around the tent.

"So what is it?" I asked.

Camilla sighed.

She sighed again and put her book down but didn't speak. The quiet made me nervous, so I started talking.

"What is the deal with Shing, anyway? Why is he so touchy about this Vijay guy?"

Camilla put the book down and turned off her lamp. "No one ever told you?" she asked in a quiet, serious voice.

I felt as if I'd triggered a silent alarm. "Oh, um, no," I said. "You don't have to—"

"You really didn't know? I hope you don't freak out—it's kind of awful." She paused, and I could hear her breathing.

"Vijay was Shing's club recruit—his friend from college— he was a doctor, a rheumatologist. Anyway, he and Shing were buddies, and they were always clowning."

"In the picture I saw, Vijay was wrapped in a rope." It felt like a confession, that I'd wondered about him all this time.

"Well, he did stuff like that. You should never mess with ropes—if they're attached—"

I *know*, I thought, but I didn't say anything.

"Anyway, he drove Alan crazy, but he was always so quick on the trail, and he was always helping everyone out, and he was a *doctor*, so no one felt like they could yell at him for doing dangerous stuff."

"Like what?" I asked. "I mean, besides playing with gear."

"Oh, body surfing in waterfalls, clowning in caves, he and Noah had these duels—anyway, that wasn't what happened: it was an accident, could've happened to anyone. Canoe trip, two years ago. Lots of fair-weather club members. Noah's day pack came unstrapped and fell into the rapids, and Vijay reached for it and fell out—no big deal by itself, but he got sucked under this massive drainpipe and lost consciousness, broke his collarbone and his jaw—"

She recited the damage in a steady tone, almost noncha-

lant. I inhaled deeply but still felt thirsty for breath, the
image of Vijay, underwater, the thin line between safety and
accident smudged.

"And Noah did CPR; and Shing's phone didn't work, so
he hiked out—ran through the woods, six miles—and got a
helicopter in; and Vijay was in the hospital in Maine for a
few weeks. . . . Noah and Shing stayed with him. And at first
it seemed like he'd be okay, except for some internal bruis-
ing, and he'd lost a little memory: the trip, what happened,
and odd things . . . like his birthday party the year before,
and Peru. . . ."

She stopped again. "Damn," she mumbled. She was trying not to cry. "But after he was transferred to the Brigham
in Boston—they took him all the way by ambulance—he got
worse. He had to have surgery to fix a problem with his
lungs, and he had some kind of clotting problem, and then it
was really fast: a few days and he was gone."

She stopped for a moment, breathing deeply.

"Shing won't talk about it," she finished. "He thinks it's
his fault somehow."

I was shivering, though I wasn't cold. All for Noah's
day pack. I'd been blind. I thought of following Camilla
and Noah through the duck-under. We could've died in
that cave. We could've gotten lost when I was the deficient
trip leader, could've been buried in avalanche, could've
tripped on that glacier and hit the rocks. We were fragile
as eggs.

"So that's the story," said Camilla.

"That's awful," I said. Then the reflexive, "I'm sorry." I ran
my finger up and down the open zipper on my sleeping bag.

I hoped she wasn't closing up again, but I didn't want to
grill her on all the club members, only a few feet away in the
other two tents, asleep while the stealthy mosquitoes sucked,

or lying awake in their own conversations. As Camilla paused, I heard the low current of Noah's voice.

"We all miss Vijay, but Shing's really sensitive about it," she said. She cleared her throat and forced a small laugh. "And by the way, he has a crush on you, I think." A new subject, like another color.

"No way," I said. Shing in his motorcycle jacket, rescuing me from a boring snow day. He teased everyone, though. Besides, I wasn't allowed to be interested.

Vijay was dead. Why hadn't they told me? Would I have ever come on another trip? Not if I'd known from the start, I thought, but now I was hooked. And I knew how to be careful enough. No doubt Vijay had, too.

"What about you, Hannah?" Camilla was trying to move the conversation out of the deep end.

"About me?"

"Shing says you have a mythical boyfriend."

"Oh, I have a boyfriend," I said. The words didn't conjure Ben. I was still thinking of Shing and the lost Vijay. There was a snore from one of the other tents. "And a screwed-up family," I continued. "The usual."

I told her about my parents' divorce, about Ted and Marla when we were kids, Ted reciting Latin, Marla's girls'-school years, reluctantly letting them into the tent so Camilla wouldn't think I was closed to her. I didn't mention my father, or Ben's moving-in plan, or Abby's pregnancy, or Marla's stick-figure boyfriend. From this distance, they felt less urgent. Older news had more weight. Even Dad's lupus stayed outside, lingering in the woods. As I was speaking, I started to feel good, as if by sharing the stories, they became just stories, not the history I carried on my shoulders like a pack.

"So," I finished. "What about you?"

"Family's boring, really. Mom lives in Wellesley; Dad died last year. My older brother used to sell drugs, but now he's a surfing cop in San Diego."

"That's a mouthful," I said.

"And I broke up with my girlfriend two weeks before this trip. I thought it didn't bother me, because we'd only been together for about three months. But now it's hitting me that she's really gone. Vivian." She said the name deliciously, ambrosia in her mouth. "It was short, but kind of intense."

We were both quiet. A mosquito buzzed and Camilla's bag made slippery noises as she swatted. Then Shing and Nicky started a snoring war, their gravelly breaths announcing sleep in the quiet windy woods.

"I'm sorry," I said again.

Camilla laughed. "Who am I kidding," she said. "It's always kind of intense."

Dad died last year. She'd let that roll on into the next news. So much information, after so much quiet. Soon enough, I'd have that history too, my father gone. My fingernail caught on the zipper as I flicked the teeth. The nail tore as I pulled, and it hurt.

"Thanks, babe," Camilla said. She patted my head. "You didn't know, did you?"

"Um, I guess I'm kind of oblivious," I said, laughing lightly.

"Well, I don't wear my sexuality on my forehead. I suppose I wanted to get to know you first."

And maybe that meant she knew me, at least a little. It was like a sip of water, hearing that. And I was thirsty.

It was raining when we woke. I'd been restless, waking to each night noise, envisioning accidents, and Vijay, whom I'd never met, but whom I felt I'd lost nonetheless. Camilla slept beside me.

The morning was gray and muted by the drone of drops on the tent fly. My teeth felt fuzzy and our clothes and bags were damp. We had a fast uncomfortable breakfast of everything we could eat uncooked, since Alan and Camilla couldn't get the stoves started in the rain. While Noah and I picked raisins out of the bag of instant oatmeal, Shing and Nicky debated over our route. Shing wanted to go an extra quarter mile to a view of Mount Rainier, but Nicky argued that we wouldn't see anything in the rain.

"Meanwhile," Linda interrupted, "we're getting soaked. Let's go. An extra half mile won't kill us, and maybe it'll clear. And I'm ready to go." Rain pattered on her pack, which she was already wearing.

Up again. I shook the garbage-bag cover off my pack. The straps were wet and sap-sticky. The rain kept drooling down. Morning monotony, step after step. I ached. I wasn't ready for a whole day of plodding, and no matter how I tried shifting my pack, tightening and readjusting straps, stopping to reorganize, something inside it stabbed my back. I caught up to the end of the group. Noah was last, and I focused on his orange socks. It seemed like forever, following Noah's orange socks, but when I peeked at my watch, the sharp thing in my pack stabbing again as I lifted my arm, it had been less than an hour.

At the viewpoint I got out my camera. The rain had settled into a fine spray. I took a photo—Shing and Camilla standing at the edge of a cliff, against a gray background. Shing clowned, holding Camilla's ponytail like reins. He was too close to the edge, and as I clicked the shutter I wanted to tell him to be careful.

"Hey!" Shing yelled, as I was stowing my camera. I felt

the word in my stomach and looked up, afraid to find empty space where he'd stood. But he was still with us, pointing. At the top of the sky, the gray had peeled back, revealing the dramatic profile of Mount Rainier. It looked presidential, royal, like a figure you recognize from a childhood of myth and history lessons.

"Mount Aix!" said Alan, pointing at another glorious peak above the fog. Light peeled the fog down farther, cleaning the sky.

"Mount Y and Mount Z!" said Shing, as long ridges came into view.

We had chocolate bars to celebrate, the fancy imported kind Shing bought with his own money. My new knowledge made me feel awkward around him, but I had to stop lingering, because there wasn't enough space in our little group for awkwardness.

By the time we made it to the campsite at Big Basin, I was feeling my blisters with every step. As we descended into the rainy bowl, we were walking close to each other's heels, a pack of mild misery. But we heard talking as we approached, and there were six tents in the clearing. We had company.

They shared their boiling water for tea, and a woman named Lila offered us fireweed stalks to chew. We sat down by their fire, beneath a tarp that kept the ground dry below. They were all dry and looked warm and comfortable in sweaters and blue jeans. It was like coming onto a fairy clearing; they left their substantial, sturdy stoves going so we could use them, never mind using up the fuel.

I watched Noah watching Lila, whose sweater rounded her tightly. Her eyes were bright green with long lashes casting shadows on her cheeks in the lantern's glow. A young man with a wide smile, Jay, wearing a baseball cap and a black turtleneck, offered us coffee. Real coffee, whole beans milled in a battery-operated grinder and poured, cup by cup, through a portable filter. I took him in while I drank: short sandy hair, square-cut jaw, skin so clean I wanted to touch him. The coffee was delicious and masked the faint metallic taste of the freeze-dried broccoli stir-fry. We were enchanted, our wet weary group squeezed under the tarp with the dry and happy, their colors lightening our day's fade into black-and-white and grainy gray.

Lila told us they'd stayed in the cirque for three days, despite their limited permit, because it was so beautiful they couldn't convince themselves to get back on the trail. And then it started raining every evening, so they'd settled in. They looked gorgeously rested.

After dinner, there was talk—it was as if we'd been starved for words, alone in our group, and we ate up conversations, Shing's cheeks dotted with perfect rounds of blush as he talked to a woman from Marin County, whose hair was bound in a braid that fell below her hips, her eyelashes invisible blond.

"You've got another week or two?" Jay the coffee guy smiled at me. Even teeth.

"I don't want to count," I said. "Though I wouldn't mind a shower."

"You guys have to stay here for a few days. When it clears, it's incredible. Dazzling. I've decided to retire and move here."

"You seem kind of young to retire," I said.

The perfect grin. "I could live anywhere," he said. "With a coffee shop, that is. I'm thinking of opening my own."

"I don't see one here," I said.

"Perfect opportunity. But my girlfriend would kill me."

She would have long red hair, I thought, freckles and

round bow lips. He grew up near the Jersey shore, he told me, and moved to San Francisco after college.

Jay yawned. Noah was over by the trees, his square head-lamp lighting tree, nylon, metal, tree, as he set up a tent.

"I've got to go," I said. "Thank you for the coffee."

"Watch for rainbows," he said. It would've sounded corny anywhere but here.

In the morning's bright fog, there was no trace of the group from San Francisco. Maybe it *had* been a modern-day fairy circle, I thought, casting the necessary magic to ensure we'd make it through the evening. But then, where their tarp had stood, I found a blue plastic cup filled with coffee. Deciding it was meant for me, I took a sip after setting up the stove. It was cold, but tasty anyway.

I put on dry socks, and felt warm at last. Camilla and Nicky straggled out of our tent, and we walked down to the stream to wash our faces and collect water. As we trod the slippery stones, leaning down over the cold stream with our plastic gallon expansion containers, the sun chased the fog from the basin and the sky cleared.

At the edge, a rainbow. We were circled by ridges and peaks. I could almost taste the view, rich as ice cream.

"They sure took off fast," said Nicky.

"Look," said Camilla. I lifted my head from the almost-filled water jug as a band of elk shifted, silent, across the sea of grasses at the bottom of the basin.

Thirteen /

By popular vote, we decided to spend the morning at Big Basin before trimming a leg off the journey and moving on to another campsite. The spot was gorgeous, the light, the elk, the jagged-rimmed mountains that held us in the green. As soon as Linda suggested it at breakfast, I was longing to lie down in the middle of the field on my foam pad, letting the light of morning glide across my face while my body rushed the materials of repair to my tired muscles and bones. Even my blood felt thin with exertion; a night's sleep hadn't been enough.

Camilla and Shing took off on a day hike right after breakfast. Alan and Linda went to nap in their tent, and I gathered my things quickly, my blank-paged little journal, pen still wedged in the rings where I'd placed it when I packed, and my sleeping pad, sleeping bag, and a sweater to use as a pillow. I wanted to give the couple space; I'd seen them looking at each other after breakfast, *sex* written on their expressions.

Noah and Nicky, their climbing shoes draped in lace necklaces on their chests, announced they were going on a bouldering expedition. Arms full, I waded out through the grasses, across the stream, and into the field. I found a flat rock and lay down. I was tired, but not sleepy enough to drift off yet, so I took out the journal and held my pen above the blank page.

I didn't know the date. It had been so long since I didn't know the date; a particular, lovely lost feeling made me shiver. It was August, I knew that much, but I didn't know the day of the week, the items due tomorrow, the birthdays requiring cards, the calls to return. All I knew was this exquisite place, the quick-shifting golden light, the small color points of Nicky and Noah as they parted the grasses, passing through the field.

Being alone was as luxurious and exotic as a wedge of mango on my tongue. No one requiring conversation, decisions. No one in the space beside me, sharing my air. And the ache in my legs was all about accomplishment. Lying on my back, I watched the round-bellied clouds chase each other across the blue.

Then Noah woke me.

"Sleeping beauty," he said. I'd been dreaming about swimming, cutting through cold water with my arms spread out like an angel. All my exposed skin tingled from the rough brush of the wind.

"Mm," I said. His cheeks were bright, and it took me a minute to remember we were parked in paradise for the morning.

"We've got to start packing up." He sat down beside me,

his leg resting against mine. He was wearing shorts, and the sinews of his thigh were defined. Noah the anatomy lesson. He chewed a piece of grass.

"What's that?" I asked. "Wild wheat?" There was sleep in my eyes, and I felt creased. I was back inside the necessity of conversation, but it was automatic, and I didn't mind so much.

"Actually," said Noah, "I have no idea what it is. Some kind of grass." He grinned and put his hands on my cheeks, warm hands, like a grandparent holding a child's face. It felt wonderful, but it also was invasive, and I sat up quickly. I wanted to be touched, and more, but not by Noah. At least, probably not by Noah. The warmth between my thighs was an embarrassment.

"Can't we stay?" I stood and gathered my things, then followed Noah, my sleeping bag trailing me like a security blanket.

"You could put it to a vote," he said.

I didn't want to move. I stuffed everything into my pack, grasses clinging to the sleeping bag, burrs scraping inside my socks, and heaved the beast onto my back. Follow Linda, follow Linda.

"It's only two and a half miles to Mud Lake," said Linda, as the sluggish forms of the others scuffed the trail with dragging steps. I wondered why she felt compelled to be group cheerleader; Camilla was in charge of navigation. I appreciated and resented them both, as the sensation of tearing spread along my arches.

Mud Lake sounded soggy. Where had Jay the coffee man and his San Francisco cohorts gone? Had they traveled this way, speeding through the tunnel of glorious view on their descent? Out. Showers, telephones, airplanes. Part of me never wanted to go back, and part of me couldn't wait to cram my backpack into a closet and sleep for a week.

We followed a long ridge. When I looked back on Big Basin it was small enough to hold inside my hands. I could feel accumulated sweat and dirt on my skin. We kept going. A rock field. I walked carefully, thinking about keystones. Like an arch, a rock field could collapse into a landslide if a single balance stone was shifted. My father taught me about keystones when I was six, sitting on a stone wall at the Arnold Arboretum, asking him what kept things together.

What kept things together was the desire not to fall apart: that was what my father the artist told me. I was terrible for leaving him, even though he'd left me, left all of us. A daughter's responsibilities were greater than that of the parents. Could that be true? To forgive, over and over. Like Marla, always trying to piece things together, confident she could build, repair. Ben was probably right when he told me I shouldn't go on the trip. I wanted his arms, wanted to sleep between them.

What if I played the switchback game with my father—what would he imagine in his future, and what would I tell him of mine? Now all his possibilities were limited. I thought of his commands and comments: *get married, don't get married, I guess that's one way to squander your talents.* My father was disappointed, but mostly in himself. For all his insistence and displays, it was what he hadn't done yet that plagued him.

I stepped in Camilla's footprints. She'd taken Linda's place in front of me and was singing "A Hundred Bottles of Beer on the Wall" in an annoying drone. Then her ankle folded. I watched its peculiar slow motion, and she fell on her hands on the rocks, one leg dangling over the edge of the trail, as if contemplating a serious fall.

"Shit," she said, her voice pinched.

I tried to help her up, but she pushed my hands away. Shing turned and picked her up, too fast and strong to be rejected.

"Cut it out," said Camilla. "I'm fine."

But I watched her as we started again: her hands were scratched, and she held the palms pressed together to stop the bleeding, and she limped, leaning so heavily on one side I thought she might fall again.

The forest changed as we moved back into the trees, which were low but not the miniature trees of the alpine ridge. Trees just a little taller than me. As we continued, and the light dipped into the hollow of the world below us, I pretended I was one of those trees. Big Basin had made me dreamy. And lazy, and aware of what it felt like to keep moving. So when we found our campsite among the people-sized trees, I was only too happy to set up a tent with Noah and Nicky, join the battle to get the stoves started, eat reconstituted coq au vin, the texture of cardboard in mud, and climb inside my bag to sleep.

I heard Noah saying good night to Nicky, and Nicky insisting that he wanted to sleep out under the stars.

"Pretty foggy stars, Nick," said Noah. "It looks like rain."

"Then I'll melt."

"Okay, buddy."

Buddy. It sounded so plain and desirable. I wanted a buddy. Nicky and Noah shared climbing history, counting on each other to hold their bodies in perfect suspension between rock and earth.

Noah shuffled in his bag. Our lights were off, and he shifted and turned, sighed and scratched, his body beside mine. Since we'd left Big Basin, all I'd wanted to do was to stop and sleep, and here, inside my cocoon, I couldn't. Noah turned again. Sighed. Peeled half out of his bag and rolled over. Whacked my face with his big naked elbow.

"Hey!" I shoved his elbow away. My cheekbone burned. At least he'd missed my eye.

"Sorry," he said. "It's just so crowded in here."

It was a joke, but I didn't realize it until a whole circle of silent seconds had passed.

"I'm sorry," he said again. He started shuffling around. His sleeping bag zipper opened and closed.

"Can't sleep?" *Obviously*, I thought, as I asked.

"Must be all that resting today."

"You weren't resting. I was the sloth," I said.

"Nick and I took it slow. Do you think he's getting soggy out there in the fog?"

"He'll come in," I said. I didn't want him to, though.

Another circle of silence. The tent smelled like dirty socks.

"When we were in the cave," I started.

"Cave? What cave?"

"I mean, this spring, Spider Cave, when we got lost—"

"Don't remind me," said Noah. His voice was soft; he sounded like he was carrying sleep on his tongue.

"I was wondering. I mean, do you think we take enough precautions? I mean, do you think these trips are really safe?"

"What's safe, Hannah?" His voice was rough but not unkind.

"I guess nothing," I said, wanting him not to be annoyed, wanting that sleepy voice, his song voice.

He shuffled.

"Camilla told me about Vijay," I said.

"You didn't know?" Noah rolled over close to me.

"Nope, no one said anything. . . ." I let my words fall around us like spent leaves.

"Hannah," he said. I could feel the heat of his breath on the top of my head.

I waited for him to say something else about Vijay, that he didn't want to talk about that either.

Instead, he leaned down and pressed his mouth into mine, his lips tentative. There was a soft sound on the tent, the shush of snow. I let his mouth stay, for a few seconds, and then I turned slightly, so we were still close but no longer touching. My lips stung from the contact, and all the threads running through me were pulled taut with guilt and longing. I'd stopped him, though; I'd had to stop him.

"What are we doing?" I whispered.

"Oh," said Noah. "Never mind." Then he laughed, a single note. "I mean—I'd hoped you had *some* idea."

Something started pinging against the tent. Hail. Then cold filled the space, the unzipping and rezipping, and Nicky flopped on top of both of us, and drops and still-frozen pebbles of hail spilled across us. Noah's arms slipped back inside his bag.

"Wake up," said Nicky. "It's warm in here, and it's hailing outside." He wormed between us. "Make room for Daddy."

All night, listening to the plunk of hail on the tent fly, the percussive occasions of a frozen pellet striking a metal pole, I pretended to sleep. Nicky snored, on and off, and Noah's breath was steady, but too fast for dreaming. Nicky slept between us, certain as a highway barrier, keeping the traffic contained in its separate directions.

Fourteen / We were back in the van again, and Camilla's ankle, swathed in ice from the general store in Forks, was propped on the seat back in a bundle of sweatshirt. We'd cut our descent short, emerging at Bumping Lake and riding a ferry back to the trail to our campground.

"I'm not going to let a stupid ankle stop me," said Camilla, from her queenly posture.

"Fine," said Linda. "But we'll go to the Hoh before Rialto Beach and Ozette. Get a good night's sleep. Then you can recover at the campground while we go on the guided path—"

"Tourist land," moaned Nicky. "I want peaks."

"We know you do," said Shing. He hadn't shaved in days, and his face was peppered with fine gray and black bristles. Noah hadn't shaved either. I could still feel the soft scratch of his cheek against mine. I shouldn't, I thought, looking at

him, then out the window as the timber fields and lumber-
yards blurred by.

"Don't change the plans because of me," said Camilla.
She counted two Tylenol out of her little metal pillbox. "Has
it been four hours yet?"

"How should I know?" Nicky squirmed from his position on the floor. All of us cramped in the van; it was worse
than a family vacation.

"Yes," said Linda. "And all we're doing is changing the
order, not the plans."

The van hit a pothole and Camilla grabbed her ankle and
moaned.

The Hoh rain forest was a tourist attraction, but one with a
trail to follow through the mossy-scented, deeply shadowed
woods. Camilla stayed at the campground, where RVs and
trailer pop-ups and the drone of radios and burning meat
odors dwarfed our little tents. She sat by the Hoh River, her
ballooning, bluish ankle resting in the water. I'd been
tempted to stay with her, to watch the water move and stay
still, but she insisted that everyone go.

I stopped at the pay phones by the visitor center and got
out my calling card again.

"Calling your boyfriend?" Nicky pressed his face against
the glass from outside. I turned away so I didn't have to see
his squashed mouth.

At first, my fingers worked through the digits of my
father's number, but before it started to ring I hung up. I
didn't want him to growl at me; I didn't want to hear him
telling me to get on with my trip and quit making him promise to postpone death. I didn't want his machine, either, giving me no information at all, so I called Ben instead, at work.

"Mr. Shepard isn't available," said the watchdog secretary.

"It's . . . his . . . um, it's Hannah," I said.

"I'll tell him to call you."

"You can't. Just tell him I'm okay, okay?"

I left the booth sweaty. Nothing was wrong, I told myself. Nothing could've happened in this short time.

"Enough love chatter," said Nicky, but he gave my arm a brief stroke, and it helped.

The trail was wide and groomed, winding between the tree giants. Linda and Alan stopped at each educational sign, and Nicky jogged around the path, lapping us as we meandered. Noah was walking with me, but we hadn't had any time alone since the tent. I didn't know how I was supposed to walk beside him. I knew it was a mistake, even if I wanted to remember his mouth on mine, even if I kept thinking about it. We'd been gone too long. I was lonely, and I'd fought with Ben, and I was mistaking new friendship and mystery and lust for something else. I willed Noah not to be so beautiful, to stop smelling like ferns and cinnamon. I was embarrassed to be near him, in the great space of the whole outside.

The trees filled the sky with thick reddish bark, with green clouds of needles, stories up. Our path looped back, crossing the river on a sturdy broad bridge, so civilized. It looked like the outdoors, but there were families with bright pink hats and all-terrain strollers. A woman walked past us in sandals, trailing a wave of fake-rose perfume.

Shing walked with Noah and me, restless. He carried his video camera and taped the woods, Noah—who stuck out his tongue—and me. I frowned.

That night we had turkey burgers and grilled fresh corn and summer squash and red peppers, and even a bottle of

Chardonnay, provisions from the stop in Forks. Noah didn't eat much. He lay on his back during dinner, not even sitting up to sip wine. I wondered if we were pretending nothing had happened between us.

"How's that ankle, honey?" Nicky handed Camilla a plastic cup of wine and a plate of premade potato salad.

"Picnic food rocks," said Camilla. She dug in. "It's going to be better enough to hike tomorrow," she said, as she chewed.

"We'll drive to Rialto in the afternoon," said Linda. "But we won't start hiking again for another day. It still looks bad."

"Gee, Mom," said Camilla. "Thanks." But she wasn't sneering, as best I could tell in the light of the campfire and the glow cast by the trailers and campers in the sites around us.

I fell asleep between Shing and Nicky. The sound of televisions from the trailers drowned out the river, the bugs' whine, the trees swaying on their hips, and even the snoring on either side of me.

In the morning, Noah didn't come out of the tent for breakfast. I assumed he wanted to sleep late, though Noah was usually up pretty fast, at least when we were on the trail. After we ate, fresh oranges, kiwi, and a cantaloupe Nicky scooped out into pastel orange moons with his spoon, Alan went in to confer. We pretended not to be straining to hear; Camilla hummed a little, and Shing picked stones from his boot soles with a stick. Not only did I want to know what was going on, I wanted him to tell me *first*. I wanted not to want him. I sat stewing, my stomach working noisily at the fruit I'd eaten too quickly.

When Alan came out, he sat down by our feast's wreckage of peels and half-filled bowls.

"Someone has to take him back to Seattle," he said. "I

think we should rent a second car. I could go and then meet you all midway on the Ozette loop."

"What?" said Camilla. She let her propped-up ankle fall off a boulder and didn't wince.

"His back is out. He said he knew it's been about to go for a few days, but sometimes it passes. He thinks it's from setting up that bear bag, pulling on the rope—he's thrown it out before. Remember when we all had altitude sickness in Peru, and Noah wouldn't come out of the lean-to?"

Linda gave a halfhearted laugh. From what I'd heard, Peru had been perfect, all intended peaks bagged, all sights seen, and everyone, I'd assumed, in perfect health.

"But it's worse this time," said Noah, from the tent. I'd assumed he couldn't hear us. "Sorry, guys."

"I'm going," said Shing. "It's only three more days until we all have to go anyway."

"I can," said Linda.

"I suppose I could go," I said. It would be safe enough; he'd just be lying on the backseat moaning over the bumps. I wondered how he'd manage the plane and what would happen on the other end. Would he get someone to pick him up: his mother, his stepfather driving a Lincoln Continental? I imagined Noah in a white bed in a white room, convalescing, painkillers fogging those bright eyes.

"I can't drive," said Camilla. "But it sounds like Nick and I will be the only ones left." She hopped over to the tent and unzipped the door.

"This sucks, Noah," she said. I saw her lie beside him. Noah whispered something. I tried not to feel jealous. My back itched where I couldn't reach.

"No," said Shing. "I'll go."

"You can find us on the beach loop?" Alan was unfolding a highway map.

"Of course," said Shing.

Alan sighed. "We really should stay paired. Shing and I should go."

"No," said Camilla, giggling from the tent. "Noah and I are having an affair. My wounded ankle and his wounded back are the price of our passionate escapades. I'll go with Shing. It'll give me time to heal, and then Shing can carry me and my pack around the loop to meet you."

"Argh," said Nicky, flapping his red wool socks on his hands like puppets. "It should be me and Shing, because we're the fastest, and we can catch up easiest."

"I think we should draw straws," I said.

"I think this is silly," said Alan. He started loading the van with Noah's things.

In the end, Shing and Alan went, with Linda along to drive the van back from the car rental in Forks. The rest of us waited for her by the river until afternoon, playing Pooh-sticks: throwing sticks into the water and watching them race past stones. We ate the rest of the fruit and pretended we didn't feel like a family, falling apart.

We'd gone from frozen highlands to the deep red and greens of the forest, and now we were by the sea. I felt slightly sad and slightly frantic, like a kid at the end of summer camp: disappointed by all the unfinished pinecone forts and lack of horseback rides, tired of swimming in the algae-dense lake and eating bad food, the lingering crush on a counselor heavy as the water above my head after a leap off the dock into the deep end. A crush. Noah was gone and, with him, all the wrong possibilities. I couldn't wait to go home to Ben—and I couldn't imagine facing the ordinary days. Facing work, facing my father.

I heaved my pack on and started. Camilla limped only slightly, with most of her gear distributed among our loads.

My pack felt worse than ever, with one of the little metal rings that held bag to frame rubbing into my side through my shirt. We followed a boardwalk, crossing the swampy ground, our boots thudding against wood. Day hikers passed us, their packs small as cereal boxes on their backs, their sneakers bouncing along.

Camilla's injured foot rasped along the wood as she hobbled. My own feet felt steamed in their layers, hot with friction and exertion. The air was thick with salt, and finally the boardwalk spilled us out onto the sand.

I felt silly, and lethargic, and sad for Noah, who'd been telling us about sea stacks for months. They were even more bizarre and beautiful than Noah had allowed. Stone cut away by tides, they were towers, monuments to the ocean, carved by water and gravity. And the early afternoon sun lit them from behind, so they looked like great blue fingers pointing at the sky.

"Good," said Linda. "We need low tide to cut across." She pointed along the sand. A stone arch stood on the beach, beckoning us like a magic kingdom's door. We stood for a minute, letting the salt air lick our faces, and then we started our long march across the sand.

"This is hard," said Camilla, her limp magnified by the rotation of ankles in the sand.

"It *is* kind of challenging," said Linda, walking behind her and reaching out to steady her from time to time. Camilla shrugged her off.

"This *bites*," said Nicky, but he sped on ahead. His pack rattled with cooking gear.

We'd been walking on the beach for an hour, but the stone arch still loomed a mirage's distance away. We weren't far from the shoreline cliffs, but if the tide came in we'd have to swim.

Walking through sand was so hard on the feet and calves it felt like penance, as if I were filling my moral bank with currency. It also felt ridiculous. There weren't even any peaks at the end of this day, just a campground where the cliffs sloped into shoreline, and sleep, and then another day of sand hiking. I tried to enjoy the sounds: seabirds, the water folding on itself, the silvery wind against my rain jacket. My skin was sticky. It was like a spa—I tried to imagine this was a spa and that a salt air treatment would improve my complexion. I decided spas were not my thing.

The mirage grew clearer, and then we were almost there. Camilla was leaning against Linda now, a three-legged sand race. Water sponged into our footprints. Then we were passing under the arch, and it did seem magical up close, the bluish stone, moist and seemingly supple as flesh when I touched it, the pin-dot holes, tiny animal tunnels, the surface glossy.

"Not much low tide left," said Nicky. He lifted Camilla's mostly empty pack from her shoulders and loosened the straps, sliding it behind his own. He was now bigger around than he was tall. Linda and Camilla fell behind me, and as Nicky rounded the shore's curve, I felt like I was alone on the beach, watching the sun droop, the water climb back inland. This time wasn't as peaceful as it had been at Big Basin, despite the hum of the water and the long stretch of view.

I'd have to face them all soon: my father, Ben, my mother, Marla, and Ted. And now Noah was something, someone—I had to consider him too. Unless I let it go. Unless I could trick myself into believing our kiss was just a mirage, an imagined object that faded in the light, instead of growing solid with proximity.

It was harder to set up camp with only four of us. I hadn't realized how carefully our team was balanced. On regular trips, four or six or eight were different during the day but felt the same at set-up and mealtimes. Nicky tried for half an hour to ignite salt-saturated kindling; finally he got it to light by burning a few blank pages from my unused journal. Our campground was a carved curve in the shoreline, a bluff overlooking the ocean, with the long white corpse of a fallen tree lying on the beach below, a perfect spot to sit and watch the tide fill in the sand and stones.

Fifteen /

We almost didn't make our flights. Shing was flying standby and couldn't get a plane until an hour after Nicky, Linda and Alan, and I; Camilla's flight left the half hour in between. The van stalled twice, once in Forks, where starting it up again wasn't such a trauma, and once on the highway right beneath the first Sea-Tac Airport sign. It didn't want to go home either, Nicky joked, as Linda and Shing worked under the hood in the breakdown lane and traffic whooshed past. The highway felt exactly right: we were going back to the ridiculous pace of things, the frantic to and fro, the tunnel of days that didn't include stopping to watch elk make their way across the field.

Shing needed his cell phone after all; we had to call the rental's towing service and a cab from the roadside. Then we had to call a second cab to fit all our gear and bodies.

"Roaming charges," he grumbled, dialing. I leaned over and checked quickly to see if he had any messages. No envelope icon. No emergency calls for me. I breathed in a deep draft of poisonous highway air.

It was hard for me to panic—even when it started to rain and the cab's trunk wouldn't shut and black smoke rose from the van's open hood. At the airport, we sprinted across the terminal, backpacks on, checking them in at the gate so we wouldn't be left behind.

On the plane, everything slowed down. The group was splitting already. Linda and Alan were in another section of the plane, up front and on the left. Nicky disappeared somewhere over the wing. I sat in the last row, the crushed middle aisle, no window, so passengers waiting for the bathroom leaned on my seat back and caught my hair in their fingers.

I was in the world again; I did my best to breathe steadily, to avoid panic. I worried about what I would find when I finally got home. I was still away, though; from this distance I could see Ben differently. Sometimes he made my worries smaller. Sometimes he made me smaller, though maybe that was my fault, for pushing so hard. I could see him at the museum, in my apartment, bringing a forkful of mushroom omelet to his mouth. I saw his passage through days, that I was making him wait, all power and control. It wasn't how I meant for it to be, but from far away I realized that's how he must see it. When I got home, I'd ask him to move in. Ben, with his soft mouth, asleep beside me. I did love him, despite my father's best attempt to make me think he wasn't worthy. That's what all Dad's bluster was for—to make me look for cracks, to make me worry about my choice. Ben *was* my choice.

This was a good thing. This was going to make us both happy. I thought about using the airplane phone, but there was no privacy; all five seats across were stuffed with uncomfortable bodies. Soon enough, we'd get there.

———

No one was waiting.

I hadn't specifically told anyone my arrival time, though I'd left the date and flight number on a note on my kitchen counter before I rushed out of the apartment. It seemed like years ago.

I got a ride from Logan with Alan and Linda, who had left their car in long-term parking. I felt sapped, making my way through the gray-carpeted corridors, my gear stacked onto a cart, straps stopping the wheels at every major intersection. No one to greet me, just the long sweltering tunnel of the carbon monoxide zone outside baggage claim, the bus to the parking lot, the tunnel, city night, Charles River Drive, and the quiet chirping of Brookline. Everything was bright. Streetlamps and windows dulled the night with their own artificial moons.

Ben, I thought, turning my key. Ben. Time to tell Ben my decision. Ben and Hannah, True Love Always. My apartment smelled green; the plants were alive and strange in their pots among the white walls. So much white. And no one, no human sounds, just the satisfied hum of the refrigerator. I was hungry, but too tired and afraid to look for food. I hadn't emptied the fridge before I left, I couldn't bear to look inside for fear of liquid lettuce and milk turned to curd.

Call me, said a little note by the neatly stacked mail.

I sat in the middle of the living room floor with my phone. A few tears worked their way out of my eyes, but I cleared my throat and stopped them. Maybe I should've called from the airport, I thought. Maybe he was worried. I'd written four postcards, to Ben, Beth, Lora, and Ted, but forgot to mail any of them. I'd meant to in Forks, in the half day we'd planned in Seattle before leaving, but they were lost to our changing schedule.

First: a shower. I wouldn't know what to say to anyone if I didn't have a shower first. I scrubbed, graying my white washcloth with layers of sweat and dust and sunscreen. I was steam-cleaned, cooked like a clam. In the mirror, I examined my leftover welts and scrapes and burns and pimples.

Then I lay in the living room, the couch feeling absurdly cushy, as if I were lying on another person. I was alone after all this closeness, too much closeness. I missed the crush. Even though it was half past one, I called my sister.

Her number had been disconnected. How, in two and a half weeks, had Marla disappeared? Had she secretly eloped? My throat felt swollen. As dumb as I thought Reed was, I didn't want to have missed Marla's wedding. I imagined Ben there, wearing his tuxedo, and my mother in a purple suit. My father. My father. It was too late to call him, so I looked up the new apartment number and called Ted.

"Too late," he answered the phone. I couldn't breathe.

"Ted?"

"Oh, Hannah, it's you."

"What's too late? That sounds really dire."

"That was meant for—well, never mind. Abby and I have a kind of thing going."

"A thing? How's Dad?" Finally, I was asking out loud.

"He's not bad. Marla's been incredible since she took over."

"Marla? Marla took over?"

"She moved in with Dad and is taking care of him. She's also taking all these ridiculous classes. The Art of Preparing Fish and How to Influence Your Coworkers, though she doesn't have any. I'm too tired to tell you about it."

"The treatments?"

"He's doing better. I've got to go back to sleep. I was dreaming of the rain forest."

"I saw the rain forest, Ted. Temperate, of course, not tropical. The Hoh. We had to take a sort of easy day, because Camilla hurt her ankle, but then we went hiking on the beach—"

"Hannah, it's too late. I'm glad you're home. Dinner at Mom's this weekend. Good night."

And Ted hung up on me. Dinner at Mom's. As if I'd never left. *I've been gone*, I said to the walls.

I called Ben.

A woman answered, a woman I didn't know. I held the phone away for a second, thinking about hanging up.

"Um, is Ben there?" I asked.

"Oh. I'm not sure."

Not sure. That's promising. Where else would he be so late? "Well, can you check?"

There was a long sigh, and then a rustling. I thought I heard knocking. A muffled laugh. I didn't like this.

"Hey, it's late," said Ben.

"I know, but I missed you."

"Oh, Hannah! Where are you? God, it's Hannah!" I wondered for whom he'd made this last observation.

"Who was that?"

"Who was what? Where are you?"

"Home. The, um, the woman."

"Oh. Fish's girlfriend, Betty."

"Betty? I didn't know Fish had a girlfriend." I'd been gone two weeks and the whole world had changed.

"You're home. You're home? Well, welcome home." I wanted him to come over, but I wanted it to be his idea. I wanted him to ask. I willed it. The phone hummed.

"Yes, just got here. I mean, a few minutes ago." My hair was wet against the couch cushions. The apartment smelled strange. Like waxes and cleaners, the faint odor of the plants' green. Suddenly I was very, very tired. I had to go to work tomorrow. I didn't have a trip to look forward to, and eighteen messages on my machine, and I couldn't bear to listen to one.

Ben sighed. "Well, would you like to get together tomorrow night? I mean, after work. I have a lot to do, but I'll be free after eight."

He was not dying to see me. I was dying to see him, to declare my intentions, to give him half my meager closet, to make room for his beautiful carved oak chest in my bedroom. And he could wait, to see me, to hear that I wanted him. Whoever he was.

In the morning: an alarm. I'd set it, but it was still a shock, the Spanish pop cutting in and out, disturbed by Brahms from the next station up on the dial. I lay in bed. I'd pushed my head under the pillow and hadn't woken once, all night. Bright white, the room, the bathroom. My toothbrush was crusted over from lack of use. I rinsed it, and my mouth, and looked at my blotchy face in the mirror. Today I would have to go to work.

Too hungry and too late to wait, I braved the fridge. It was clean, cleaner than I'd ever left it, and there was a reasonable-looking loaf of bread at the front. No sign of liquid lettuce; it had to be Ben's work. The apartment was blighted with holes where he usually stood, the mornings when he was here. I wasn't used to being alone anymore. No one to wrestle with the stoves, no one to complain about the oatmeal. I wondered about each of them, Camilla and Nicky and Shing and Linda and Alan. At least the last two had each other. And Noah. I didn't want to think about Noah.

I put on a blue linen suit, dressing up a little more than usual. I hoped I wouldn't get fired, not today. But then, if it happened right away, I could come home and take a nap. I rode the T, my blisters burning in my blue pumps, feeling like a great big bruise. I felt restrained in the skirt, my chest cramped by my jacket. The air was thick and humid; everything smelled too strong: the sewer vents, the hot sidewalk like tar and gum and crushed grass, the coffee carts like burnt toast and cigarettes.

My boss was not around. I didn't look for her. A chorus line of "Hey, Hannah"s greeted me as I passed down the hall to my cube. I remembered when Agnes, the intern, had gone to Hawaii, she brought back macadamia nuts, and even my awful boss carted in saltwater taffy from Cape Cod. I hadn't thought of my coworkers once, not even to write a postcard.

My office was terribly bare. Nothing new in my in-box. I had 329 new e-mail messages, but most of them were irrelevant. Thirty-six voice mails, but then the box was full. The familiar mouse funk was almost a comfort, as I sat down and started sorting through the messages. Listen and delete, listen and delete, listen and delete.

"Hey, Hannah," said my boss. She was leaning on the doorway, wrapped in a dark red silk skirt, her eyelids frosted lightly to match. I wasn't scared of her, but I did feel like I was waiting for a jury's delivery of verdict.

"O-Two barely survived without you, so I handed it over to Agnes."

"Agnes? Intern Agnes?"

"She's been promoted. You were gone."

"Okay."

"But I've got something new for you. Hair Salon. It's called Hairy Business, out in Needham. We're thinking some nice orange seats. And really bright lighting. And bathrooms.

Your spa bathrooms had so many *woes*. So I hope you're rested up and ready for it. Specs due at the end of the week."

The end of the week, I thought, was the day after to-morrow.

"No problem, boss," I said.

I took the folder and went back to listen and delete, listen and delete. I hadn't been fired, but a hair salon wasn't exactly my territory. In Needham. Shuffled out to suburban strips. My trip was over. Listen, delete.

"So. You don't have to worry about your old dad. I'm growing hair on my nose and my throat's dry, but I lived, as promised."

His voice crackled in my receiver. My father had called me. I turned my back to the cube's opening and dialed his number.

"Hi," said Marla.

"Marla? Oh, right, I heard you moved in while I was gone?"

"Hannah! Lease ran out, and it was the thing to do. He's really getting better. I mean, no one knows how long he'll last, but the steroids seem to be helping. Or delaying the inevitable, anyway." She emitted a sharp bark. Our father's failing kidneys were worth a chuckle. But she was the one who'd moved in, and I was the one who'd gone away, so who was I to say anything about nervous laughter?

"Can I talk with him?"

"He's asleep. Or else he's making coil pots. Coil pots everywhere. He makes these incredible long snakes on plastic bags in his room, and then keeps slicking them down until he's done and ready to wrap. Cool shapes, like elephant trunks and vines, and he uses slip, so they'll hold things, maybe even liquid. It's new for him."

"Oh." I pictured him on the floor, werewolfed by the drugs, his face red and hairy, slicking clay snakes in hopes of making pots that would hold things, after all. Marla was changing him. Or else disease was.

That had been our project together, coil pots. I was allowed a wad of clay the size of an apple. I would spin it between my palms, letting the gray stain my hands, until I had a long thin snake. If I worked fast enough, it wouldn't crumble. But usually, Dad had to patch it with slip when I spun it around on itself to make a pot. I never wanted the snake fully smoothed; it seemed sacrilegious to erase all the work of that body.

"So, welcome home. You coming to dinner on Saturday?"

"What about Reed?"

"What about him?"

"I mean, I half expected you'd be married by now."

"He's on a job in New York. He might be the hand model for a ring ad."

"Great, Marla," I said.

I got off the phone and braved the e-mail. Then I called a friend at another firm to find out if she had some generalized specs for hair salons.

The Adventurers' Club was just in my imagination, my overwrought blissful imagination. It was night, and I was on a purple floral-sheeted bed in a white room with windows looking out at the window eyes of all the other buildings. The mountains were just in my head, as were the six rolls of film I'd sent in to be developed. Now, with bathroom stall sketches spread on my pillow and the mechanical pencil out of lead, I imagined they might come back squares of plain color: the greens and whites of hallucination.

I couldn't wash off the polluted air in the shower, but I

tried, for half an hour. I wasn't hungry. But I was more exhausted than I'd been on our eleven-mile day. Sitting in the swivel chair at my desk was uphill. Worse than uncountable switchbacks and, despite the nest of other workers, very lonely.

Home was better. The colors were bright and too clean, but I wasn't tired of comfort yet. I wanted to share it.

Ben had left one terse message on my machine, "I'll be really late, sorry." And whenever I called, the rings rolled over to his voice mail.

The laundry beast in the corner of the room was laughing at me. It shook its muddy gaiters and sweat-grayed T-shirt arms at me. The wool sweater with orange-cheese-powder splotches seemed to shimmy slightly under the mushroom of halogen lamplight.

"You ready to talk?" I asked Ted's machine. My voice was alone in his apartment, or Ted was screening me out.

I refilled my pencil and stared at the fax of my friend's salon plans. Probably I should quit tomorrow. I could move out of my apartment and set up a tent by Walden Pond. Eat sassafras root and chicken of the woods. Maybe Ben would come. My Ben. If he wasn't with Betty.

The phone. I couldn't get used to how loud it rang, a crying sort of sound, a little scream, an even metal sob.

Maybe it would be Ted, or my father; I'd asked Marla to tell him I called. Maybe it was Ben saying he'd decided never to come back to my arms. *You spent too much time outside*, he'd say. *You need to look in more often.* I let the machine answer.

"H," said Noah's voice. Since when did he call me H? My face burned with memory. "I'm walking again. And we've got a planning meeting this weekend. Kind of a barbecue thing, at Camilla's mom's. She has this enormous place on the Charles in Wellesley. We can canoe, if you're up for it. Six. Call Camilla for directions."

Then my door opened, and Ben came in. He was paler than I remembered. And shorter. His dark hair looked waxed under the lights, and he was tired. He moved like an older man. Through the bedroom door, I watched him walk in. He threw his keys on the counter and looked around. Entirely comfortable in my space.

"Hey, Hannah?"

I lay on the bed, pretending to sleep on my bathroom stall plans. If I let him talk first, he'd know what to say. With my eyes squeezed shut, I could remember the feeling of sliding down the slanted wedge of space in Spider Cave. Cold and silt and darkness.

Ben sat down beside me and started to pet my hair, lightly, as if it were an animal he was afraid to rile.

"I missed you," he whispered.

"Me too." I rolled over and kissed him. And the comfort factor was greater than any shower. My body's memory took over. Ben's tongue traveled over me, stopping at the bruises and blisters. He nipped me where my skin was still solid.

Only once, as he held his hand behind my neck and kissed me, pressing his mouth against mine so I could feel his teeth, I did think of Noah, how long his arms were. I wondered how we'd match up, having sex, where he would fit. I opened my eyes and looked into Ben's. Ben, I thought, Ben, Ben, Ben. He was exactly the right size, and his knee inside my thigh hurt just a little, how I liked it.

"Want to tell me about your trip?" Ben was still looking at me, though I'd turned off the lights. Outside light leaked in, the city's orange pollution glow, the slivers of artificial suns from the other apartments.

"No. Not now. Want to move in?"

"Yes. After our trip to my sister's this weekend."

"Mmm," I said. I wasn't ready to think about it, the juggling balls of Club Meeting, Family Dinner, and Trip to New Jersey competing for hand space. Something would fall; I couldn't hold all three.

Instead, I lay back on the cleared-off sheets, breathing in Ben's scent, pretending to sleep, while graph paper diagrams of toilets crumpled themselves in my night-lit imagination.

Sixteen / In the woods, there wasn't much scheduling to do. Sure, there were issues of light and dark, of shelter and food and sleep, but which party to attend and when to set the salon's drywall and will the next stage sink designs be on time and when to visit the ailing father and when the boyfriend's sister in New Jersey weren't on the agenda. Probably, that was why I started to dream in the greens and browns of the forest. Probably, that was why I picked up a mostly patched Lemon from Holy Motors and made little charts, counting the days until the next Adventurers' trip.

Every day I felt a little heavier. I let go of the longing during daylight hours, but at night I was back by the sea stacks, smelling the Pacific Ocean, back in the frozen glory of the crevasse, only my feet didn't hurt in my memory's invention.

Air conditioners mumbled to themselves all along my street as I walked out for work, and the T held the cumulative odors of all the bodies passing through until the collective anxieties and lateness and arguments made the ripe air unbearable. I got off a stop early and walked to the office under Back Bay's thick green maple skies, my short heels scraping the sidewalk, quiet beneath the griping of car engines and buses sighing at the curb.

The barbecue was rescheduled for the end of August. I suppose I was relieved, because that left only one scheduling error: my family versus Ben's. I sat at work while my ugly hair salon plans ground out of the mammoth printer down the hall. Ben had already started packing, and I'd already let it go for two days, and we were supposed to leave tomorrow. He was glowing with our new status. Ben the Good, wearing the crown of the man who would be my king. He worked late every night but came back to my apartment and walked around as if he was proud of the floors, the walls, now that he was moving in. He'd told Fish and Mark and even Fish's girlfriend, who would be happy to take Ben's room and convert it into a walk-in closet for her enormous collection of coats: vintage fur and leather and plastic and faux snakeskin.

I couldn't say no to my family. I hadn't seen my father yet and had only succeeded in leaving messages with his new answering service, the ever-present Marla.

At lunch, I wandered along Newbury Street to meet Ben at the Public Gardens. He had a whole hour, which would be three-quarters eaten by travel to and from the museum, but it meant fifteen sweaty minutes of watching the swan boats plow through the ponds, holding hands, sharing a cone of lemon shave ice. And it meant I had to tell him about my family dinner usurping his sister and the new baby.

I stopped at my favorite independent bookstore, where banners announced GOING OUT OF BUSINESS. Of course, I thought, as I mulled through bargain bins of nonfiction, sadly fingering the spines. *Lupus and You: Living with SLE* was sitting unapologetically next to *How to Plan Your Own Funeral.* I took the lupus book to the counter and paid $7.99 to learn all about Dad's disease on the sticky August grass.

I could hardly read it; it seemed like cheating. As usual, Dad only wanted us to know his version of things, his side of the sickness story. But the book agreed in general: he was dying. If he'd found out sooner, started on the drugs when he did find out, he might have had a decent chance. But since his kidneys were already clogged from filtering out compounds from the disease, his prognosis wasn't good. The body was attacking itself.

I remembered watching my father at an opening of a group show, one of three or four I could remember. There'd been a few solo shows, too, though I couldn't recount the chronology; they blended into the lost time of fighting and family division. At the show I remember, I was eight and wore a dark blue wraparound skirt because my mother said you had to wear a skirt to art openings. My father hovered by the objects of his greatest attention. Had he felt successful? I'd believed he was; I'd been painfully proud of him. My father hunched by the glass shelves, peering into the reds and silvers of the glazed pieces, the dull of those fired unglazed. I watched people making the connection between his work and his corporeal self; they nodded, they shook his hand. He was paler than the white ceramic clay. He was also on display.

How was I supposed to be with my father, now that he was dying? It wasn't easy before. Now our time together was not only unpredictable but also heavy with impending finality.

Ben sat down on the grass beside me. His face was red

from the heat; sweat spots spread from the armpits of his striped button-down.

"Hey," he said. A wide, weary grin.

My voice spilled out into the heavy air. "I can't believe it. I should have said, but I can't do it, this weekend."

Ben's face didn't change.

"It's not because I don't want to, it's because my family has this thing."

"Oh," said Ben. "Your family."

"Please," I said. "I said I'd go. I just feel like I'm not allowed to say no, after being gone—"

"Yes," said Ben. "You were gone." His eyes were on the lupus book in my lap.

Gone was good, I thought. *I miss gone.*

"I suppose"—he sighed dramatically—"I could ask Kate if next weekend's okay." He reached over to the book, touched the cover. His finger made quick sticking noises on the laminate.

"I want to meet them, I promise."

"I know." He still wouldn't look at me, so I took his hand. I wasn't sure what I wanted, but quiet acquiescence wasn't it. More drama seemed appropriate. After all, we'd scheduled this trip months ago. It was the one thing he'd asked for, that and moving in. That and me.

He wanted me, and that was a responsibility. The air was too thick to breathe, thick with city, the exhaust of trucks, buses, and cars, the exhalations of all the disappointed people on the streets.

"Aren't you mad?" I asked, fishing for his glance with my eyes. Ben watched a woman holding her twin girls' hands like balloon strings as they danced her toward the bronze Make Way for Ducklings ducks. He watched a sugar ant climbing a grass blade, a swan pecking at a still-wrapped sandwich tossed among the cattails.

"No," he said. "Disappointed, though."

He was too big, and too mature, and maybe I didn't even deserve him.

Ben came with me to the family dinner. My father held court on the couch, and Marty made two chickens, apricot-glazed and coriander-and-yogurt with a crispy skin, and three kinds of potatoes: baked, mashed with buttermilk and chives, and casseroled. We ate in the living room, so my father wouldn't have to get up. I felt like I was waiting for an audience with the king. I kissed him and examined his face. No hair growing on his cheeks or forehead, but he was ruddier than usual and had a ring of acne around his nose: side effects of the corticosteroids. It was weird, inspecting my father. Before, I don't think I would've noticed his skin. Now, it was all outward evidence of his body's inward battle.

I'd expected Marla to be by his side. But for most of the dinner, she was out in the garden arguing with Reed. They stood by the bird feeders, Reed in a black T-shirt, Marla in a short sea-green dress that showed off her perfect knees. Even I wanted to touch the backs of them, the dimples in the vulnerable pits. Abby wasn't there, and Ted wandered around the house, helping Marty and rearranging the food on his plate.

My mother kept going upstairs for books, for articles she'd retrieved from Medline. She watched my father, as if she could see the complexes his liver had filtered, the inflammatory cells inside his body through the skin.

"Tell me about your trip," said my father.

"Well." I chewed a forkful of potatoes, happy to provide some diversion. "The ice climbing was probably the hardest part. And once I got us lost—" I tried to tell him, tried to share the scent and the exertion making my legs shake, but it sounded dull, an itinerary.

"I read a new study on oxygen deprivation," my mother interrupted, as I tried to explain how altitude made everything feel heavier.

"Sometimes I think that would be the best way to go," said my father. "Suffocation."

"Not funny, Wolf." She stood up and started up the stairs again.

"Where are you going?" Dad looked like a sulky child.

"Oh, I've got something else on the steroids. It's mostly graphs, really, but I thought you might be interested."

"Where are *you* going?" Dad asked Ted, who'd sat down for a whole minute and was up again.

"Hmm," said Ted. Dad turned his attention to the food, then my mother's article, and the subject of adventure was lost.

Going home I realized the worst part of the whole thing was that it didn't really matter that I had been there. We could've gone to Ben's sister's, and nothing would've been any different. It wasn't about me, and I wasn't helping anything. My father was going to die; there was nothing I could do about it, and unlike Marla I was no better a daughter for the tragedy.

We left Boston the next Friday. Ben picked me up from work in his VW, and our bags lay side by side on the backseat like two sheep in a barn stall. He'd brought piles of presents, things he couldn't resist in the Children's Museum shop and some things he'd seen online.

"They were all on sale, Hannah," he said. "Look at this!" He showed me cloth blocks with pictures of dogs and disembodied hands, a rubbery barbell that made weird noises when you dropped it, a set of fuzzy rings with a detachable squeaky head, and a stuffed wolf from the endangered species exhibit. There were things for six-year-old Ricky and four-year-old Elizabeth, and baby Hannah, now four months old. He'd put the wolf on the seat so it could look out the window.

Ben drove fast, and we were at his sister's house in under four hours. Ravensnest, New Jersey, was a perfect little town. The streets hissed with sprinklers; the neighborhood looked a lot like Newton, Victorians and Dutch Colonials hidden behind long rows of hedges. Spent lilies and irises lay across the little metal fences holding flowers from lawns.

I was afraid that they wouldn't like me, that I wouldn't know what to say, that I'd scare the children and break something in the perfect yellow house. But when we walked inside, there were toys all over the living room, and Ben's sister, Kate, and her husband, John, were draped over the couch, watching television.

"Everyone's asleep," she said, kissing my cheek. She smelled like lilacs. I didn't have time in the embrace to kiss her back. Kate's eyes were enormous and blue and innocent, with a perfect ring around each pupil. I watched her looking at Ben and felt oddly jealous. John waved from the couch. He was fleshy, built as solidly as a snowman, but appealing, with wide boyish brown eyes.

We sat up that night, drinking fruit-flavored beers from Texas and eating cold pizza. John perked up as we settled in, a cut flower in fresh water, but after about an hour, he looked longingly at the blank TV screen while Ben and Kate crowed over a pile of recent photos of the kids. They passed them to me, and I tried not to smudge them. Kids, cute kids. Sitting kids, standing kids, crawling kids, eyes wide or half-shut for the flash. I tried to hide my yawn.

John laughed. "Hannah and I are going to bed," he announced. I imagined his mouth on mine, a brief unbidden fantasy. "I'll show you the guest towels," he said.

The guest room had its own bathroom, and the lemon-colored hand towels matched the comforter. I lay on the queen-size bed, listening to the whine of the central air. I could reach the window from where I lay; I lifted the blind to look out at the night. The glass was warm, and when I unlatched the windowpane and pulled it up, I heard the rhythmic mating calls of cicadas, half-dollar-sized insects filling up the night with their buzz of need.

The morning was loud and bright. Ben had closed the window when he came in to sleep; he'd eased off my shoes and wrapped a blanket around me. Now he was watching me, his face intense with anticipation.

"They're up," he whispered.

I rolled over and read my watch, taking the biting band off and leaving it on the whitewashed wicker table by the bedside. Six-fifteen. Too early to get up, unless there was somewhere to go.

"I'm not," I said, peeling off my clothes and getting under the sheet.

I tried to go back to sleep while Ben dressed.

"Okay if I go?" He kissed me and shut the door behind him, not waiting for my answer.

I listened for a while. Baby voices, cries, a coffeemaker rumbling its digestive noises. Silverware banging, the sweet bready smell of pancakes. Two men's voices: Ben and John in a conversational fugue, and Kate, laughing. Two kids and a

new baby asking for breakfast or her breasts. Who was
cooking, and how could she laugh through all that need?

I got up and dragged my exhausted self into the shower
and went down to see if there were any pancakes left. Of
course, John had left some batter in the bowl and the griddle
on, just for me.

By midafternoon, we had been sitting on the leather
couches all day, eating pancakes and becoming unavoidably
acquainted with the sight of Kate's breasts. They were enormous with milk, and veins like rivers on a map ran down the
sides. The nipples looked painfully red, but she didn't seem
to mind.

Kate fed Hannah in her long lap, with pillows propping
up the soft infant body. The baby wore a cotton gown with
elastic at the bottom and didn't do much other than eat and
cry and sleep and waggle her limbs from her position on
the couch. But she was fascinating. When she did open her
eyes, you wanted to be the object of that perfect attention.
She stared without looking away. Mostly, she looked into
Kate's eyes.

When she wasn't nursing, Ben or John held her, doing
embarrassing little dances to soothe the crying. Then Elizabeth and Ricky came back from swimming lessons, diving
out of the carpool van and trailing towels and goggles on the
paint-green lawn. I watched the noise of their motion from
the window and wondered when we'd go somewhere.

"Hey, Hannah, can you hold Hannah for me?" John held
out the package of baby. Everyone was watching, even
Ricky. I took the baby, afraid I wouldn't hold her right. But
once I had her in my arms, I felt okay. She was warm and
moved, amazingly, squirming in the nightgown, her pea-
sized toes gesturing as if she had something to tell me. At
first she kept her eyes closed but moved her mouth in a series

of beeps and whines. My arms cramped up after a few minutes, and she started to fuss. So I swayed, like I'd seen the others doing. It didn't feel as goofy as it looked.

She stopped fussing and stared right at me; I felt as if she could see me more clearly than anyone, baby Hannah, staring and staring as if decoding secrets no one would ever know about me, even me. She looked at me as if deciding whether I was fit for motherhood. I didn't even know if I was a fit daughter. I couldn't determine her verdict, even when she moved her perfect mouth, suckling the air, and Kate laughed and finished her mouthful of cold pancake.

"I guess she wants more milk," she said. "And I'm the milk machine." This didn't sound particularly funny, but Kate laughed again, and when I gave her Hannah, she looked like a woman from a dark Dutch painting, enlightened by the bliss of having the means to fulfill such need.

My cramped arms felt slightly bereft.

Finally, we were in the car again, and my bottom was sore from all that sitting. At first, Ben recounted his highlights: holding Hannah, how Ricky had wanted help with his computer game, how the house looked great, how Kate seemed so happy. All I could think of was how hard it must be on Monday morning, all alone with three kids. John would walk to the train, unencumbered by diaper bags and strollers and shoulder spit-up, and Kate would be alone with the second-to-second tasks of caring for all those children. I wondered how often she loved it, and how often she wished she could get into a suit and go out to lunch with a client, elegantly spearing chicken salad with a lean designer fork.

Or maybe she never thought about it.

"I can take over for a while," said Ben, as we crossed the Tappan Zee Bridge. The flat wide Hudson spread out beneath us. Light filled the car and I turned up the air-conditioning.

"We just left," I said, squirming to get comfortable.

"You seem antsy," said Ben.

"I'm not."

We didn't say anything as the road passed through a great split in a shelf of granite, blasting scars at the tops where the trees leaned over.

I thought about the perfect town, open-faced families strolling the avenues, in love with the contents of their carriages. I was far from ready to think about having children, but I wondered what Ben had already decided for himself and where I fit into that decision. I remembered how exhausted Kate seemed, losing sentence streams as she sat on the couch, nursing, as she stooped to tie Elizabeth's shoelace.

How she'd watched me when I held Hannah.

"Careful," she had said, her eye bags hardly concealed by a quick brush of orangey makeup. "Babies are contagious."

And it scared me, the physical memory of baby Hannah, her fingers hooked around the neck of my T-shirt, her milky scent, the whole of her fitted into my grasp. They *were* contagious. I could want this, I thought, the amnesia and the pleasure of it. It looked much better than designing toilet stalls and oxygen spas.

I thought of Noah. I'd let him kiss me. I looked at Ben, who was jiggling his leg and playing with the lock button on his door. He was ready to say something, but he was so careful; he'd wait until he knew it was the right thing to say.

"Did you—well, I mean, you had an okay time, right?"

I sighed and almost missed the exit for I-84. Put on the blinker, changed lanes, ignored Ben's blurts of worry as I drove. It was annoying. He was picking at me, unconsciously, and I supposed I wasn't driving as carefully as usual.

"Sure," I said.

More quiet. All the cars on the highway, like river water. My pack was sitting in my apartment. Our apartment. I wondered whether Ben would mind if I kept going on my trips. If I had kids, could I take them camping? Or would I sit in the living room like Kate and John, an island in the sea of what they'd wrought? I didn't know what I wanted. I'd made it to twenty-six without any pure desire or direction.

Ben pulled the lock button up. Down. Up.

"Ben." I said it sharply.

"What?"

"I can't be like your sister."

Ben laughed, a ringing sound. Then he touched my knee. Through my cotton dress, his hand felt warm and heavy.

"Well, I can't be like your brother."

"Thank God."

"Besides, I wouldn't want you to be." He stroked my knee and I felt like a young woman again. Potential motherhood slipped by along with Connecticut. He hadn't been wondering, at least not the way I had.

I pulled off in Waterbury, so Ben could drive and I could stretch my sorry, weary underside.

Seventeen /

Ben was irritating me. He wasn't *doing* anything irritating, at least on purpose, but the sheer fact of his living in my space felt invasive. When I brushed my teeth before work, there he was in the mirror, trying to check his shave; when I slammed around the apartment in lost-key desperation like a puppy scenting a scrap, he sighed and pointed to the TV top or the basket of laundry. He watched me eat, a gesture I'd once found touching, but which grew humiliating as the novelty wore off. And he'd decided he needed to go on a diet, sitting in the couch's lap on a Saturday with a pile of books, choosing which fad to follow. I told him I didn't think he was fat. I told him diets didn't work. Both truths. He watched me eating mocha swirl ice cream with fudge sauce and about half a pound of jimmies. Because his eyes were counting the calories, I had to eat quickly, and it didn't taste good under all that scrutiny.

I loved him, I was sure of it, but the more he said he

wasn't pushing me to be anything in particular, the more I worried he really did want to make me into his sister.

Besides, my father was dying, and I wanted to sulk about it alone. I resented it when Ben was still at work and I didn't know when he was coming home, so I didn't know how much of a private funk to fall into, and how much to worry he wouldn't be home in time to make me feel better.

I was full of selfishnesses.

Marla, on the other hand, hardly ever called, so it wasn't until Ted filled me in that I learned Reed had left her and moved to New York, letting her keep the plastic mood ring he'd dispensed for her at the Stop & Shop but not the ring she'd forked over the down payment for at Shreve Crump & Lowe. In fact, Reed had cashed in Marla's deposit. He claimed it was a loan, that the engagement wasn't really off. I could practically hear my mother sighing across town. Oddly enough, I wasn't sure what kind of sigh I felt in my own chest. Sure, Reed wasn't right, and Marla had been so full of planning for them, and it had been easy to resent her pettiness. It put a filter on the unbearable brilliance of her beauty. But now she was taking care of our father, happy in her nurse-nun role, with its own brightness of will and patience and compassion. I didn't know what to think; I only knew I felt guilty for my own lack of light.

The club barbecue was on Saturday. It was Wednesday, and the week stretched on, long and humming with late-summer heat. There were no trips scheduled for an entire month.

I hated the heat, I hated the hissing of the air-conditioning in my office, I hated my newest project: a paint store. There was nothing whimsical or even vaguely interesting about it. Just shelves, storage, adequate lighting, low budget. They rejected my plan to paint the walls like color strips, complete with the odd evocative color names: Marionette Green, Movie Star Blue, Moon Maroon. It was in a cruddy corner of West Roxbury, off Route 9 in a mini-mall, and the walls would be white.

Ted called me all the time, at work and at home, when Ben hadn't come back yet and I was looking around my newly strange space. The pile of cuff links in the drawer with slippery black work socks. Ben never wore cuff links.

Sometimes, Ted just said "Hey" and then waited for me to guide him through the conversation. His work was slow, for once, and he was nervous about Abby and the baby, and sometimes she let him come along on the appointments to hear the heartbeat and sometimes she cried with him, about how she wished they were still together. But when he said he wanted to live together again, she crumpled her handkerchief on her belly mountain and shook her head, no. But she let him feel for baby kicks, and she let him take the only ultrasound picture to keep on his bedside table in his dingy studio near Fenway Park.

I didn't understand Ted, why he wasn't more direct about what he wanted, why he didn't tell her he'd do anything, singing dopey songs about it on one knee. With me, he was almost whimsical about his great desire to reconcile. With Abby, I pictured him as nervous. He probably stuttered some Latin into his sentences. He probably didn't say what she wanted to hear, because he was afraid he didn't know. But I knew he knew. He knew Abby, even Abby altered by the hormone waves of pregnancy. He was inexplicably afraid. I wanted to slip into the shell of his body for a day, so I could fix things for him. Everything was clearer from the outside. He was going to have a child, and despite all the opportunities this afforded for mistakes, I thought Ted could do it. All he needed to do was try to find middle ground, to show he was willing to make some changes for this enormous one. Why

couldn't they compromise, buy a house in some less expensive
suburb, let Abby stay home and make homemade baby food?

This is what our parents had taught us: we were practiced
in being left, but we didn't know the rules for hanging on.

Noah wasn't at the barbecue when we arrived. Ben was
holding a plastic bag of raw chicken breasts in one hand and
my hand in the other. I wore a purple sundress and sandals
and felt like a fraud, dotting on lipstick and smearing it with
Chapstick. Pretending I didn't care how I looked.

Camilla stood by the fancy gas barbecue, wearing cutoffs
and a T-shirt I recognized, complete with wear holes in the
shoulders, from our trip.

"Whoa, girl," she said, as Ben handed her the chicken.
"You're gorgeous."

"So are you," I said, but I felt the fierce blush climbing
my face from my neck.

"Careful what you say," said Camilla. "I'm *dangerous*."
She shook Ben's hand and turned her attention to the meat.

"It's Hannah!" Nicky was swinging on a tire swing that
stretched its arc from the green expanse of lawn over the wide
bow in the river. Redwing blackbirds called out their claims on
the cattails. I was overdressed. Ben, at least, was wearing tai-
lored shorts and a polo shirt. I poured myself a soda and sur-
reptitiously patted my mouth clean with a paper party napkin.

Camilla wiped sauce onto her thighs and stabbed chicken
and steaks with a long fork. She grew up here, I thought,
watching, as Ben and I sat on lawn chairs with Alan and
Linda. Alan was telling Ben about volcanoes, pitching an
exhibit for the museum, painting lava into the hot afternoon
air. Camilla grew up here. I wondered what her parents
thought when she came out, what they'd said. Had her father
known before he died? Had she been close to him? Had she

known how to let him go? She wasn't who she was to get attention, but the family constellation must have modified its orbit to circle her, at least for a while.

"What about you, honey?" asked Ben.

I felt Linda and Alan's attention as he put his hand on my thigh. What were they talking about? Why hadn't we gone on a trip this weekend? I needed to get out; I needed to leave everything for a while. I was already losing the pure vision of distance, the bliss of the purely essential, sleep and food. My soda was too syrupy. The scent of burnt meat was nauseating.

"Not sure, honey," I said. "Sorry, I wasn't listening."

"We know all about it, Ben." Alan grinned, sharing the secret of my difficult personality. I laughed too loudly and walked down to the river, sitting on the bank. I broke twigs off a fallen branch and played Pooh-sticks with myself. Then Ben sat beside me, put his arm down on the ground, circling my back, so I felt his heat, but we weren't touching.

Only when I looked up, it wasn't Ben—it was Noah.

"Hey," he said. He brushed an invisible object from my cheek with two sure fingertips.

"Oh," I said. "Have you met my boyfriend, Ben?" I pointed, nervously.

Noah chuckled. It was an odd laugh, broken into syllables of sound. We both looked across the lawn. Ben was chatting with Nicky and Camilla.

"We never talked," I said.

"Ah," he said. "The *talk*."

I didn't like his smirk. I could see, in the corners of his mouth, that it had all been about the chase.

My hands were sweating. With him beside me, all that height, so he knew me from a different perspective than I ever would, seeing me from above, like a bird or a god, I couldn't pretend we hadn't kissed. I was a cheater and a selfish brat.

"How's your back?" I asked, for something to say.

"Okay," he said. "I don't mind if we don't talk, it doesn't matter to me. I've got a new girlfriend, by the way—she was my physical therapist." He smiled and leaned his arm in so it grazed my back.

Asshole, I thought. *It doesn't matter to me.* All my Pooh-sticks backed up into the same eddy, like lost logs on a river. I got up and went back to Ben. From a distance, I squinted so Noah's form was small enough to disappear in a blink, like a speck. I enjoyed the rest of the party on the surface, jokes about mac 'n' hack, passed photographs.

I didn't look at Noah, even when he said, "Hannah was our finest navigator," with a superior little chuckle. Maybe he meant well, but I was busy hating him.

"Hey," said Ben, driving us home. The night concert of insects and birds flooded our open windows. "Those pictures were amazing. I really should come along on a trip. How about that next one? Vermont? It sounds manageable. And if I lose some weight, maybe I can keep up with you—"

"You don't have to lose weight, Ben, you're fine as you are."

"But I want to. I mean, it's for me."

"Okay."

"And kind of for you. I mean, you're always *going*, Hannah."

"What's that mean?" I rolled up my window and turned on the air-conditioning, even though his window was still open.

"Never mind," said Ben.

Never mind? *Never mind* and *It doesn't matter to me.* I was on a roll tonight, I thought. Obviously what I do and say is very important to men. I wasn't prepared to fish Ben out of his private sea; I was just too tired.

To make myself feel worse, when I got home I called my father. Marla answered, as usual.

Ben had to go in to an installation at work, and I was relieved, because I felt too raw, too exposed. I needed a break, so I went to my father's apartment in Watertown, driving Lemon along Commonwealth Avenue, through Newton, watching the joggers and feeling glad I wasn't one of them, in the horrible heat, the pavement sweating the last dregs of August, burning their feet through the fancy forms of their soles.

Marla looked the same, but she did seem calmer. She said nothing about Reed, and so for once I was interested. We sat on my father's old couch, the blue velour sectional with bald patches that used to live in our living room. Marla, Ted, and I used to fight over the ottoman and arm-wrestle with our elbows wedged between the cushions. It looked old. There were stains on every section.

Marla made us tea, despite the heat, and a single window air conditioner whined and blew its tepid breath on us. I thought a fan would be better but didn't say so. I sipped my tea and listened to my father. He looked okay. The acne was gone, but he was gaunt. The apartment smelled of clay, but the cigarette stink was gone. Marla's work, I was sure.

"So, I'm finally working the way I want to—just in time to die." He chuckled.

"Cut it out, Dad," said Marla, but fondly.

"Okay. Anyway, I'm making these bowls with faces on the bottom. You could use them for cereal and get cornflakes up their noses. But it's best if you put water in them, so the liquid distorts the countenance. It's kind of like these photographs I saw last year at the New Museum in New York. All about the distance of different media. A photo of a woman standing in front of a camera. It's kind of a stretch, but you two went to college; I'm sure you get it."

"Hmm," said Marla. She smiled. She was making pfeffernuese from Marty's recipe, because Dad loved them. She had powdered sugar on the front of her green apron. She'd look great in a toque, I thought. She leaned down to pour Dad some more tea and stirred in his sugar, without looking resentful, not one bit put out as he gestured toward the bowl for another spoonful. She looked calm and wise, and I was happy he had this, and jealous that it was something I could never be for him.

It was petty, but watching them, I couldn't bear the angel glow any more. I felt mean.

"So, Marla, what's the scoop with your fiancé?"

She didn't pause. "Reed wasn't right for me," she said, a slight smile sweetening her mouth. "You tried to tell me, Hannah, and I couldn't hear it. But he wasn't right. Now I'm working on figuring out who I am. Then maybe I'll be ready for a real relationship."

It was right out of a book. I wondered if she'd taken a class, How to Tell Your Family You Broke It Off with the Boyfriend They Despised. How to Save Face After Being Dumped. But Marla didn't need either of those. She was being honest, even if her words lay couched in the language of self-help psychobabble.

When I left, I kissed my father. His cheek was familiar, the scratchy feel under my lips. And I kissed Marla at the door.

"He looks good," I said. "And so do you. You are so good for doing this."

"It's for me too," she said. "But he's not in great shape. He just wanted you to think so. He made me hide the tank."

"Tank?"

"Oxygen."

"Really?"

"He's dying, Hannah. I mean, it looks like he has at least a few more months, maybe even a year. So that gives us a chance to hang out with him, to say whatever needs to be said."

"God, Marla, what would that be?"

"Oh, I don't know. Normal stuff. Like *Butt out of my life* and *I love you.*"

"Eek," I said.

But all the way home I felt his rough cheek against mine when I kissed him. And I wasn't sure there was anything really left to say, anything I knew well enough to speak truly. *Butt out of my life* and *I love you.* If only it were that easy. I longed to go back and I wished it were over, that we could leave things as they were: clean on the surface.

Ben came home very late. I'd read the entire last weekend's Sunday *Globe*, distracted and trying not to agonize about what I should have said to my father, about where Ben might really be. Trying not to recall the sensation of Noah's bare arm brushing my back. In the National section, I flipped past an article about trees and protesters and loggers and Washington State, and then flipped back to it. The black-and-white photo showed relief inhabitors, coming to take over the tree platforms of other long-term protesters. A dozen people living in trees to keep them from falling to the ax—or the chain saw, as it were. A face in the photograph made me look more closely at the dots of black-and-white, and closer still. It was Jay, the coffee man from the campsite at Big Basin. He had grown a beard on his smooth-skinned cheeks. *Anywhere with coffee*, he'd said. I still had the cup he'd left behind. I wondered how he'd get his beans to a fifty-foot-high platform in a tree. And I envied him. He was doing something important and exciting and outside.

When Ben finally came in after 1 A.M., I pretended I hadn't been waiting. I picked up a book and feigned deep interest. I sighed and yawned and pretended to be relaxed. I was sweaty and my jaw ached with tension.

"Hey," he said, dumping his keys on the table and flinging socks and shoes. "Sorry."

He didn't sound sorry. He smelled of cologne and I asked him when he'd started wearing it.

"It's from being in a room with Jessica Velmer. She wears so much perfume it clouds everything."

"Who's Jessica Velmer?"

"Exhibit designer. She's a pain."

"Uh-huh," I said. I had no right to be jealous, and it gnawed away at my stomach. Jealous of Marla, jealous of Ben and Jessica Velmer, even jealous of Ted and Abby, who ought to figure it out. Maybe having the baby would do it. I didn't believe in babies to save marriages, but maybe that new warm form would define things for them, clarify what really mattered.

"Daughter," said my father, on the phone. I squirmed in my seat. It was still a new enough habit that it startled me when he called.

It was late on Monday, and I was at the office, where a file on my computer had been corrupted and I wanted to drive a stake through its nasty silicon heart. I needed the file, a budget proposal for the paint store parking-lot expansion. Until I recovered it, I couldn't go home. Home was crowded anyway.

"I wanted to tell you something, but I didn't want to say it in front of Marla."

Ah. It was pathetic, but I felt a happy surge. Secrets. Secrets even from his savior, the glowing Nurse Marla.

"Dad, sure. What is it?"

"I've changed my mind about your fellow, Ben?"

My *fellow*? A leaf of hope crumpled inside my chest.

"You can marry him if you want to. I was being selfish to say you shouldn't."

"Dad." I felt the leaf in my throat, trying to choke me. "He hasn't asked."

"I mean, now that you're living in sin, you might as well think about it."

How did he do this? How did he find exactly where to press to make it hurt? I did love Ben. But this wasn't right for now. Maybe he was trying to give all his future fatherly advice. Maybe he was the wrong one to give advice in the first place. What did he know?

"Um, Dad, I'm kind of busy."

"You should have said so, Hannah. But I'm glad I told you. In fact, I feel much better. I may even have a cigarette before Marla comes back from class."

"Don't," I said. But I wasn't entirely convinced he shouldn't.

"That's my girl."

I couldn't fix the file. I got error messages and a hopeless, annoying *ding*. And Ben wasn't home. I kept thinking, *About your fellow, Ben*, remembering my father's voice. What if Ben gave up on me? What if he was the only one my father ever approved of and I lost him?

I took the T home, pacing the car to avoid a drunk who was wandering behind me, mumbling obscenities and making a hawking noise in his throat. Lemon was parked on the wrong side of the street, a ticket flapping in the hot breeze, under the wiper. And I had to move it again, or get another ticket, a pile of evidence of my negligence, my neglect. I was getting exactly what I deserved. In my apartment, the logging protest article was still staring at me from the coffee table. I picked up some maps and traced the contour lines.

Then I dialed Camilla's number and got her machine.

"Just wondering if you wanted to go on a little trip," I said, surprising myself as the words came out. "I've got to get out of here. New Hampshire? I was looking at the map—Franconia Ridge or the Baldies look great. Anyway, maybe this weekend? Call me."

I stared at the phone for a second after hanging up, chewing on a fingernail, looking at the map. No one really needed me here. My father had Marla, my mother had Marty, Ted and Abby were living out their own drama, and even Ben had survived without me when I was gone. I remembered how he'd said Jessica Velmer's name, how my father's voice graveled out *your fellow, Ben.*

I had to leave them before anyone left me first.

I stuffed as much clean gear as I could find into my pack. I grabbed some crackers and peanut butter, slipped on some shorts and a T-shirt, collected a road map of New Hampshire, the trail maps, and my boots. On the back of an Eastern Mountain Sports receipt, I scribbled a note to Ben.

I have to get out for a while. Don't worry, I love you.—H.

It took three tries to get Lemon started, but once she was going, and I was driving west along the Massachusetts Turnpike, then on Route 95 to 93 north, I felt the cool breeze of escape through the open window. Trees scrolled by, and the bright lights of cars and trucks, going places, traveling the distance between where they were and where they planned to be. Maybe I was doing the wrong thing, but my skin tingled with the thrill of freedom. I was escaping, alone at last, and fully in charge of navigation. I crossed the Massachusetts state line and thought, *out, out, out.* I started singing, letting all the songs on the radio and all the songs I could remember fly out the window as I sped up the turnpike toward the cool green north.

Eighteen /

I spent the night camped in my car by the trailhead for the Baldface Circle Trail. Not really camped, more like parked, my feet stashed under the dash and my front seat partway reclined, because Lemon's seats only reclined partway. I still had most of Camilla's tent in my pack—an unsorted result of the summer trip—everything except some of the stakes and the fly extension poles, but once I drove into the little dirt lot, around midnight, the dark was a deep pool where my headlights ended, and I wasn't brave enough to get out and set up a proper camp. There was another parked car, a rusted yellow Ford, and I was nervous about the possibility of its owners appearing. Despite the sureness of my flight, the long clean beam of knowing I had to go, I wasn't where I was going yet, so I felt the need to stay tucked inside Lemon where the doors locked. I ate a chicken sandwich from a fast-food drive-through, the lettuce greasing my fingers and lap when it slopped out. I had a half-filled water bottle and I drank it all down: water from Forks, Washington. It tasted of plastic.

Then I tried to sleep. All along the drive I felt elated by my departure, easily navigating until I was in Franconia Notch, where I chose my mountain, North Baldface, as quickly as you selected your best friend for your team on the playground in third grade. Never mind that I didn't know this particular best friend all that well. I knew enough to trust her: that the trail led up to a ridge connecting two mountains, North and South Baldface, and that you could link up to Emerald Pool. Like choosing a friend for her funny name and her long brown braids, it was perfectly logical.

My floor mats were damp and the seats felt bumpy. I didn't sleep well; I heard every car pass on the road and an airplane rending the air miles overhead and something nocturnal, a skunk or deer or maybe a porcupine, prowling in the shrubs, then meandering leafily into the stand of skinny young birches beside my parking spot. Each teeny noise woke me, and I tested the door locks, mentally executed the steps of bolting over the gearshift to the driver's seat so I could start up and go if anyone tried to get in my car. I slept with the keys in my hand, denting the skin of my palm into pink submission.

In barely rosy morning, I woke from my final two-hour piece of sleep, a brief suspension of my fear, filled with dreams of uselessly pressing the brake pedal, of climbing a glacier roped too tightly to my father, limping and linked to an oxygen tank, to Ted, to Ben, who was eating potato salad. I was exhausted and a little less sure. Where was I going? Would Ben worry? I wanted him to worry. I didn't want him to worry. I wanted a break, and I wanted to be alone and unavailable for a while, like the Washington trip, only without the dangers of all that company. I wanted a sliver of my hour at Big Basin, stunned by light and colors and peace. I needed it right away, and I needed to go by myself. But I had left a thread or two behind, and for a minute, looking out at the dappled birches in the morning, I considered going home. I could be there in time for an evening's worth of work. What would they think at the office when I didn't come in to print out the toilet stall for the paint store, the parking lot plans left jammed in my computer's memory?

The fantasy of my boss, left with my computer, was enough to wake me fully. I was here; I had supplies and gear; I might as well go for a hike. I stuffed my sleeping bag back into its sack—its sleeping bag condom, as Nicky called it— and opened Lemon's door to the New Hampshire dawn. The air was cool and clean. The birds were up already, a woodpecker drumming its territory on an oak tree, chickadees like clocks in the birches. I took a reconnaissance trip a quarter mile up the trail to the stream, a Charles Brook tributary, and filled two bottles with water, dropping in the nasty-tasting pills I'd bought for cases when the filter didn't work. I didn't have a filter, anyway. I wondered, briefly, how much gear I was missing, without the whole Adventurers' team to plan for me. *With* me, I reminded myself. I could plan some on my own.

I'd stopped at an all-night convenience store when I'd pulled off the highway in North Chatham, and now I crammed the loot I'd bought into my pack: two oranges, oatmeal, an apple, a box of instant rice, and a tube of imported tomato paste, which I thought was a brilliant invention if it was any good; we should have had some for flavor in Washington. I had a chunk of cheese and the gorp ingredients: nuts—I'd gone upscale and substituted almonds and cashews for peanuts—and M&Ms and raisins. Mixing them into a bag

and sampling, I felt as if I was already under way. Fine caloric
food: what to eat when the energy mattered.

Then I was hiking along the trail. One foot, one foot, an
easy rhythm. With no one else to keep up with, I started out
at a leisurely pace. My pack was heavy with all the water,
with a whole tent, with two boxes of matches in case one got
wet, with my own stove and a canister of fuel. The air
smelled sweet, and I could feel the chill behind the fading
bank of summer. Fall. It seemed too soon. I'd been waiting
for the summer trip, it seemed, only days ago, and already
summer was closing in on itself like a collapsible fan.
My shoulder straps rubbed my T-shirt in a familiar way. My
back still had bands of sore skin from our beach hike. My
boots still held grains of sand in the soles. I was shedding
Ozette onto the Baldface Circle Trail.

It wasn't exactly quiet. I could hear a chain saw, and the
low hum of the road, and the arguments of jays and finches.
One foot, one foot. I was tempted to go back, to stop and
eat, or to stop and watch the forest happen—leaves losing
their hold on branches and falling to the ground, the exclamations of chipmunks shifting and snapping twigs as they
ran, the light tipping across the trunks and igniting the silver
birch bark.

One foot, one foot. It was happening already—I was forgetting who I was supposed to be and traveling the necessary
distance to see clearly. And it wasn't: I was a woman alone in
the woods, shouldering a bunch of junk along a path. I
wasn't sure I would be brave enough to keep going on after a
lunch break. I looked at my watch: 7:32. I'd been walking for
one hour. The trail turned north and started out of the paper
birches and along the Charles Brook, which grew wide and
shallow and cut a notch in the earth. I climbed higher and

higher above it, following the trail. Then the path swung away from the water, but I could still hear the mumble as it spilled over rocks. The trail looped back around to a narrow suspension bridge, wide enough for one. I thought of my early Adventurers' trips, of the fear of falling and of falling itself, my wet boots, scraped palms. Of Noah in the cave, in the tent. I blushed as I started across the bridge. I couldn't believe I'd been so foolish—Noah was as bad as the boys in high school, holding real and invented tragedies up like bait for girls who wanted romance and drama, who wanted to save somebody.

But as a friend, he wasn't so dangerous. Opacity. His glints of emotion weren't to make me fall in love, they were his protection, the glasses he wore so no one could see his eyes. How could I have missed it? He'd never really wanted anything other than to see how far I'd go—testing the powers of his beauty. So careless with other people. How could I have not suspected from the first meeting? Of course I suspected. I'd been susceptible to his generous hands, his proximity. I hadn't done anything wrong, really. Except that I was guilty of wanting to kiss him. And maybe there was some reason for that. Maybe I was careless too; maybe I needed to pay attention to what I was running from.

Ben. I thought his name as I stepped along the bridge. Then I stopped and watched the shallow water while I swayed slightly. I thought of Vijay, how a simple accident, a single mistake, had killed him. If I slipped, no one would know, until someone came in or out of the woods this way. It wasn't likely to be soon, midweek, end of season. I knew how to be careful. I wouldn't make any mistakes. I was alone in the woods, I was the only one choosing which way to go, and the only one around to sort out a fall.

———

I didn't let myself stop for lunch until I came to a junction at five miles. It was a good morning's work, and my back was slick with sweat. The trail had climbed out of the birches and up above the stream; then I'd had switchbacks for a mile of pines until the trees shrunk with altitude and the vista started to open below.

I sat on a long wide rock, soaking up sun. I drank the bitter water and ate gorp, cracking the candy shells and sucking on the chocolate, feeling the oil from the nuts against my tongue as I chewed. I could see the tops of trees from here, the flank of the mountain green and silver where the birches stood. A lake lazed along the horizon. It was a low view but still a kind of dessert.

I studied the map, triangulating, though I knew where I was because of the junction. I used the lake and the bumpy-nosed peak to the east and stuck my finger on the map where I was standing: between these two lines. There was no one to show my work to, no one to tell me which route we'd take next. So first I chose one route, then another. I said it out loud: Bicknell Ridge. The air had a plain answer, a soft breeze. A chipmunk climbed the rock beside me and squeaked, snatching a fallen almond and darting into the low-bush blueberry. Blueberries! I suddenly saw them and started collecting in my bandanna. Some were overripe from sitting on the bush, but I took as many as I could, eating one for each one I saved.

The summer before Marla was born, we went to Maine for a summer, renting a cedar cabin beside a pond for two weeks. My father brought shiny, easily dented paint tubes and an easel and set up on the rotting dock every morning. Ted and I practiced climbing trees and came back from a morning's pretending to be circus performers with sap smeared on our shorts and shirts and in our hair. Our father

made us peanut butter and honey sandwiches to put in our
shared backpack—I always made Ted carry it—and we sat
on the limbs eating peanut butter and honey on skinny-
sliced bread, tossing chunks of lunch through the needles
and yelling, "Here, moose, here, moose!" One afternoon my
father stopped painting for long enough to take us on a hike
around the lake. Mom came too, leaving her medical texts in
the cabin, and halfway around we stopped in a patch of blueberries and tried to pick enough for a pie, filling bandannas
and pockets and hats. But as the air cooled, the black flies
swarmed, and we ran back around the path, screaming. Even
my father yelled "Bugs! bugs! bugs!" half alarmed and half
amused by the dramatic flight.

The next day my mother found a bakery in town and
bought us a wild blueberry pie and we ate it, pretending the
filling was the squashed loot from our pockets.

It hadn't all been argument.

I decided to continue along the ridge. Still unsure how
long I planned to stay out, it seemed the route with the most
possibilities and the best way to see where I was going.

Everything seemed slower alone. The trail, the day, ticking
along. I checked my watch, every fifteen minutes or so,
because there was no one to tell me when to stop. I kept hiking past dark, not because there was any site in particular
along the ridge where I intended to camp, but because once I
stopped moving I'd have to sit with myself for the night. I
was better company in motion.

As I set up the tent, the woods creaked and rattled, and I
realized that the coat of bravery I wore in the group was
missing. No one else's body odor or body heat. I tied the
tent fly to some low branches since I didn't have the poles; it

fanned out like a great wing around my diminutive nylon
house.

No one else to help cook or to cook for. I ate some cheese
right from the block and more gorp. I drank the last of my
water and scrubbed my teeth with my finger and a clean corner of bandanna; I'd forgotten a brush and toothpaste. Then
I zipped into the tent and fell asleep, fast and hard.

I woke up because something was making a shuffling
noise. At first I was confused, looking for Ben beside me;
then, once I remembered I was in a tent, for Camilla or
Linda. Just the still tent, the hissing of the wind, a single hoot
from an owl, and something shuffling. I turned on my flashlight and swept the tent. Something in the corner. Something
in the corner moving. I thought it was moving. I moved the
light away, in an odd belief that what I couldn't see couldn't
hurt me. More shuffling. I flashed my light on it and away.
Gray, the size of a rabbit. It was coming toward me. A baby
porcupine? A baby bear, with mama close behind? I stayed
still, thinking out my escape. Then I looked again, holding
my light firmly on the form. It hadn't come any closer. It
wasn't actually moving. The rustling came from outside,
vegetation brushing against the tent. The object wasn't alive.
I slid over to it and grabbed, my heart still beating fast.
Camilla's sock, gray wool, knee length for extra warmth,
hunched upon itself like a sleeping rabbit.

I wished the humor of it would guarantee me a good
night's sleep. I did laugh out loud, but still, I woke for all the
noises, the wind sweeping under the wing of the tent fly, animals crushing leaves and underbrush as they made nightly
hunting or foraging rounds. The thud of acorns, sap-sucked
twigs clicking through branches to the forest floor. Night
noises that sounded dangerous. I could go home tomorrow, I

told myself, to my apartment with locks and keys, windows and walls and doors.

I had a short stretch of sleep between new light and the bright green beam of midmorning. I woke up hot and almost rested, my head heavy with unfinished dreams.

I purified more stream water and cooked myself breakfast, tasting the sweet air as I pumped my stove and started it on the first try. I made oatmeal and sliced apples into it. I didn't pick out the raisins. Conserving the purification tablets, I boiled more water to kill any nasties living inside, and made hot chocolate from a sugary, salty mix with mini-marshmallows that reconstituted and slid satisfyingly across my tongue. It was good, knowing I could go home now; I felt tall and brave. I'd spent the night alone in the woods, and I'd hardly been scared.

Now that it was light.

I packed up camp, whistling a little song to the birds. Then I sat on my backpack with compass and map and realized I had no intention of turning back. Tracing a route along the lines of the map, dotting the view spots with my finger, I knew I fully intended to keep on going.

Nineteen / After the third day, things got easier.

There was a natural rhythm to being alone, to moving, to stopping. It felt less like a race and less like I had weights of resistance strapped to my legs.

During the day, I noticed colors and shapes. At a morning break, I watched the light tapping the flanks of mountains, and the leaves themselves, single ovals, pointed, lobed, the million fine points of needles, a tree all starts and stops. The shades of green: the deep black-green as I moved through white pine and pitch, the red undertones of cedars, the gray standing lichens tipped with red soldiers or white hats, rocks tinted green by the webby spread of flat lichens slowly digesting stone.

At night, it was noise I noticed. Even before dark dripped through the trees, the bird sounds grew more particular, *pee-wee* and *ti-whit, ti-whit*. I tried to match shapes with forms, but the light was too grainy by the time I remembered, and the calls became voices only, telling me who owned the trees. And wind, buffeting, cluttering, rolling back upon itself when it came into the clear space of my campsite between the trunks. Because I wasn't making so much noise, talking all the time, and because I wasn't trying so hard not to listen, the way I did through my days in the real world, I heard the important sounds of small things: mice ticking through the dead needle blanket on the forest floor, insects complaining about their birth and needs, impending death. I heard the sound dark makes, filtering into the trees, a quiet whistle, almost inaudible; I could only hear it when I was still, regulating my breath, turning my head to the side to stop the clamor of my thoughts.

Already, the nights were growing colder, and already, I was starting to run out of food. I'd eaten all the rice; I'd cut the tomato paste tube open and licked out the inside. Water was less of a problem, because I boiled some every morning, and by the time I broke for lunch at a view spot I'd chosen on the map, the water had cooled enough to gulp. I took long breaks at lunchtime, and naps, to make up for the times I woke at night. Even the nervous waking had acquired a sense of habit; now sometimes I woke to an owl, a flurry of leaves letting go, or pines shuffling their fingers like a pianist stretching before practice, and I could slow my heart after a minute of hard listening. No people, only the outside. Somehow, I was more afraid of people than anything else in the woods. People were unpredictable.

As I grew braver, I didn't have to be in my tent before night slipped like a cap over the treetops. Each morning I planned my track along the ridge, to a peak, and I stopped to measure where I was by the points of landscape: Franconia Ridge, Mount Washington, Carrigan, the cliffs of Cathedral

Ledge and Whitehorse—mountaintops, lakes, an occasional road wrapped through the knuckles of the White Mountains. The map was as familiar as my keys had been in my other life.

Once, on the trail, I heard the shuffle of other hikers across the woods. Men's voices. I clambered off the trail and into the trees, convincing myself I was just looking for a spot to pee. I crouched behind a boulder, fingering the rough spots of lichen, the cold contained in the stone, until the voices passed. I didn't want to see them, or for them to see me.

After five nights or so I wasn't sure exactly what day it was. I went back over my map, trying to count the days backward. It didn't matter. What did matter, what got me up each morning in the happy chill of morning, was knowing it was wrong, that I was inflicting injury, that those who had no choice about caring for me—my family—and Ben—who did—would notice.

I fully intended to go back, when the right time to go back made itself clear. It wasn't like waiting for a biblical sign, I needed something like an alarm to wake me. But then again, maybe if I never went back, I thought illogically, my father wouldn't die.

My food was running out; that seemed pretty obvious, and the season was turning, the nights were already colder. I had never experienced a fall like this, and sometimes, when yellow screamed into orange and red stood in patches alone, I could hardly stand not telling someone. But still, I wasn't ready.

I was out of cheese and water pills, crackers and oatmeal. At lunchtime, I counted out six M&Ms and three nuts. The raisins were gone. All I had were a few nuts and some candy and a single orange in the bottom of my pack, and I took it out and smelled it but I didn't eat it, not yet. Noah's book had taught me some things; I could picture the pages for a few plants I found, so I knew they were safe. Wild raisin, which had seemed dowdy, doubtful, and stingy to me before, gave me great handfuls of sweet-tasting flesh, clusters of blue-black bliss. I ate them after my last cracker, a shock of sweet like dates. After I found them twice at campsites, I got too eager, and started to eat something close but not the same viburnum. I could hear Ted. "Is that *Viburnum cassinoides*?" It wasn't. I bit into a bitter fruit of arrowhead and remembered the book had suggested exactly that mistake as I spat it out.

But being hungry was exhilarating too. It was like running. And sometimes, when I was moving along the path, thinking slight thoughts about the stones on the ground ahead, I started to jog a little, to feel the rush of resistance in my muscles, the ache. But my joints didn't like it, with all the weight of my pack, so I resumed a brisk walk.

One afternoon I camped early, because hunger wasn't feeling so good, and because I couldn't walk without stopping to scratch a brand-new patch of poison ivy or poison sumac that blistered the back of my calf. I wondered when I'd gotten it. I missed company. I didn't want it, but I missed it. I missed Ben, but I felt like I was ruining things, irrevocably, the longer I stayed away. I thought of him only in the melancholic past tense, the nostalgia for our early days together. It was as if I was practicing for a death, playing that childhood game of imagination: what would it feel like if Mom died, or Dad did, or Ted; how would they feel if *I* died—the game I'd played when they were getting divorced. Imagining something worse that would capture our attention, something that might force us to feel, Ted and Marla and me, instead of floundering along hoping not to get wounded in the lashings as the boat tore apart.

We wanted my father. I wanted my father. This was why it was my job to invent diversion, still, in a crisis—because my normal life couldn't hold enough of his attention. A minuscule mean part of me envied my brother his problems, because they attracted my father's focus. As long as I could remember, he was looking away—to his work, baby Marla, his battle with Mom, even the wood and plaster needs of the house. But once he must have held me as Kate and John held baby Hannah. Once, I must have captured his attention, and my mother's too. Once I was the center of all that diffuse energy, a star in the blurred Blue universe.

I supposed, striding along, strong-legged, my insides warm and my skin cold to the touch, that I missed my family, missed sorting out how I belonged to them and how they belonged to me.

My campsite had a clear view of the ridge behind me, and I sat with my feet in the stream, cooling the blisters and running my wet bandanna along the patch of itch. I boiled water and made tea with velvety stalks of sumac. They were so soft in my fingers I thought of baby Hannah's fingers, and then, tingling, I realized there was a very great likelihood Abby had had her baby by now. Ted's baby. Ted.

I was hungry and bored. I counted out four M&Ms and felt in the bag. I only had three left. I ate them all. I left the stove, boiling my water, and looked for more wild raisin, more blueberries. I felt the hunger in my center scrabbling like a small animal trapped inside a giant box. I watched a spider making minute progress across a stone and wondered what it would taste like. I didn't know enough about spiders to risk possible poisons. But then I saw a tiny ant dragging the corpse of another. Before I could think myself out of it, I pinched them both in my fingers and put them into the back of my mouth. Swallowed. I didn't gag, as the fluttery food slid down my esophagus, but I certainly didn't feel full once I'd eaten them. Ants wouldn't make much of a meal.

I started back to my site where I could rinse my mouth with water. As I came out of the trees I saw a strange flare around my stove and started running. I had left the map under a rock, but the wind had blown the corner too close to the flame, and it had caught fire. I pulled it to the ground and stamped on it, extinguishing the blaze, pure instinct. I turned off the stove and set the water pot on a rock to cool. Then I started shaking. I realized how stupid I had been; I could have started a forest fire. I could have burned my camp, the trees, I could have been trapped in the flames myself if I'd left the stove long enough for the fire to spread.

I breathed slowly and wrapped my arms around myself until the shaking stopped. Then I folded the sooty remains, useless for where I was now, and tried to memorize what I knew of the trails, tried to remember the map I'd looked at every day. I knew I'd looped the ridge, and had gone west and north. I should have invested in the laminated topo, which might have been more fire resistant. I should have remembered to put it back in my pocket. I never should have left a burning stove; I was lucky the map was the only damage. I still had my compass, but without the map, I didn't know exactly where I was going or where I'd been.

It froze that night. When I woke in my tent I heard a cracking sound, something new. I was still hungry, and for once, the noise didn't scare me; I was curious. I dressed and got out of my tent. Moonlight filled the spaces between the trees, pouring in where it could reach. The smallest eddies splitting off from the stream were freezing, and as new water flowed in, the ice crackled. Shards lifted like miniature icebergs. Frost sparkled on the ground. I wondered whether I could last through the fall, through early winter. There wouldn't be enough to eat; I'd have to come out soon. It was too exquisite, the gloss of frost on the floor of fallen leaves, the moon spilling over the cold woods. I dragged my sleeping pad and bag out and lay down, unable to sleep for all that beauty.

In the morning, I had finally fallen asleep, but rain woke me. I pulled everything into the tent, realizing how lucky I'd been so far. Rain. I remembered our Washington trip. When it was raining, you couldn't think about anything else. When it was dry, you forgot.

For the first time, I thought without trepidation about being found. They would have no idea where to look. I tried to remember what I'd said in my message to Camilla, whether I'd mentioned New Hampshire in my note. I'd left so abruptly, running away like a child. But back then, I hadn't thought that far ahead: to being sought, to burning my own map, even to staying out past one round of dark.

I was cold, and unwrapped the emergency blanket, pulling it around me in my damp sleeping bag, around my soggy clothes. I put on my wool hat and two pairs of wool socks. I felt my body working, trying to make enough heat to keep from shivering. I was really hungry now, and I sat inside my tent feeling pitiful. The rain's thunk on the nylon and the ground was a soothing sound, but I was too hungry to enjoy it, too quiet from all my time alone to be soothed. I thought of Ben, and for the first time I tried to imagine what it was like for him to try to love me. With my bumpy family, with my moods, as Marla called them. My energy, my leaving, always leaving. It couldn't be an easy thing, and I wondered how long it would be before he let go. I did tell him things, but not enough, or I wouldn't be here, in the woods, without him, wallowing in a dry spot in the wet world, mapless, being selfish.

It felt like a discovery. Selfishness. What everyone carried. Self-centered. How we are born, all needs, and unaware of the separateness of people, our parents, the providers for those immediate requirements: food, carrying from here to there, holding up our heads. Baby Hannah, looking at me, trying to see what comforts and entertainments the world provided, learning whom she could trust. This is where I hadn't finished becoming an adult; I was still watching to see whom I could trust. My inconsistent parents had fooled me at first into believing I could trust them, and then I couldn't. They were no worse than I was: fallible, self-centered. They'd suspended themselves for long enough to make us, to make us need them. And then they'd committed the most obvious act of parenthood, the most important one: letting us go.

But the people we chose, we had to trust them and stop practicing this pattern: need, release. I had been watching Ben for all the signs of separation, when I should have been watching for the places I could stick. It wasn't about Ben, exactly. He didn't have to make up for anything. It was me; I needed practice at attachment. I lay inside my tent holding my sleeping bag to my chest, happy with discovery, bereft over all I'd done to try to lose him.

It rained all morning. I dozed and shivered in my tent; I tried eating some acorns I'd collected the day before, but they were too hard to chew. Finally, the downpour calmed into a misty spray, and I took down my camp, stuffing the bag and tent into my pack and then sitting by the stove while my water boiled, eating the last orange, shivering slightly. I boiled some acorns and stuck them into my pocket. It was cold despite a feeble drip of sun, the last boundary of summer spilling off into the long cold valley of autumn. I drank some water before it cooled, burning my tongue. I would try to go back; I'd follow the trail I was on, I'd try to remember where I'd turned, I'd use my compass for general direction.

I thought of my parking spot with sudden longing. I wondered if they'd towed Lemon by now, if she'd start. At the bottom of my pack, my wallet was probably moldering. I had at least forty dollars in there, and a credit card. I thought through what food I'd eat, oily French fries, hot soup. I wanted minestrone: salty carrot cubes, slippery pasta. I was hiking fast, my boots squishing along the trail, my socks soaked and an occasional trickle of accumulated sweat and rain spilling down the back of my neck.

I was losing altitude as I cut along the ridge. My ears popped and the trees grew taller: woods, sweet-scented and misty, swallowed my views. I made a turn, pretty sure I wasn't getting lost. If I didn't know my way for certain, at least I could pretend. I could listen for a road. I would get out someday. I stopped and studied my map's remains. I could also wander for a long time before I found a road, another person, a restaurant. I was very hungry. It had to be the right turn.

It was midafternoon when the sun suddenly found its way out of the maze of fog. Steam rose from the loamy banks of fallen leaves as the rain evaporated. It was like hiking through a sauna, and I peeled off my jacket, tying the sleeves around my waist, zippers burring against the nylon. I stopped to pick some sorrel and to try the boiled acorns. Just enough fuel to keep me going. Then I heard the strangest birds. Deep-voiced birds, quarreling birds. Birds that spoke and shuffled loudly in the leaves.

They weren't birds; they were people, and the voices were familiar, but I wasn't sure whether to trust my ears. The acorns tasted like boiled dust. I chewed and stood still, letting the voices grow louder. I scurried farther off the path, trying to stay quiet as I knocked raindrops off the leaves of the underbrush. Crushed sassafras, a sharp scent.

I crouched behind a trio of birches, trunks nearly grown together at the base, glimpsing flashes of color through my silvery-branched viewfinder. The voices were coming up another trail, about to intersect with mine. A woman's voice, several men. One of them, I was almost sure from the cadence, was Shing. I wanted to run but stood still. Two other voices, another woman and a man, were approaching from another arm of the intersection. They met in the middle, a crowd.

It was almost like fear, as if I were standing backstage waiting to make my entrance, all my lines puddled at my feet with the laces of my costume, my face frozen. They were people I knew, six people collecting at the intersection, a divisible group: Nicky beside Linda and Camilla, Shing standing; he looked huge beside the narrow form of someone I never remembered seeing in the woods. Marla. Here for me. She wore jeans and a bandanna on her yellow hair. Without makeup, her face was clear and serious. And beside her, his arms gesturing like wings, his voice low and steady with authority, was Ben.

"I'm not ready to give up on this side," he said. "We have to look a little longer. Her note was on the back of the receipt for this topo." He held an unfolded map in one hand, a compass in the other, and I fought back the powerful urge to run to him, yelling.

"So you've said, Ben. It helps, but that map covers a huge area. We should try South Baldface," said Camilla. "To-morrow?"

"Okay," said Linda. "I'm good for another few miles here. I'll take the yellow blazes. Nick?"

"Yeah," said Nicky.

"What do you think?" Marla looked at Shing. I couldn't see her expression.

"Hey," I said, pushing through the birches. I was still holding a clump of wood sorrel.

"Hey!" I said it louder, and they all turned. Unbearable, the stage I'd set for myself.

"Hey!" I said it a third time, and strode toward them.

"Looks yummy," said Nicky, pointing to the greens in my hand.

But as I came close enough, I could only see Ben. His denim shirt was drenched and he wore a red rain slicker tied around his waist. That beautiful dark hair stood up in back; it needed a trim. Ben's freckly hands, his skin; I could almost smell the clean mint as I moved closer, not quite running, and he stood square on the trail, his sneakers splattered with strips of leaves. Ben looking at me, not a rescuer, not my hero, but exactly whom I'd been missing.

Epilogue /

The centerpieces were edible. Ted made them, though I offered a design consult, happy to have something to do with my hands while I waited for Ben to arrive. Bunchberry, mayapple, yucca flowers, the waxy-white clusters hanging around the outside with a not-quite-obscene fecundity. We had daylilies and nasturtiums, their orange faces like little lanterns among the greens. Since they were a surprise, Ted and I laid out our ingredients on the black-and-white floor squares in the ballroom, away from the caterer-filled kitchen, where my mother and Marty reigned and worried over the quail and wild mushroom risotto, the timing of Marty's grand cake, a *reine de Saba*, a queen of chocolate. My mother's instructive tone echoed up from below.

Abby and eight-month-old Lily were coming later. Ted and I sifted through the loot of leaves and shoots and flowers we'd collected on our day trip to the Blue Hills, wearing sweaters and digging for corms and enjoying the sweet spring air, the hordes of field-tripping students snapping twigs as they flowed down the trails. I took the day off from my new job: working with Ted, managing his office, and writing up preliminary designs for overflow projects. Ted had more work than he could manage, and I had time for classes in architecture at Harvard Extension. I still wasn't sure about graduate school.

They were getting along, Ted and Abby, and she let him stay over at the beginning to help with Lily's night feedings, but now that Lily was sleeping through the night, and crawling manically around the apartment, dragging the string of her pull-toy dog in her perfect purse of a mouth, Abby preferred that Ted pick her up for visits, most of the time. He had his own car seat and crib, he had a high chair in his cramped new place, but he wanted to come back. It weighed on everything we did together when I saw him, longing for them both, for the neat package of family. And sometimes Abby seemed ready to relent, he said, and sometimes she seemed happiest when he was leaving to go home.

"Whorled loosestrife," said Ted. "*Lysimachia quadrifo-lia.*" He plucked at the yellow petals as if bringing out the red dots in their mouths.

"What do you think Dad would think of this?"

"The violets in the centerpieces?"

"Of course not." I slid a handful of purple flowers, their stems wrapped in wet paper towels, across the checkered floor.

"He liked Shing. I think he probably knew."

"Maybe if you *insist*," I said. "Maybe she wouldn't be able to resist you. Maybe tonight. I'll take Lily out to look at the cardinals, and you can talk with her."

"It isn't anything new," he said. He tossed some droopy

greens with closed-up yellow flowers into the reject pile. "It's all about trust. And I can't undo our history. But now that she's stopped nursing—well, things in bed are pretty good." He sighed. "Anyway, what do *you* think Dad would think of this?"

"Of the centerpieces? Pretty good. Of Shing and Marla? He'd have an announcement of some kind to upstage the engagement party. He'd be getting married again himself—"

"Never," said Ted. He plucked a clover head and sucked at the bottoms of the purple flowers.

"Kids," said Ben. He was standing at the door, wearing a tuxedo. I brushed green refuse off my long purple skirt and stood up to meet him. I didn't know yet, what we'd be together, but I'd stopped swimming upstream just to prove the current wrong. I knew about getting out; now I was working on coming back in.

"Hi," I said. With yellow-stained fingers, I put a nasturtium flower into my mouth and one into Ben's. The petal slipped against my tongue, the softness tempering the sharp peppery taste. I looked out the window, past the edge of Ted's hedge maze, at Abby and Lily out on the lawn, wrapped together in the necessity of arms. Marla ran through the cherry grove toward the house. She wore a pink nursing uniform from her work-study rotation, a long garment bag with her dress trailing behind her like a sail. The windows were open, letting in the rustling of the trees, quick-chickadee calls, my sister's laughter, and the tiny messengers of pollen and seeds, riding the shaft of late-afternoon light.

Acknowledgments / My husband, Joshua Rosenberg, was this book's invaluable first reader and is the most supportive, compassionate partner I could ever desire.

Thanks to the many branches of my family. I am grateful for such encouraging friends, and relied especially on Marcia Worth-Baker, Harlan Coben, Veera Hiranandani, Moira Bucciarelli, Erika Tsoukenelis, Patricia Dunn, and Cynthia Yoder for their insights. My sister, Claudia Rose, provided expert climbing advice. Thanks also to my old friends from the Environmental Science Program.

I am indebted to Elaine Koster, my agent, who is a joy to work with and to know, and to my editor, Jennifer Barth, for her faith, energy, and eagle eye.

I referred to the very useful *A Field Guide to Edible Wild Plants: Eastern and Central North America*, by Lee Allen Peterson (Houghton Mifflin Co., 1977), and *Mountaineering: The Freedom of the Hills*, 6th edition, edited by Don

Graydon and Kurt Hanson (The Mountaineers, 1997). Of course, any inaccuracies in the novel are my own.

This is a work of fiction; the people and events in it are invented. Some of the places may be real, but I wouldn't go without a map.

My love and gratitude to my friends from the once-proud Explorer Post 507, long may the brown-and-yellow flag wave in our memories.

About the Author / GWENDOLEN GROSS completed an M.F.A in poetry and fiction at Sarah Lawrence College. She is the author of the novel *Field Guide*, which will be published this spring in paperback by Harvest.